ON A ROLL

BETH BOLDEN

Copyright © 2021 Earl Gray Publishing.

All rights reserved. No part of this publication may be reproduced, distributed or transmitted in any form or by any means, including photocopying, recording, or other electronic or mechanical methods, without the prior written permission of the publisher, except in the case of brief quotations embodied in critical reviews and certain other noncommercial uses permitted by copyright law. For permission requests, write to the publisher, at the address below.

Earl Gray Publishing LLC

www.bethbolden.com

beth@bethbolden.com

Publisher's Note: This is a work of fiction. Names, characters, places, and incidents are a product of the author's imagination. Locales and public names are sometimes used for atmospheric purposes. Any resemblance to actual people, living or dead, or to businesses, companies, events, institutions, or locales is completely coincidental.

Book Layout © 2023 Beth Bolden

Book Cover © 2020 AngstyG Book Cover Design

The people in the images are models and should not be connected to the characters in the book. Any resemblance is incidental.

Ordering Information:

Quantity sales. Special discounts are available on quantity purchases by corporations, associations, and others. For details, contact Beth Bolden at the address above.

On a Roll/ Beth Bolden. -- 1st ed.

PROLOGUE

Two years ago

There was nothing Gabriel Moretti enjoyed more than the squeaky-clean, sparkling-with-possibilities, fresh-start feeling of every food truck season. He stood back and admired the new sign emblazoned on the side of the truck. It read, in a fun bright green script, *On a Roll,* which was not only an adorable name that totally referenced the mobility of his truck, but his specialty. He'd originally begun with his nonna's famous meatball and red sauce recipes, and then boosted his popularity by putting everything together on one, soft, garlic butter-slathered Italian roll.

Nonna's Kitchen on Wheels had been a perfectly serviceable name, especially when he'd still been a Southern California spinoff of his family's famous chain of Italian restaurants in Napa. But the meatball sub had become famous last season, and he'd spent the short Los Angeles off-season prepping for a new name that matched his bestselling item.

Truthfully, there was *barely* an off-season in LA. The weather made food trucks viable most of the year, but a lot of trucks took

Thanksgiving through February off—the first big food festival officially kicking off the new season each year.

"Hey, Gabe. That looks *real* good."

Gabriel looked up and saw Tony Blake, both a friend and fellow food truck owner, standing, arms crossed over his chest, admiring the new logo on the shiny stainless steel side of the truck.

"Thanks," Gabriel said. He was trying very hard not to be overly proud of himself. But he *was*. His family had all said this food truck thing was never going to work out, not for him anyway. "People want to eat at a table with a knife and fork," his oldest brother, Luca, had insisted. "They don't want to chase a truck around."

Gabriel had never been prouder than when he mailed a check to Luca, paying off almost all of his family's investment from the last season's profits.

No—that was not completely accurate.

He'd never been *happier.* Because the food truck doing well and not only supporting him, but allowing him to put money into the bank? It meant he could stay down in Los Angeles and away from all his mouthy, interfering, and unbelievably nosy family.

Gabriel loved each and every one of them, but they were a hell of a lot easier to deal with when they were several hundred miles away.

"I think changing your name was a great idea," Tony said, meandering closer as Gabriel put the finishing buff on the already shiny side of the truck. "But you might want to rethink what you're changing it to."

"What?" Gabriel glanced up. "What are you talking about? This name is *perfect*."

But Tony just shrugged. The concerned look in his blue eyes was a lot more worrying than his casual attitude. "Maybe if you don't mind sharing a name with another truck." Tony pointed across the busy festival lot, to where trucks were parked on the other side. And sure enough, to Gabriel's incredulity, there was a food truck—shining white, with a crisp red logo painted on it—that proclaimed that it was *also* On a Roll.

"What?" Gabriel gaped. "That's not . . . I mean, I *did* the research. I spent months finalizing the name!"

Tony shrugged again. "At least you guys are serving two very different things."

That did not make Gabriel feel any better. He still felt like marching right over to the other truck and giving them a piece of his mind. After all, he'd done meticulous Google searches, making sure that there were no other trucks with that name in the Los Angeles area. When he'd looked into it, there hadn't even been any trucks in *California* with the name he'd eventually settled on.

And yet, there one stood. Taunting Gabriel with its fresh paint and bright red logo.

"What are they even serving?" Gabriel asked, filling his voice with scorn so that Tony wouldn't hear the disappointment. He'd worked so hard last year, and even during the off-season, when a lot of food truck owners actually managed a vacation. He'd done it all so he could say proudly that he'd succeeded where his family had expected that he'd fail. He'd done it for space and for self-respect, and he'd gone into this season with so much hope and optimism that he'd felt like the sky was the limit.

Well, the sky was looking a hell of a lot closer to the ground now.

"Looks like some kind of healthy crap," Tony said. "Wraps? Something like that. Dairy-free. Vegan? God only knows."

"So he likes vegetables?" Gabriel would have to be living under a rock not to know that the hottest trend was food trucks that served food you didn't feel guilty eating.

He liked vegetables just fine—as long as they were cooked into his meatballs with lots of butter and cheese.

"That's probably a good guess," Tony said. "We could go over there and find out?"

"I have stuff to do. Sauce to finish. Meatballs to cook." Gabriel shoved his hands into his jeans pockets. "Maybe I'll go over there after the dinner rush is through and do some reconnaissance."

"Yeah"—Tony nodded—"might be better to be less confrontational about it." Which was laughable, because Tony was one of the most hot-headed people that Gabriel had ever met. And he was *Italian.*

Tony wandered off, losing interest, the way he probably assumed Gabriel was doing, back towards the food truck he co-owned with his brother, Wyatt.

But Gabriel was definitely not smart enough to leave well enough alone. He already knew that basically nothing was going to prevent him from going over there *right now*, but he hadn't wanted to do it with Tony looking over his shoulder, cataloging every word of the exchange for juicy gossip later.

Tossing his cleaning rag into the truck, Gabriel stomped over to where the copycat truck sat.

It was only a third of the size of Gabriel's own, barely big enough for one person. And that person poked his head out of the front window just as Gabriel arrived.

The opening salvo Gabriel had been preparing as he stormed over died in his throat.

The guy was *young*. Maybe even younger than Gabriel. And he was goddamn adorable.

Dark blond hair, shaggy and in need of a trim fell over one grayish-blue eye. The guy's nose wrinkled, his forehead crinkling cutely as he regarded Gabriel.

"I'm afraid we're not open yet," the guy said. "But if you're hungry, I'm sure I can find you something."

He was also *nice*.

Gabriel did not want him to be nice. He wanted him to be rude and bossy and just as fucking pissed off as Gabriel was.

"Hi," he said shortly. "I'm good, thanks. But you might want to consider changing the name of your truck."

"The name?"

Gabriel had never found confusion on any single creature to be so goddamn appealing. Somehow this guy managed it. While also, simultaneously, being an enormous pain in Gabriel's ass.

"Yes," Gabriel said, none-too-patiently. "The *name*. You know, the exact name that you copied from *me*."

That last part was technically not true. They'd both probably done their research off-season, and figured they were in the clear. But Gabriel had a feeling that this guy was soft (and new, if he was going by the look of the brand-new truck and the fact that Gabe had never seen him around before), and he could get under his skin and get him to change his name more easily if he came out swinging.

"I didn't copy my truck's name from anyone," the guy said primly. But with an undertone of steel that belied all that adorable confusion.

Had Gabriel read him wrong? He decided he didn't care, and forged ahead, recklessly.

"Yet, somehow we have the exact same name," Gabriel said, pointing across the worn grassy field to his own truck, slightly less shiny in the morning sunlight but still *his*.

"Oh, look at that," the guy said. Unconcerned. "Well, I hope there won't be any confusion."

"There won't be," Gabriel said between clenched teeth, "because you'll be changing your truck's name. Tomorrow."

"Really?" The guy looked skeptical. "I really don't have plans to change it, especially since this is the first day."

"It's your first day?" Gabriel said. Not that it hadn't been obvious from the pristine truck. There wasn't even any mud on the tires, for god's sake.

The man's eyes narrowed. "You *know* it's my first day, which is why you're over here, trying to bully me into changing my name. Well, I won't. So you might as well save your breath."

Gabriel flinched, like he'd just been punched in the face. He had not expected *that*. Not from the guy who was still smiling at him so sweetly.

"This isn't over," Gabriel said.

"I expected that it wasn't," the guy said firmly. "I'm not exactly thrilled either, I'll have you know. First day out, and already someone making trouble for me."

"Making . . ." Gabriel wondered when he'd lost control of the conversation. Maybe . . . *maybe* he'd never been in charge of it in the first place. He'd just thought he was.

"Making trouble," the guy confirmed with a sharp nod. "And *no*, I appreciate your concern, and I share it, but I won't be changing my name. Goodbye."

And before Gabriel could argue, the blond man had turned around, clearly done with the conversation, and with him.

That stung.

However, Gabriel had no intention of taking any of it lying down.

The next time he ran into the blond guy with the identical name, it was a week later, and Gabriel had discovered a few things about the copycat.

1) He was not only new to the food truck scene, he was new to Los Angeles. Nobody Gabriel talked to had ever heard of him before. And thanks to being friends with Tony and his brother, Wyatt, Gabriel knew or knew *of* a whole lot of people.

2) The *wrong* version of On a Roll already had five reviews on Yelp, and a 4.9 rating.

3) One person had already confused the two trucks, because one of those reviews was *his*.

4) The guy's name was Sean Cooper.

5) Gabriel had already spent more time obsessing about Sean than he was willing to admit to anyone. He'd found the copycat's Twitter account and Instagram and had proceeded to follow both, only to tweet himself that if you wanted the *real* On a Roll in LA, you had to come see him.

Sean, annoyingly, had not responded to the bait.

"You should just change your name back," Tony said, as Gabriel stirred his tomato sauce, AKA his nonna's "gravy," in the enormous pot on the back of the stove.

"I do not want to change my name back," Gabriel said between clenched teeth. "I asked you if you had any advice. That's not advice. That's a knife in the back."

"Hey!" Tony said in mock outrage. "That's not fair. I'm trying to help here."

"What you're trying to do is take his side," Gabriel muttered. "He's been here a *week*, and already everyone likes him better."

"I don't think that's true," Tony argued.

"I saw him having a real friendly chat with Ash," Gabriel said. Ash was *his* friend. Ash should be on *his* side. But instead, Ash had been talking and laughing between lunch and dinner with Sean.

And it was definitely not because Ren, his cousin who helped him at the truck, had proclaimed them a "cute new couple." No sirree, he was definitely not jealous. No way. Yes, Sean might be a little cute, a fact that Ren had pointed out half a dozen times already, until Gabriel had really wished that he could fire him. But Lorenzo was his cousin, and Ren's dad, Stefano—his father's younger brother—would never forgive him. And Luca? Luca, his oldest brother and officially now the head of the family since his parents had retired, would be down in LA in a flash, and the last thing Gabriel wanted was to deal with Luca's profound inflexibility.

Okay, Luca was now the *second* to the last thing Gabriel wanted to deal with. The first? Definitely Sean Cooper. Sean was a complete asshole, even if he was an inadvertent one, and he was *going* to change his mind. Gabriel was going to make sure of it.

"Ash was trying to be welcoming and nice," Tony said. "You know, after *someone* marched over to Sean's truck and tried to intimidate him when he said he wouldn't."

Gabriel refused to feel guilty. "You're just disappointed you weren't present for said intimidation."

"It's alright," Tony said. "Maureen, who runs the fish and chips truck? She was parked right next door and heard everything."

Gabriel grimaced. "Of course she did."

"Hey, if you're going to be weirdly threatening just because the guy's got the same name as yours, you're gonna have to expect everyone to be talking about it."

"I wasn't . . ." Okay, he might have been. But who could blame him?

"Listen," Tony interrupted him. "You're the more established guy on the circuit. You had a lot of success last year. You put a lot of time and effort and money into rebranding. Maybe if he was also selling Italian sandwiches, make a big deal out of this, but now? You gotta let it go."

There was no way Gabriel was letting it go.

"I just wanted to say that," Tony said, before shoving his hands in his pockets and wandering off.

Gabriel had five minutes alone with his sauce, before Ren showed up.

Ren was, to put it mildly, a complete pain in Gabriel's ass.

He was still not over the fact that along with the investment his family had made in the food truck, they'd also decided that if Gabriel was going to strike out on his own, he might as well take the most annoying member of the family with him.

Lorenzo Moretti—or Ren, as his family and friends called him—sauntered in, an innocent smile on his face that didn't fool Gabriel for a hot second. In his experience, Ren was a complete and total brat, and wouldn't know innocence if it came up and bit him.

"I saw your friend outside," Ren said, leaning against the back counter.

Gabriel was not stupid enough to think that Ren meant Tony. Especially because if he'd been referring to Tony, he'd have said something like, *your really hot friend who I'd love to hook up with.* When they'd started the season, Gabriel had thought that was the most difficult situation he'd have to deal with: Ren and his endless crush on Tony.

"Your blond friend," Ren added slyly. "He looked like he missed you."

"Like a hole in the head, probably," Gabriel muttered. "I didn't realize he was going to be here today. He wasn't on the list they released a month ago."

"New and exciting truck? Yeah, I'm sure they added him after," Ren said, opening the tiny closet in the front of the truck and pulling out his navy blue apron, emblazoned with the new logo that Gabriel had spent so many hours laboring over.

Gabriel made a face.

"He might be new, but he's not exciting," Gabriel insisted.

Ren shot him a pitying look. "You just keep telling yourself that."

"I am," Gabriel said. "And I'm also going to figure out a way to convince him to change the name of his truck. We can't *both* be On a Roll. What if someone has a hankering for a really good meatball sub, and then they accidentally head to his truck and end up with a mouthful of weeds? That's a problem."

"It's not just weeds," Ren sniffed.

"Oh, so you're an expert on his menu now, huh?" Gabriel asked. Of course Ren had tried the competition. He'd sampled the food—and flirted—with nearly every truck owner they'd ever run into. At least all the queer male ones.

"He's cute," Ren said. "Maybe not as cute as Tony, but he'd do in a pinch."

"I didn't think blonds were your type," Gabriel said, rolling his eyes.

"They're not, but he gets under your skin, so I'd be happy to make an exception."

"Ugh," Gabriel complained. "You suck."

"Yes, yes, I do, and really well too," Ren teased.

"Ew."

"So that's a no, you don't want me to hook up with the cute copycat and use my extensive persuasive powers to convince him to change his name?" Ren raised an eyebrow. "I thought you'd jump at that chance."

"No, you didn't," Gabriel said. The only thing that would be worse than Sean existing, would be Sean hooking up with his cousin.

"Okay," Ren said, laughing. "Fair enough."

"What I *need* you to do is get the caprese stuff prepped, and the veggies prepped. I'm going to make meatballs in a few."

"Veg is already done," Ren said. "I finished it already."

The only other reason why Gabriel continually resisted his urge to fire Ren—other than a fierce need to avoid his elder brother—was that Ren, when he put his mind to it, was actually fairly efficient.

He did spend more time flirting than taking orders, sometimes, but he was good with prep. Quick and kept his head down. Most of the time, anyway.

"Oh good," Gabriel said. He turned off the burner under the sauce.

"You're leaving?" Ren raised an eyebrow. "I thought you were making meatballs."

"I am. I'm . . . I have something I need to do first."

"Go badger the poor copycat?"

"No," Gabriel insisted. *Yes.*

"Alright, then. Have fun," Ren said with a smirk.

It was not *fun,* Gabriel thought as he walked across the field to where the bright white and red logo of Sean's truck was calling him like a beacon. It was a necessary action, born of frustration and annoyance.

He was definitely *not* looking forward to seeing Sean again.

No way.

Sean was outside his little truck this time, setting out plasticware and cleaning off the stainless steel counter under the window. He was slim, but his hips curved under his jean shorts, and that annoyingly jaunty white apron, which Gabriel hadn't gotten quite a full look at, was tied precisely around his waist.

The logo was annoyingly right there, right in the center of his chest. Gabriel found he couldn't quite look away.

"Oh," Sean said, after glancing up, "it's you again."

"Gabriel," he said through gritted teeth. "It's Gabriel Moretti. You know, the guy you copied."

"I didn't copy anyone," Sean said, seemingly still unconcerned. "You *just* changed your name, which you failed to mention last time we spoke, by the way, and I'm brand new. It's just . . . a rather unfortunate coincidence."

"Rather unfortunate?" Gabriel thought it was a hell of a lot worse than that.

But Sean just shrugged. "We're serving such different things. Does it really matter?"

"Yes, it matters!" Gabriel said, trying very hard not to explode. "I've got a reputation, and I've worked hard for it and . . ."

"And you don't want me borrowing it just because we have the same name." Sean gave a sharp nod. "I understand. Except that *I* work plenty hard too, and maybe, in a few weeks, or a month, it'll be *you* trading on *my* name."

"That's never going to happen," Gabriel scoffed.

"Maybe. Maybe not. You'll have to stay tuned to find out," Sean said lightly. He turned to go back into the truck.

"That's not . . . *no*," Gabriel said, and before he could stop himself, he reached out to catch Sean's arm.

Sean shrugged it off easily, even though he was a few inches shorter, and definitely didn't seem to have the same muscular bulk that Gabriel prided himself on. "I'm afraid," Sean said with complete disdain, "you don't get a vote here. Not at my truck. And not in my life."

Okay, so that confrontation had not gone quite as Gabriel had expected.

He had also not expected to return to his own food truck, and after making about a thousand meatballs, check his phone only to realize that Sean had followed him back.

He'd also had the nerve to tweet, "Looking to stay on track with your new beach body? Make sure you visit the other On a Roll for more diet-friendly options."

Gabriel couldn't pretend it was insulting—he made zero apologies for his meatball subs. They were delicious but that was because they were full of carbs and cheese and meat with a high fat content. Still, it was annoying to see that Sean had already picked up a way he could market his own truck more effectively.

"You're glaring again," Ren said as Gabriel formed meatballs with an ice cream scoop, setting them in long rows on the baking tray.

"I'm not glaring," Gabriel said. But he was. And he knew exactly why.

"Is it because of that cute guy?"

"The cute . . . *what*?" Gabriel exclaimed.

Ren rolled his eyes. "You know he's cute. I've seen you staring at him. You know, when it doesn't look like you'd like to punch him in the face."

"No." Gabriel shook his head vehemently.

"I'm just saying. So he's got the same name as you. This is a big city. Lots of food trucks. You guys could co-exist peacefully, if you wanted to. But clearly you want to get under his skin."

"He got under mine *first*," Gabriel insisted. Did he completely believe that? Well, *mostly*. He hadn't been lying when he'd told Sean that he was worried about the problems of having the same name. It would have been so much easier if Sean had just recognized that right off the bat, and agreed to change his.

But he hadn't, and he clearly had no intention of changing his mind.

Gabriel was just going to have to change it for him.

Right after the lunch rush, he enacted the first step of his plan. He pulled out his phone, quickly composing a tweet, challenging the food truck community to vote on which On a Roll truck was better.

Maybe, Gabriel thought, it was a low blow. He was going to get more votes, because it was *his* account, and because he'd spent so much longer in the community. He was well-known, even if most of that reputation had been earned when he was Nonna's Kitchen on Wheels. Sean was brand new.

Maybe it was time to remind Sean that he *was* brand new.

Almost immediately, as he settled down outside, on one of the tables set in the festival clearing, to eat his plate of meatballs—yes, even *he* avoided carbs sometimes—he started seeing retweets and replies, and just like he'd expected, every single comment sided with him.

And maybe he stoked the fire a bit higher by responding to some of them, agreeing with a lot of the comments, often giving a whole string of praise emojis after. He loved his customers. They were so fucking loyal, Gabriel was touched by it. This was the kind of thing that Sean needed to *see* so he'd understand that this battle wasn't one he could win.

Gabriel was always going to come out on top.

And maybe he got carried away and tagged Sean on a few of the replies. Maybe he shouldn't have called him an imposter.

His finger hovered over the tweet, wondering if he should actually delete that one. But before he could, a shadow crossed over his vision, blocking the bright California sunshine.

Gabriel glanced up and supposed that he shouldn't be so surprised to see Sean standing there, a tight-lipped glare on his face, his arms crossed over that perfectly pristine white apron.

He wanted to mess up that apron.

He wanted to take it and tie Sean up with it and defile it.

Maybe Ren was right after all. This guy had really gotten under his skin. Maybe if Gabriel hadn't been so attracted to him, he could've let the name thing go.

But probably not.

Gabriel already knew he was the kind of guy who didn't "let things go." It was the Italian in him.

"I can't believe you did this," Sean said, gesturing towards Gabriel's phone. "Couldn't you just leave well enough alone?"

"No?" It was like this guy didn't know Gabriel at all; and then it occurred to Gabriel that he really didn't. "Listen," Gabe said. "I'm Italian. I'm loud. I'm obnoxious. I'm passionate about stuff I care about. I definitely am not good at compartmentalizing shit."

"And?" Sean said.

"What I mean is that I was here *first*. You're new. This whole Twitter thing proves it. Why can't you just change your name?"

"Why should I?" Sean challenged.

"I changed mine. And it really wasn't a big deal. I don't get why you're so determined not to. It'd probably help you, too, to not be tied to my obnoxious Italian ass for all time."

Sean didn't say anything right away. Just stared at Gabriel like he had two heads. And even though he was clearly pissed off, *yeah*, Ren was definitely right. He was cute.

Gabriel didn't want to think it, because Sean probably hated him now.

"I just don't want to, okay? I have my reasons," Sean finally said. "And," he added, his voice going cold and hard, "I'd appreciate it if you could take that whole thread down."

"Oh," Gabriel said innocently, "is it making you look bad?"

Sean's mouth dropped open in shock.

"Actually, it's making *you* look bad," Sean said.

Gabriel had just stabbed one of the meatballs on his plate with a plastic fork. One of his moist, delicious, red sauce-covered meatballs. He froze, meatball speared by the fork, and felt his brain go blank with frustrated rage. Sean didn't want to tell him why he wouldn't change his name *and* thought that Gabriel was making himself look bad?

He'd never pretended to have anything other than a terrible temper.

He was Italian, wasn't he?

Truthfully, he was actually pretty laid-back most of the time, but when he lost his chill, he usually lost it big-time.

This time was no exception to that particular rule.

Later, he wouldn't even remember throwing the meatball and watching with gloating satisfaction as it slammed into Sean's chest, emblazoning his red logo with an imprint of greasy red sauce. It hit the ground with a juicy *plop*, the only sound that Gabriel could hear over the roaring in his ears.

Sean stared at him in shock, then looked down at the red smear on his chest, and then at the meatball on the ground, and then back up to Gabriel.

"You . . . you . . . *you*," he stuttered.

"Yeah," Gabriel said. "Now we *both* look bad."

Out of the corner of his eye, he saw Tony approaching the scene, trepidation written all over his face.

"What the fuck is going on?" he demanded.

"It turns out that not only are my balls delicious, they make excellent missiles," Gabriel said.

Sean's brows slammed together and he looked completely, totally, incoherently pissed. Gabriel thought that if he'd been in Sean's shoes, he wouldn't have felt much different.

But maybe, *maybe*, it would be enough to convince Sean that it wasn't worth it to tangle with him.

Sean nudged the meatball with the toe of his black Converse. "You're disgusting," he muttered.

"I mean . . ." Tony trailed off.

"Don't you dare say he's right," Gabriel said to his friend. Maybe he'd crossed the line, but if he got what he wanted out of it, it might be worth it.

"I'm right," Sean said, and then, suddenly, his blue eyes were pinning Gabriel in place, not just flat and pissed off, but blazing hot with passion and indignity, "and if you think this is going to scare me off, you'd better rethink that whole plan."

After Sean turned and stormed off—probably to try to get the stain off his apron, which Gabriel could tell him was going to be a total waste of time—Tony turned to him. "What the fuck were you thinking?" he asked. "He's not . . . he's not a bad guy, Gabe."

"Are you really going to vouch for *that* guy?" Gabriel asked, rolling his eyes. "Really?"

"I'm just saying he's not the enemy. Maybe you guys don't need to be enemies."

"That ship's already sailed," Gabriel said. "And you know it."

CHAPTER ONE

Sean Cooper couldn't quite believe that even though so much time had passed, he could still feel that goddamn meatball.

Before that moment, he'd been laboring under some kind of wild delusion that maybe he and the hot Italian guy could be friends. He'd needed friends in LA—he'd been brand fucking new to the area, and lonely, and looking for friends. But from the very beginning, it was clear that Gabe hadn't been looking to be friends.

The tweets that Gabriel had sent that day had been the beginning of the end. But the *end* end of it? Definitely the meatball missile.

Technically, it hadn't hurt. It'd stained his apron, of course, and he'd never been able to completely get the red shadow out of the stark white cotton. But sometimes, when Sean came face to face with Gabe, like right now, when they sat across from each other at a table in their favorite bar, the Funky Cup, there were moments when he swore he could still feel it hitting him.

Time might have passed, and maybe he'd never changed his truck's name, but neither had Gabriel, despite many threats to the contrary. Even though they'd kind of uncomfortably settled into the same friend circle, and the same food truck lot, they were always more apt to argue about something than agree on it. And that, Sean thought, sometimes felt more like habit than anything else.

Gabe argued because he liked to. And Sean argued back because by this point, it was sheer reflex.

Maybe he could've stopped it. Milo would've told him long ago that it was a waste of his time. But then, Milo wasn't around. Hadn't been around for awhile now, and Sean had occasionally, especially in the last six months, found himself not really caring that Milo might not have liked what he was doing.

He'd long since stopped blaming Milo for leaving him.

The spot in his heart, the one that always belonged to his husband, still stung every once in awhile when he prodded it especially hard. But mostly, he was a little embarrassed to admit that, with a lot of goddamn therapy, he'd mostly gotten over Milo's death.

Milo would always be a part of him, but he wasn't around to be a part of Sean's life anymore. Sean had to make his own life, now.

And for better or worse, that life now included Gabriel Moretti.

"I can't believe that everyone's still intact," Tony muttered as he slid into the seat next to Sean. He pushed over a bottle of beer towards Sean, and another towards Gabe.

"Hey, there's been no meatball-on-man violence for some time now," Gabriel said. *Boasted.* Like it had been some feat of his self-control to not chuck any more meatballs in Sean's direction.

Sean rolled his eyes. "He didn't say anything stupid for . . . *well*, now we're back at zero, but before that, he was up to almost twenty-four hours."

Tony didn't laugh, and Tony almost always found their antics humorous. The miniscule but insidious part of Sean that had worried for the last two years that his steadfast refusal to change his truck's name would come back to haunt him began to get antsy.

He'd worried this might happen before they were both invited to the Food Truck Warriors lot down by the Coliseum football stadium. But that had gone through without a hitch. But now, there was some kind of look in Tony's eye that Sean hadn't seen since the very beginning.

Since Gabriel had chucked a meatball at him.

"I'm . . ." Tony cleared his throat. And couldn't look at either of them. "I really hoped that it would never come to this, but I think . . . well, *we* think, actually, that it would be better for overall guest experience, if we didn't have two trucks with the same name."

"We?" Gabriel echoed Sean's own thoughts, even the disbelief practically identical.

"Ryan and I, well, and Wyatt, too," Tony said.

"So they sent you to play nice with us," Gabriel bit off.

"I sent myself," Tony's voice was firm. "I thought it might be better coming from me, since I know we're all friends here. I want to help you guys succeed. Just the same as I know you want the lot to succeed."

Sean told himself to stay calm, even as he felt his heart begin to race. "Why now and not six months ago, when we all joined the collective?"

"It wasn't a problem then. We didn't think it'd be a problem. But . . ." Tony winced. "It kind of is, guys, and I know you're not blind to it. There's a lot of confusion, even though we've set you up on opposite sides. We went through your Yelp reviews, and there's a lot of cross-posting. Lots of customers *don't* understand that there are two On a Roll food trucks, and they don't realize they're both in LA, and they *definitely* don't get that they're both semi-permanently parked in the same lot."

Sean didn't know what to say to that. Tony *wasn't* wrong. But he also, more today than he had been two years ago, was absolutely determined not to give up his truck name to Gabriel.

Not just because it was Gabriel and he was kind of a smug asshole sometimes. But because Sean had made a promise to someone who deserved to have that promise honored.

"I'm not changing my name," Gabriel announced. And god, he *could* be a smug asshole. Sean didn't even feel a tiny pulse of guilt for thinking it.

"I'm here to talk about it with both of you," Tony said gently. "You *and* Sean. It's a decision you guys are going to have to discuss on your own. Maybe you'll both need to learn to bend a little."

"Bend a little?" Sean echoed. "How is that going to work? We can't each have the name six months out of the year."

"No," Tony said. Hesitated. "But surely there's something you two can work out."

"And what," Gabriel retorted, "you're here to be our referee?"

Tony threw up his hands. "Hey, if you guys hadn't proved on at least one occasion that you needed it, I'd be happy to walk away. *More* than happy, trust me."

"Yeah," Gabriel said. "I know Lucas is here, so trust me, as someone who has walked in on you two *more than once*, I understand you'd rather not be coaching us through it. And," he continued, his voice turning thoughtful, "maybe you shouldn't be."

"What?" Tony sounded surprised. Like he'd expected more of a fight from Gabriel than from Sean. And truthfully, Sean was just as shocked. Yeah, he'd been pretty stubborn about the name thing—but he had *reasons*. Gabriel was just being stubborn about it because he *could*.

"Yeah," Gabriel said. "Just . . ." He turned to Sean. "We can figure this shit out, right?"

Sean was not as easily convinced. "If this is just a ploy to get me one-on-one and away from Tony's pacifying influence, you have to know by now that it's not going to work."

"It's not. I swear . . . I just . . . it's fucking embarrassing, okay?" Gabriel admitted. "We can't even talk about this without Tony being afraid we're going to lose our shit. *Tony.*"

"You're the one who used *me* for target practice," Sean reminded him.

"Hey," Tony said a moment later. "I just got that."

"Yeah, we know you got your shit together," Gabriel said to Tony, "but maybe it's time you let us take care of ours."

"Well, I've been *trying*," Tony said. Then glanced over at Sean. "What about you? Are you really with him on this?"

Sean wasn't sure he believed Gabe either. Of course, after the meatball incident, they'd stopped arguing about the name. They'd argued about everything else, instead.

Had enough things changed in two years that they could find a solution to the problem that was satisfactory for both of them? Sean didn't really believe it, but otherwise what were they going to do? Flip a coin? One moment everything would be fine, and then the next, Sean would be forced to give something up that he had zero intention of *ever* giving up. It wasn't like the name of his truck was his last tie to his husband. It wasn't. But it felt like the most important one.

This was what Milo had wanted for him. This was something they'd both worked for, before Milo had passed. Sean wasn't going to let it go.

Maybe two years of discovering just how stubborn Sean was might be enough to convince Gabriel that it was time to give in. Not likely, but *possible*.

"I don't see any other way we can do this," Sean said.

"Okay," Tony said uncertainly. He was clearly not convinced either, but while he was also their friend, he was also technically the owner of the ground they parked their food trucks on—an arrangement that over the last six months had made everyone a lot of money and brought tons of success. Nobody wanted to leave. And while he'd not exactly *said* so, Sean had a feeling that this was a watershed moment. One of them needed to change their name, or one of them was out.

Tony had known Gabriel first. Gabriel was still really well-known in the community. Sean had made a lot of inroads in the last two years, but if Tony had to pick someone, Sean was pretty sure it wasn't going to be him.

He was better off negotiating with Gabriel, as awful as that idea was.

"Something needs to change by September first," Tony said. "That's the first home game at the Coliseum," he added, referring to the home football stadium of the University of Southern California—the lot was situated only a few blocks away from the stadium entrance, and they already knew on game days, they'd be overwhelmed.

"Alright," Sean said. "We'll figure something out." That gave them a little over a month to either make a decision—or kill each other. Whichever came first.

Tony stood. "Good luck," he said. "I'll be around if you decide you need a referee." And then he was gone, leaving the two of them alone.

Sean couldn't remember a time they'd ever been alone. Their friends had probably gone out of their way to make sure of that. Not sure if anything would still be left standing if it was just the two of them.

"Not for this," Gabriel said, and the underlying intensity—the *intimacy*—in his voice made Sean's hand freeze on his beer bottle.

He glanced up, and Gabriel was staring at him, those dark eyes reflecting his tone. More than once during the last two years, Sean had been reminded of his very first reaction to Gabriel.

Tall. Big. Broad. Beautiful.

It had been the first time since Milo that he'd seen a guy and felt that instantaneous moment of attraction. Then Gabriel had opened his mouth, and the moment was gone, but it *had* existed.

Sean often remembered it at the worst possible times. Like right now.

"So," Sean said, clearing his throat. Trying not to think of how dark the corner of the bar was, how the flickering candle on the table was reflected in Gabriel's eyes. How the light turned his face into a Renaissance masterpiece. "How are we going to do this?"

"All business," Gabriel teased, but the edge of his voice was almost . . . *sweet*. Like he thought Sean's attempt to be professional wasn't annoying, but cute.

Something that Sean never expected from Gabriel was sweetness.

"Did we have something else we needed to talk about that *isn't* business?" Sean wondered.

"No, but we have time. Over a month," Gabriel said, taking a sip of his beer. "What's the rush? Maybe we'll negotiate better if we get to know each other first."

"You mean that you want to charm me first so that you'll get the upper hand." He didn't really think that was true—Gabriel could be difficult and frustrating and slippery, but Sean wasn't sure that he'd do something so underhanded. He wasn't a *bad* guy. Sean had learned that much by watching his friendship with Tony and Lucas and Ash and Tate blossom.

Even their own relationship, while still combative, had lost the sharper edges in the last few months.

Gabriel shrugged. "The best negotiation is one where we both get what we want."

"I'm not sure how we can do that," Sean admitted. "We both want the same thing."

"Do we?"

Sean made a frustrated noise. "You know we do. We've wanted the same goddamn thing for the last two years, and you even threw a meatball at my chest to try to get me to cave. So don't start, okay? I'm not stupid. I know exactly what you're after."

"Do you?" Gabriel's mouth curved into something dangerous. Or maybe that was the unwanted attraction to him blooming inside Sean.

"You want to win," Sean said.

"Maybe we can figure out a way we can both win," Gabriel suggested.

"Based on what I *know* we want, I find that hard to believe," Sean said. Then hesitated. This was exactly why Tony hadn't wanted to leave them alone. Had wanted to play referee. He hadn't thought they could do this on their own. Maybe he was right. But then, they'd never actually *tried* either.

Gabriel drained the rest of his beer and set it on the table with a decisive click. "I need more alcohol for this," he muttered, standing up. "You want something?"

Buying rounds was a routine thing that their friend group did when they came to the Funky Cup. Sean was sure that Gabriel had bought him a drink before—but never *just* him. It didn't mean anything, he told himself firmly, but his heartbeat accelerated anyway. "Anything you're having is fine," Sean said, anticipating that Gabriel would come back with another pair of beers.

Gabriel nodded, and walked off towards the bar, where their friend Jackson was tending bar as he did most nights. Sean decided he would take advantage of the momentary reprieve to try to get his—well, it was his dick, wasn't it?—under control. Maybe Gabriel was undeniably attractive. Maybe Sean hadn't had sex in four years. Maybe their combative interactions often had an almost flirtatious edge. But none of that meant anything. It certainly wasn't going to mean that he was going to pant after Gabriel like a thirsty puppy dog.

He was better than that.

He was sure of it.

Then Gabriel returned, and slid a squat glass filled with amber liquid across the table.

"What's this?" Sean asked, shooting the glass a suspicious glance.

"Manhattan. Jackson's special recipe," Gabriel said. "I figured we could use something stronger than beer."

"Trying to get me drunk?" Sean wondered, even if he knew that wasn't true. Gabriel wouldn't want to cheat to win; he'd want to win free and clear.

"Just thinkin' that maybe we might do better if we were both a little more . . . relaxed?" Gabriel said, shooting Sean a lopsided, almost bashful smile. "Sometimes our edges are a little . . . sharp?"

"My edges are sharp?"

Gabriel leaned forward, and Sean swallowed hard, suddenly, painfully aware of how close he was. How little Sean would have to move to press their lips together. "Don't even pretend you don't know. You like cutting me, I can see it in your eyes. They really shine when you land a particularly good blow."

"Oh." Sean didn't know what to say to that. It was *true*. He was sometimes a little bit too proud when he came up with a particularly excellent retort.

Gabriel settled back in his chair, cradling his glass in those big, capable hands. Sean had watched them, way too many times, rolling meatballs, stirring sauce, serving the best Italian food that he'd ever been privileged to try. Not that he would *ever* tell Gabriel that. The man was already egotistical enough. But Ren would sometimes sneak Sean something when he was having a bad day, and Gabriel's delicious food never failed to make him smile.

"You should try your drink," Gabriel said, taking a sip of his own. "I think you'll like it."

"You think I will?" Sean wondered. "Or Jackson thinks I will?" He lifted the glass to his lips, and felt the smell of strong spirits hit him. He didn't usually drink hard liquor; normally, he preferred a light beer, or a nice glass of wine at home when he was unwinding from a hard day. But it smelled good, actually, underneath that first hit of booze. Dark and complex, with a hint of cherry.

It was smoother on his tongue than he'd anticipated, and not just the cherry, but hints of orange as well. "That's . . ." Sean cleared his throat. "That's good. Strong, but good."

"Told you so." Gabriel's grin widened. "They're actually Ren's favorite. He introduced me."

Sean glanced around, searching for Gabriel's cousin, as well as a topic of discussion that wasn't an insult or the actual matter at hand. "Is he here tonight?" It was a rare weekend evening that didn't find Ren here, holding court by the fire pits.

Sean really liked Ren; was kind of in awe of the man's natural confidence with potential hookups.

Gabriel shook his head. "No," he said. "He had a date tonight."

"Which means," Sean deduced, because he was familiar enough with Ren's habits by now, "that you'll want to postpone your return home as long as possible."

"Yep," Gabriel said wryly. "You know it."

"How long has he been working for you?" Sean was still searching around for the right topic to keep them away from *the* topic. Ren was as good a one as any. He knew Gabriel's cousin had been with him since almost the very beginning of his food truck, but he'd make Gabriel tell him anyway.

"From the first day," Gabriel said ruefully. "The guy works hard, despite all his many failings."

"I like Ren," Sean said staunchly, knowing that Gabriel did too. He just liked to pretend that Ren was a pain in his ass.

"I keep him around to make the truck look good," Gabriel admitted. "I feel like half my customers show up hoping to hook up with him, and the other half are there to try to do it again."

Sean was surprised at the rueful tone Gabriel used. Did he think … *no*. There was no way that Gabriel thought he wasn't attractive. He was just as attractive as Ren—*more*, even. He was just a little growly and difficult, and spent far less time attempting to charm the masses.

"You make the truck look plenty good," Sean said, before he could stop himself. Why did he care if Gabriel didn't think he was as hot as his cousin? It wasn't any of his business. Gabriel wasn't his boyfriend or his crush. He was barely his friend. He shouldn't care. But he did.

Gabriel stared at him. "Really?"

Sean was flustered, even though he didn't want to be. Why hadn't he just kept his mouth shut? He took another drink and felt the booze burn all the way down his throat.

"You know you're hot, okay," Sean said.

"I do?" Gabriel raised an eyebrow.

"Uh yeah, you're just as attractive as Ren. Maybe more, I don't know. I don't spend much time thinking about it." *Liar.*

Gabriel's smile was slow and sweet, and unbelievably, blisteringly sexy.

"I'm not sure I believe that," he said.

"You can believe whatever you want," Sean retorted.

"I can't believe I didn't know this about you."

"If you're thinking . . ." Sean didn't know how to finish that sentence. What he should do was change the subject. Back to something safe. Like which of them was willing to change the name of their truck.

But he didn't, because Gabriel Moretti had always fascinated him, and now he was caught.

"What would I be thinking?" Gabriel asked.

"I don't know," Sean said, and then made the worst mistake of all. He drained his drink. Felt the alcohol wash over him in an overwhelming wave.

Why had he done that? Was he hoping that if he was drunk, this would be easier?

Truthfully, everything did seem a lot clearer right now. He could see the last two years without any of the blinders that he'd clung to so hopelessly. He'd been attracted, on a deep, visceral level, to Gabriel from the very beginning. That had never really changed. He hadn't been sure if it was mutual, but from the way

Gabriel was looking at him now, it seemed impossible that they weren't on the exact same page.

He could do anything . . . *anything*.

"I'm thinking that this wasn't exactly what I had in mind," Gabriel said, "but that I don't mind it."

Sean held on to his sanity, barely. "What *did* you have in mind?"

"Well, first thing was, I hoped that you'd relax enough to finally tell me why you named your truck On a Roll," Gabriel said.

It was a reasonable assumption. There was no denying that. But it was a metaphorical bucket of ice-cold water, dumped over Sean's head. It didn't quite extinguish the warm fire in the base of his stomach that the alcohol—and *Gabriel*—had started. But it was enough to remind him that he'd never intended to waver from one unalienable truth: he was never going to give in and give up the name.

Sean stood, abruptly, the chair legs screeching across the old wooden floor of the bar. "I think . . . I think I should get home," he said. "We can talk about this later." Though he really didn't want to leave. What had he been thinking, letting Gabe get him tipsy and pliable? Letting him flirt? Flirting back? It was insane, and it needed to stop now.

"Wait," Gabriel said.

Sean turned away, the desperation on his face showed.

He didn't want Gabriel to see it, and he really didn't want to *feel* it.

Sean was across the room and through the door before he could be tempted to stay. The cool air hitting his skin helped to bring him back to reality—but not enough. Especially not when Gabriel was right behind him.

He heard the door to the bar slam behind him, and came to a halt as he sensed Gabriel's big, warm body right behind his.

Taking a deep breath, Sean wished that his head was clearer. The realization that something had *almost* happened helped. The fresh air helped.

But he still wanted it. He wanted it way too much.

He couldn't remember the last time he had wanted just for the sake of wanting. Sex just because he was horny, and there seemed to be only one person who could scratch his itch.

With Milo, there had always been affection and care and so quickly after that, *love*. And while there had been a handful of others before Milo, Sean had never felt this hard and fast pull.

He didn't know how to deal with it, and he definitely didn't know how to deal with the fact that the person he wanted so badly was *Gabriel Moretti*.

Sean wasn't stupid enough to think his sudden lust for Gabriel was a betrayal of Milo. Milo was gone and sex was sex; sometimes you couldn't help who you wanted it with. But Sean was embarrassed for *himself*.

He'd always believed, during the worst of his pain and heartbreak, that he'd at least had his dignity.

Gabriel made him want to give it all up.

"Hey." Gabe's voice was low and concerned. But still, underneath his obvious worry that he'd scared Sean off, he could hear the edge of lust.

Why hadn't he kept his stupid mouth *shut*? If he had, Gabriel might never have known that his feelings were so complicated. *He* might not have known just how complicated they were.

Sean squeezed his eyes shut. Wished he could block out Gabriel's voice, too.

"Hey," Gabriel repeated, and this time, Sean felt a hesitant touch of one of his big hands. Not on the relative safety of his shoulder. But on the plane of his back. The warmth of his hand seeped through the cotton of his t-shirt and Sean thought wildly that he wanted to know if Gabe was that hot everywhere.

If he turned around, he was going to do something that he regretted. That much, he knew.

He turned around anyway.

CHAPTER TWO

Something was happening.

Inside of him.

Between him and Sean.

Definitely something inside Sean.

Gabriel had never known Sean to run before. He'd always stayed strong, so goddamn strong. Like he had a backbone made of freaking steel. But now, he wasn't sure if the steel was bending, or it had never been as strong as Gabriel had originally believed.

Then, Sean turned around, and Gabriel realized as he saw the heat in his eyes, normally so clear, but tonight, a cloudy, hazy blue, that he wasn't bending. He was *melting*.

And he was melting right into Gabe.

"I left because this is a bad idea," Sean said, and there was a little of that inner strength that Gabe found so amazingly annoying—and so amazingly sexy. Somehow, at the exact same time.

"Yeah," Gabriel agreed. "It's a wrinkle." He'd only touched Sean briefly before, when he'd been standing there, back to him, and breathing hard, like he'd just run a marathon. Or maybe, Gabe realized, it wasn't a marathon at all, but a battle with himself. But he touched him again now, in the same place, hand resting gently over the same spot on Sean's back, and this time he didn't move.

Sean glanced up at him, licking his lips. "Discovering you've run out of lettuce in the middle of a busy day, that's a wrinkle. This is . . . a catastrophe."

That stung a little, deep down. It wasn't like Gabriel liked this situation any more than he did, but being wanted despite someone's best efforts to feel otherwise? Not as fun as he'd always imagined.

But Sean laid a hand on his side anyway, right where his t-shirt met the waist of his jeans, and those nimble fingers grazed a sliver of his skin and Gabe inhaled, sharply. He never had a chance to exhale, because Sean's mouth was on his, and they were kissing, and it was every bit the catastrophe that Sean had predicted.

It was wet and messy and absolutely fucking fantastic.

Sean's fingers slid up along his spine and curled around the base of his neck, tugging him down, deepening the kiss, tongues tangling together as they stumbled backwards.

Gabriel felt the rough bricks against his back as Sean pushed him against the wall of the bar, his thigh brushing against his hardening cock. Rubbing against it shamelessly, like they weren't on a public sidewalk, devouring each other like the rest of the world didn't exist.

And, Gabe thought dreamily, as his hands pulled Sean even closer against him, until he could feel all of that lean, strong body pressed against his, maybe it didn't. All he could feel right now was

Sean. He'd wanted him, just like this, for so long now. Despite all his annoyance that first day, he'd wanted to do exactly this, even then.

It was just as good as he'd always imagined it would be.

Actually, it was *better*.

But then, before he could start to think of what he could do next, without maybe getting arrested for public indecency, it was over.

Sean was pulling away, his mouth missing from Gabriel's, and then slowly, he dragged his body away too. Until they were standing with too many inches between them and an increasingly distressed look on Sean's face.

He opened his mouth, and instantly Gabe wanted him to close it, because he was going to say something he didn't want to hear.

But Gabriel had always considered himself a very stupid man, so he let Sean say whatever it was that was apparently more important than kissing.

"We . . . we shouldn't have done that," Sean said, then licked his lips, like he could still taste Gabriel on them. Like he couldn't quite get enough.

Gabriel already knew that he couldn't get enough. Even if he had Sean naked in his bed, it wouldn't be enough. He hadn't even gotten him there yet, and he still knew that he'd always be wanting more.

He forced himself to focus. To try to handle this right so that he wouldn't scare Sean away. So Sean wouldn't scare *himself* away.

Rolling his eyes, Gabe shoved his hands into his pockets. Mostly so he didn't try to touch him again. "Could you be any more cliche?" he asked.

"What?" Sean looked shocked.

"I mean, that is such a cliche, right?" Gabriel said. "You sure didn't seem to think it was a mistake when it was happening."

Sean licked his lips again. "Well, that was because . . ."

"Because you really liked it? Believe me, I know. I was there."

"No," Sean said. Then hesitated. Like he hadn't really meant to say that. "Actually . . ."

"Yeah, I know," Gabriel said. "You enjoyed it."

"But it's such a bad idea. What are we going to do about the truck name? We can't just tell Tony, *sorry, we got so busy fucking that we never decided who should give up the name.*"

Gabriel was momentarily very distracted by the idea of them being so busy fucking that they couldn't even do anything else. Even the premise felt solid; like if they finally got their hands on each other, that was absolutely something that could happen.

In some faraway future, if Sean lets it happen, Gabe thought ruefully.

"I don't see how they have anything to do with each other," Gabriel said.

Sean eyed him skeptically. "Seriously?"

"They aren't related," Gabriel insisted, though even he wasn't stupid enough to believe it. And Sean? *Definitely* not that stupid.

"I think they'd be hard to separate," Sean said slowly.

"Do you want to have sex with me?" Gabriel asked, even though he knew better. His fragile ego might not be able to handle Sean's answer. But then, if he was being truthful, how could it be anything else but the truth? But *yes*? He'd felt Sean's cock, a hard line against his thigh, only a few minutes earlier.

But then, there was always the possibility that Sean would lie. To Gabriel. Or to himself.

"I . . ." Sean hesitated. "I do," he finally finished. Gave Gabriel a timid glance, like he was afraid that once he'd admitted it, Gabe would press *him* against the wall and continue to ravish him.

It was a good idea. Gabriel wanted to do it more than he wanted to take his next breath. But he knew if he pushed now, *well*, it would never happen. If he was going to get Sean naked underneath him, it was going to have to be Sean's choice.

He was a stubborn, infuriating man, and Gabriel had discovered that as difficult as that made everything, it was also kind of a turn-on.

"And do you want me to have the truck name?" Gabriel asked archly.

Sean didn't even hesitate this time. "No," he said emphatically. "Absolutely fucking not."

"Then, there you go," Gabriel said with a wave of his hand. "They're not related."

"What are you saying, that we can argue about the truck name during the day and fuck in the evenings?" Sean's forehead creased in confusion. Like he wasn't quite sure he could compartmentalize that way.

Frankly, Gabriel wasn't sure he could either. But trying was better than not ever getting a chance to feel Sean the way he wanted to so desperately.

He'd thought he'd wanted him before all this, but now that he'd gotten a taste? He thought he'd go mad with it.

Gabriel nodded. "Exactly."

"Or," Sean said after a long, fraught pause, "we could try something else." He took a step closer, crowding Gabriel against the brick wall again.

"Try what?" Gabriel's voice came out in an awkward squawk as Sean's hands rested on his shoulders, creeping up towards his neck, tucking behind and tangling in his hair.

"This," Sean said, and laid another hot-as-fuck kiss on him. The kind of kiss that would keep him up late tonight, his hand fisted around his cock, as he imagined every dirty, filthy thing he wanted to do to this man.

Sean's tongue was agile and quick and also slow as molasses, sliding over Gabriel's leisurely, like he owned it. Owned *him*.

And goddamn it, Gabriel liked that even more.

One of Sean's hands trailed down his chest, towards where his cock throbbed in time with his heartbeat, trapped behind the zipper of his jeans. Ten more seconds, and Sean would know just how hard he was.

But then, Gabriel realized with a start, he already knew.

Sean's mouth left his two seconds before his hand reached just where they both wanted it to be, and then, like some kind of black magic, his hand was gone too, and Gabriel was left wound up, nearly panting, with nowhere to go.

"I could do that," Sean said.

"You think you could convince me with really, really good sex that I should change the name of my truck?" Gabriel heard how high and wrecked his voice was. "You think you could *seduce* me?" Oh, he could. So easily. They both knew it.

But that knife cut both ways, and Sean's own eyes were glassy and unfocused. As he'd been winding Gabriel up, he'd hardly been unaffected himself.

"I think I could," Sean said. "I think I'm already doing it."

He was, goddamn it.

"Even if you *could*," Gabriel said, "you're not that kind of guy. You wouldn't be able to live with yourself afterwards."

Sean shrugged.

"It won't matter," Gabriel vowed, though he wasn't quite as sure as he sounded. "I'm not going to be led around by my dick."

"Me either," Sean said, his voice hardening, the steel edge back in his tone. He took a step back and then another, and Gabriel resisted the urge to drag him back. To prove to both of them that they could keep it separate. But maybe Sean was right. Maybe it was impossible.

But then maybe *he* was right too, and they were inevitable.

"I guess we're settled, then," Gabriel said. "It's back to fighting, and not the fun, sexy, mock kind of fighting where I try to rub your dick every five seconds."

Sean's lips compressed into a tight line. "Like I'd actually enjoy that."

"I actually think you might," Gabriel said thoughtfully.

"You don't know me," Sean said. "Just because you've had your tongue down my throat doesn't mean that you *know* me."

"Right, of course not." Gabriel rolled his eyes. He extended his hand, waving it towards the empty sidewalk. "Well, I apologize. I interrupted your carefully choreographed huffy exit. By all means, continue."

Sean shot him one last scorching glare—Gabriel felt it down to his *toes*—and then finished storming off, like they'd never been interrupted by the hottest goddamn kiss he'd ever had in his whole life.

Gabriel wished he could leave it behind so easily, but he already knew he couldn't.

Sean told himself that the next time he saw Gabriel, everything would be exactly the same as always.

The flirting that had happened inside the bar and the kissing that happened outside of it had been a random aberration brought on by his longtime celibacy and too much alcohol.

The next time he saw Gabriel, he would be just as annoyed as he usually was. Then Gabe would say something rude and infuriating, and Sean would hate him like he always had.

The good and bad news was that now that they'd both joined the lot, they saw each other nearly every day. There would be no reprieve for Sean to mentally re-stuff Gabriel back into the same box he'd been in from the beginning. Hopefully, Sean thought as he locked up his bicycle behind his truck and walked up to the back door, pulling his keys out of his pocket, Gabriel would make it easy on him by saying something particularly rude today.

That'd make it . . . not exactly easy . . . but, Sean decided, *easier*.

He unlocked the back door and walked up the single step to the interior of his truck. It was small, but it was cozy, and two years in, he still loved working here as much as he had the very first day.

This was everything he and Milo had wanted to build together; the dream just looked a little different after his death, but it was still the same dream. *With the same name,* Sean thought with pride as he pulled his favorite apron off the hook in the corner.

Buried beneath it was one other—was the very first apron he'd worn in this truck. The one that was permanently stained with a big red circle, thanks to Gabriel.

Sean fingered its starched cotton fabric, and nearly put it on instead. Maybe he couldn't wear armor, but he could protect himself with the knowledge that Gabriel *was not a good guy.*

Maybe remind Gabriel too, while he was at it.

But his perfectionism wouldn't allow him to wear something so obviously stained for customers, so he left it behind, pulling on the pristine white one instead.

He'd just begun his prep for the day, when he heard an all-too-familiar voice.

The day was already warm, so he'd opened up the big window that ran the length of the truck, and flipped the little mini fan on, hoping for some circulation. Which meant he couldn't help but hear everything Gabriel said.

He was talking to Tony. Loudly. Of course, this was Gabriel, did he ever talk at a lower volume? *He did last night,* Sean's uncooperative brain supplied. *He was practically whispering sweet nothings in your ear.*

"So, did you guys work it out?" Tony asked.

Gabriel looked right over, and his gaze caught Sean's. He stared at him for a long moment, and then looked away. Aware now, though he probably had been before, that Sean was listening to every word he was saying.

"Not quite yet," Gabriel said. "But I'm working on it."

"*You're* working on it?" Tony wondered. "What about Sean?"

Sean was rewarded a thousandfold for his eavesdropping when Gabriel's face flushed bright red. "Oh, I mean, of course he is too," he said, nearly stuttering. "He's definitely . . . involved."

Tony looked confused. "Okay, then," he said. "Remember what I said."

"I know, we're going to figure this out," Gabriel said, sounding like he was chock-full of confidence.

"Good." Tony clapped him on the back, and Sean knew both of them well enough to know that Gabriel didn't really think they could, and Tony hadn't believed a word he'd just said.

Ugh.

Why had he let his cock get so carried away last night?

It had made something that was already difficult even tougher.

And that's on you, Sean's conscience reprimanded him. *You did that.*

Technically it had been Gabriel that had incited him, but Sean had been the one to kiss him. *Twice.*

If Sean could kick himself, he absolutely fucking would.

"So, you're lying to Tony now, huh?" Sean asked, before he could stop himself. Stopping himself—something that apparently he couldn't quite do anymore.

Gabriel glanced up at him through the open window. He took a few steps closer, and shrugged. "I told him what he wanted to hear. He didn't want to hear that we kissed."

His voice stuttered slightly over the last word of his sentence, and Sean felt the echo of it in his stomach. They'd *kissed*. And no matter what he might claim, he did want to do it again. He wanted to do it again, and he wanted even more.

"Actually, he might," Sean said lightly, stepping out of the back of the truck and walking around to the front, until he was face to face with Gabe. "Those guys are practically a gossip factory."

"Exactly," Gabriel retorted. "That's *our* business. Nobody else's."

And Sean realized, at the worst possible moment, that Gabriel wasn't being just protective of himself, he was being protective of . . . *him?*

The knowledge knocked the wind right out of him.

It was difficult to convince himself that Gabriel was a bad man, when he didn't *act* like a bad man.

"I agree," Sean said, and hesitated. There was an apology tugging at him, deep down, annoying and persistent. But he didn't say it out loud, because he didn't even know what he was sorry for. For claiming that he'd seduce Gabriel into changing his mind? For walking away so abruptly, *twice*? For wishing that Gabriel had followed him the second time?

None of those were apologies that would end well, so Sean did the only thing he could—he kept his mouth shut.

"I guess we still have to figure our shit out," Gabriel said.

An understatement of the century.

"Well, you just told Tony that we would and . . ." Sean trailed off. He'd been arguing for two years that nothing needed to change. He and Gabriel could always share the name, right? Never mind that they'd never done it particularly well. But it wasn't really affecting either of them. Sales were good. Even when Tony had come to them last night, Sean had mostly thought it was bullshit.

But then after he'd walked home from the Funky Cup, angry and worked up in ways that he didn't want to examine too closely, he hadn't been able to fall sleep right away.

Finally, in desperation, he'd pulled out his phone and went to his truck's Yelp page, which he tended to avoid, and then visited Gabriel's as well. And just like Tony said, there was an under-current of frustration. A few reviews claiming confusion. More reviews posted on the wrong truck's page.

He'd lain in bed and for the first time acknowledged that maybe it really *was* time.

Not for *him* to change the name, of course, but for them to figure something out.

"And?" Gabriel asked archly.

"And it's time," Sean said. "Don't ever tell him I said it, but Tony is right."

Gabriel shrugged. "We could always keep going like this."

"No," Sean said. "We need to do something." It cost him some-thing, to admit that. To reveal he'd not only been wrong, but that he'd been deliberately ignoring that wrongness for a really long time.

"Okay," Gabriel said, but didn't say anything else.

"Don't you have any brilliant ideas?"

"Oh, I'm brilliant now?"

Sean rolled his eyes. "You weren't brilliant last night, that's for sure."

"Yet," Gabriel pointed out, "you still kissed me. *Twice.*"

He had. And goddamn it, he wanted to do it again.

Sean cut that thought off hard and fast. This negotiation didn't need to be tainted by thoughts of everything he wanted and shouldn't ever indulge in.

"That's . . ." Sean cleared his throat. "That's not what we're talking about right now. You said it yourself, they're not related. And they need to stay unrelated."

"Fine," Gabriel said. "Why don't we start with your reason why you won't change your name?"

"What?" Sean supposed he should have seen it coming. But he hadn't, and the question hit him right in the solar plexus, stealing his breath.

Why had he ever thought that Gabriel would fight fair?

"You have a reason. I'm just a stubborn asshole," Gabriel said with a wry smirk, "but you? You've got a reason you're clinging to."

The last of Milo, Sean thought, even though that wasn't even remotely true. He had lots of pieces of Milo; he'd carry one of them in his heart, forever, no matter what his food truck was called. But old habits died hard.

"It's none of your business," Sean said. Even though he knew that was a lie. It kind of *was* Gabriel's business. Not only because

Milo was the reason that Sean wouldn't address for refusing to budge, but also because, before last night, Milo had been the last person Sean had kissed.

"That's not true, and you know it," Gabriel said. "I can even see it on your face. You don't even believe yourself."

Sean had never wanted to be *that guy with a dead husband,* so when he'd moved to LA, to start fresh, and to start On a Roll, he'd deliberately never mentioned it to any of the guys who had become his friends. Milo was *his,* private and inviolate, and he had no intention of sharing now, or ever.

"It doesn't matter what I believe," Sean said stubbornly. "All that matters is that it's none of your fucking business why I won't change the name, just that I won't. Not now. Not ever."

"But you think Tony is right," Gabriel stated with disbelief.

"Well, I would think the conclusion you could draw from that is pretty obvious," Sean said. Knowing he was being prickly, and not really caring. He wished that he'd put the stained apron on this morning, if only because he *knew* Gabriel felt guilty about it, and reminding him of what he'd done might have given him an advantage.

"I don't see why I'm the one who needs to give in," Gabriel said.

"Because I have a reason and you're just, as you so charmingly put it, a *stubborn asshole.*"

"Why are you allowed to keep secrets and I'm required to just give in because of a personality flaw?"

"It's the secrets that really bother you, isn't it?" Sean challenged.

"Well, *yeah*," Gabriel said. "I had your tongue down my throat last night. I think I deserve a little fucking consideration."

"Except you said that had *nothing* to do with changing the name on your truck," Sean argued. "You even went out of your way to prove it, if I remember correctly."

Gabriel glared at him, and this felt . . . well, not *better*, but at least more normal. Like always, like they hadn't figured out last night that the heat between them was actually sexual.

It's not, Sean told himself, *you still really don't* like *him. He threw a freaking meatball at you.*

"So that's it, then, I just have to change my name, no cooperation and no compromise from you? Just because you say so?"

Sean wasn't normally an unreasonable person, but after being shoved between a rock and a hard place by his own stubbornness, what else was he supposed to say? *No, I'm sorry, this is about something you'll never understand. A love that transcends time and space and life and death.*

He didn't usually make a habit of saying nothing, but he kept his mouth shut again, and that made for the second time today.

"Yes," Sean said.

Gabriel threw up his hands. "You are fucking unreasonable, you know? I'm trying here, and you're just trying to tie me up in knots."

He felt a pulse of guilt, but pushed it away. "There's an easy way to untie yourself," Sean said. "Give in."

Gabriel actually *glowered* at him. "No way. Not like this. Not just because you want me to."

"See, this is actually how I thought last night's 'discussion' would go," Sean said. He glanced down at his watch. "I'm sorry, I've actually got important stuff to do. More important than having a pointless argument with you, anyway."

Gabriel opened his mouth, and then snapped it shut again. "Fine. *Fine.* But just so you know, I'm definitely not the only stubborn asshole here."

As Sean watched him march off, temper rolling off him in nearly visible waves, Sean found that he couldn't disagree. He was being both ridiculously stubborn and kind of an asshole.

He *should* go apologize. There was a part of him that knew he should. He should sit Gabriel down, even though the lunch crowd would show up in less than an hour, and explain all about Milo and the plans they'd made when they were still so young and naive and starry-eyed.

He *should*. But he didn't.

Instead, he went back to his truck, and instead of starting the veggie prep like he needed to, he went straight to where the aprons were hung up, and grabbed the one with the stain, the one that Gabriel had branded, two years before.

Sean could still feel the weight of that stupid meatball, smacking him right in the chest. And maybe it didn't excuse every shitty thing he'd done and said to Gabriel in the past, but it sure made it easier to ignore them.

CHAPTER THREE

GABRIEL HADN'T KNOWN THIS when they'd first met, two years ago, but Sean was undeniably one of the most particular, meticulous people he'd ever known. His truck, now over two years old, was practically as shiny and perfect as it had been the day he'd opened.

So when he spotted Sean, approaching the group of them gathering near the central circle of picnic tables, wearing an apron with a telltale red blotch across the chest, Gabriel knew something was up.

"You have an accident today?" Lucas asked Sean, as he lounged between his boyfriend's legs. Tony was halfheartedly sifting Lucas' hair between his fingers, and Gabriel felt that all-too-familiar sting of jealousy. Tony and Lucas were so casually, so flawlessly yet imperfectly happy. They didn't always see eye to eye, but that didn't matter, because they always had each other's backs.

And the love? You'd have to be blind to miss it.

What did Gabriel have?

A frenemy who refused to confess his secrets, wouldn't tell him the truth, and now had pulled out evidence of his worst behavior and was displaying it for all their friends to see.

It hurt, even though by now Gabriel should have been used to it.

"This?" Sean asked, pointing to the telltale stain on the center of his white apron. "Oh, this is old. Just an old stain."

"An old stain from where Gabe beaned him with a meatball," Tony said with a chuckle.

"Ah," Lucas said, shooting Gabriel a sympathetic look. "Makes sense."

If he left now, went back to the truck and grabbed his stuff and went home, everyone would know that he was bothered by Sean wearing it.

Sean would know that he was bothered.

"Really?" The voice was low and incredulous.

Gabriel glanced back and saw Ren approaching, holding two bottles of beer by their long necks. He passed one to Gabe. "What?" Gabriel said, gulping his beer. It didn't really help. Last night had proved that booze was not the solution to the problems he had with Sean—but at least he'd take *those* solutions over these.

"He's really going to pull that out now?" Ren shook his head. "He kind of sucks, doesn't he?"

Gabriel sighed. "If only that was actually the case."

Ren's gaze turned calculating. "Oh, so you finally acknowledged that you *want* him to suck?"

"You're the worst," Gabriel said.

"Unfair, considering we've already established who actually *is* the worst," Ren said lightly. He tipped his beer bottle in Sean's direction. He'd gotten drawn into a conversation with Lucas and Tony and was thankfully ignoring Gabe.

Gabriel wasn't under any stupid assumption that would continue, but for right now, he'd take it.

"I just wish . . . I wish he'd tell me *why*," Gabriel said under his breath.

Ren shrugged. "If he hasn't by now, he probably won't. You should just change the name and get it over with. He's never going to give that up."

"How do you know?" Gabriel had always believed that over time he could wear Sean down. That belief had wavered over the last few days, but he still wanted to think it was true.

"That boy is holding on to something more important than just ornery stubbornness," Ren said. "You know it, too, and that's what drives you crazy. That he won't tell you." Ren took a drink of his beer. "Just change it. I know you have the name. I know you have the stuff all ready to go."

"Is anything a secret from you?" Gabriel complained.

"Not really," Ren admitted. "You know you're going to do it, eventually. It'd be easier to just change it now, before you take each other and this whole lot out in a war of attrition over who's going to give in first."

"I . . . I can't, okay," Gabriel said. "I just can't."

Ren's gaze turned pitying. "Oh, boy, you do have it bad."

He'd probably had it bad before, but last night? That had been the last nail in his coffin.

"I guess," Gabriel said.

"Hey," Tony said, raising his voice, pulling their—and Ren's attention, thank *God*—away from their conversation. "Anyone see that new guy who's been hanging around the last few months?"

"Dark hair? Intense gaze? Jumpy? Looks like he's used to carrying?" Ren spoke up. Gabriel wasn't surprised. Ren knew most of the regulars, if not by name, then by sight.

It also felt like he'd slept with most of them. The single ones, anyway.

"Yeah," Lucas said. "I tried to strike up a conversation with him today, but he's . . ."

"Jumpy," Ren repeated. "Yeah, I know. I actually asked him out . . ."

Gabriel groaned. "Of course you did."

Ren shot him a glare. "He's hot, in case you didn't notice, or you were maybe too preoccupied with . . ."

"That's enough," Gabriel said, glaring back.

"Anyway, he turned me down," Ren said. "But he said his name was Lennox. Just Lennox."

"First or last?" Tony wondered.

"Does it matter?" Ren retorted.

"If you're gonna be screaming it, you might want to know," Gabriel said sulkily.

"I told you, he turned me down," Ren said.

"For *now*," Tate piped in, chuckling as he walked up with a bottle of his own in his hand. "We all know it's inevitable that you'll end up popping his food truck cherry."

Ren actually looked proud of this particular fact.

Gabriel didn't know whether he was disgusted or kind of pathetically envious.

At least Ren had never been stupid enough to turn his attention to Sean. They'd never talked about it, but Ren had flirted with everyone—from Ash to Shaw, the bartender at the Funky Cup, to Lucas, at least before he'd realized that Tony wasn't exactly the sharing type—but he'd never once even tried to get into Sean's pants.

Gabriel was afraid that if he asked, he knew exactly what his cousin would say. *He's yours, he's always been yours.*

If that was true though, then why did it feel so goddamn shitty? Why hadn't Sean ever told him even one of his many secrets?

It hurt. It had hurt for so long that Gabriel was almost used to the throb of it, by now.

"We'll see," Ren said. "But yeah, no idea if Lennox is first or last."

"First," Tony said at the same time his boyfriend said, "Last." They both burst into laughter.

Gabriel couldn't help himself. He looked over at Sean. And to his surprise, Sean was looking back. Like they'd both thought the same thing at the same time, *look, they disagree all the time and they still share the same bed at night.*

Gabriel might have asked again. Might have tried to make his case again. Except that apron was yelling at him, telling him Sean's answer before he'd even asked.

He turned away, draining the rest of his beer, not looking back at the warm circle of friendly laughter as he melted into the shadows.

Sean would have to be blind to not notice when Gabriel left.

Especially after that look they'd shared.

Gabriel, as annoying as he was, was painfully transparent sometimes.

It didn't help that Sean was pretty sure he'd had the same exact thought.

Look at Tony and Lucas. They argue all the time, and they love each other so goddamn much.

Sean *knew* that he and Gabriel were fundamentally different from their very loved-up friends, but that didn't matter. He couldn't help but wonder. Surely if it was just sex . . . that could work, right? He already knew that was all he wanted, because he'd been madly, completely, totally in love, and whatever he felt for Gabriel couldn't be more different.

"Hey." Sean glanced up, and Tate was standing there, a bottle of water in his hands, and a sympathetic smile on his face. "How're you hanging in there?"

Tate was a good friend, and someone who watched out for everyone in their group. But there was an added layer of concern in his expression tonight.

"Tony told you about the ultimatum," Sean stated rather than asked.

Tate nodded. "I don't want you to think he was gossiping or anything . . ."

But Sean already knew that his and Gabriel's bickering was a source of gossip. Which was why Gabriel hadn't wanted to share that they'd done a lot more than just argue last night; they didn't need to add more fuel to the fire.

"I know, I know he wouldn't," Sean said. Even though Tony definitely *would*. Still, it meant something that Tate cared—but then Sean realized that made sense. Dating one of the most famous football players in the world would make someone more aware of who was saying what and to whom.

They'd all agreed in an unspoken vow to keep Tate's shit—and as an extension, Chase's—locked down tight. Nobody was getting anything out of any of them, no matter how many times they showed up at the lot, looking for dirt about Tate and Chase's relationship.

But he and Gabriel were a whole different kettle of fish, and Sean knew it. First of all, they'd brought the notoriety on themselves, by arguing so frequently and with such vehemence. And, besides, they weren't a couple.

Tate shot Sean a crooked smile. "Yeah, of course not. Never. Gossip is totally not Tony's style."

Sean laughed. "Maybe a little bit Tony's style."

"I still wanted to make sure you were okay. I know that two years ago, you really didn't want to change your name, and I'm assuming that nothing's changed."

"Nothing's changed," Sean confirmed.

"So what are you guys going to do?" Tate wondered.

"Gabe's just gonna have to figure out how to live with the name change, I guess," Sean said.

Tate looked surprised. "You're just assuming he's going to give in?"

"I've still got my reasons, right?" Sean said. "They didn't just go away. Gabriel's just being an ass."

"Is he?"

"Well, *yeah*," Sean said. "It's Gabriel. Of course he's being an ass about it."

Maybe Tate's worried expression shouldn't have reminded Sean of how guilty he'd felt when Gabriel had left, but that guilt was now back in spades.

"I'm sure you've got great reasons," Tate said carefully, "but that doesn't mean that Gabe should just automatically do whatever you want him to. He's got rights here, too. Maybe you could figure out how to compromise?"

"Compromise?" The idea felt ludicrous. But then the idea of kissing Gabriel had been ludicrous before last night. "How would we even do that? We can't share the name, not any-more."

"I know." Tate patted him reassuringly on the shoulder. "But you guys are both super smart, and I know you'll figure something out. Something," he added with a pointed glance towards Gabriel's truck, "that you're both happy with."

Sean wanted to tell him that was impossible. There was going to be one winner and one loser here. Sean had always assumed that he'd be the former and Gabe would just have to come around to the new state of things.

But Tate's words exposed not just the guilt he'd been feeling, but the fundamental assumptions he'd been making, and how they made him sound.

It hit him like a hard smack to the side of the head: he was always complaining that Gabe was a stubborn asshole, but when he believed that Gabe would *have* to give in, did that make him any different?

Didn't it actually make him *worse*?

Tate patted him again. "You look like you just saw a ghost."

He had, in a way. Milo would not only have disapproved of how ridiculous Sean was being, he'd have been ashamed.

Could he and Gabriel compromise? The very thought seemed laughable, but how else could they get out of this and not hate each other in the end?

Because no matter how much they complained about each other, how vehemently Sean had bitched about Gabe and vice versa, he knew they'd never really hated each other.

But they would, if this kept going. If there was a winner and a loser.

"I think I need to go," Sean said slowly. He reached up and tugged the knot out of his apron. The stupid, petty-as-fuck stained apron that he'd put on because he'd wanted to put Gabriel in his place. Shame him into giving in.

If it had worked, Sean never would've been able to live with himself.

He pulled the apron, and without a second thought, chucked into the trash.

Tate chuckled under his breath. "It's about time," he said.

"Yeah," Sean said. "It really is."

Gabriel was just locking up his truck when Sean found him, barely illuminated by a circle of one of the motion sensor lights scattered around the edge of the property. So far, the lights had kept the thefts and vandalisms to a minimum, but he knew Tony was still worried.

"Hey," Sean said.

Gabriel glanced up, and then looked away. "What do you want?" he asked.

"I want to talk."

Gabriel shrugged. "We already tried that."

"No," Sean said bluntly. "We really didn't."

"I'm not sure I'm following," Gabriel said. "Is talking some kind of sexy metaphor that I'm not aware of?"

"No," Sean said. "You said you wanted to know why I didn't want to change the name. I guess if I'm asking you to change your name, you should at least know why."

Gabriel rolled his eyes. "I've only been begging you for *years*."

"I know." Sean hesitated, trying to tone down the defensiveness in his tone. "It's just that I don't talk about it . . . about *him* . . . much."

At all, actually. Ever.

And maybe that was kind of fucked up too, now that Sean thought about it.

"Him?" Gabriel looked shocked. "What . . . *no*," he said. "I think I need a drink for this." He turned abruptly and headed in the direction of the Funky Cup, which was only a few blocks over.

"Wait," Sean said, scrambling to reach him. Gabriel's legs were just so freaking long. "Wait, I still need to lock up . . ."

Gabriel turned. "So go lock up, then," he said. "I'll meet you there."

"Are you really sure we should drink around each other again after . . ." Sean took a deep breath. "After last night?"

"You stopped thinking about it?" Gabriel wondered.

"Last night?" Sean swallowed, hoping his voice wouldn't squeak when he said the word, but it did anyway. "The kiss?"

"Yeah," Gabriel said.

Sean stared at him for a moment. He was illuminated under one of those viciously bright lights. They washed everyone and everything under them out, but Gabriel was still, unbelievably, handsome. *It's because you're just so horny. You want him so goddamn bad, that's all.*

"No," he admitted. "No, I haven't stopped thinking about it."

"Me either," Gabriel said. "So I figure that whether we drink or not, it won't matter."

It was such a Gabriel thing to say. "It might happen again," Sean hedged.

"Yeah." Gabriel smiled wide. "I kinda hoped it might."

"Okay," Sean said. "But only after we . . . you know . . . *talk.* Actually talk."

"Sure thing," Gabe said. "See you in a few." He turned away and walked off, slowly retreating from the circle of light into the darkness.

Sean took a deep breath, and as he headed over to his own truck, hoped against all better judgment that he wasn't making a mistake.

If they did kiss again, if they did *more,* he was going to have to make sure he was clear. This was just sex. They were, what did they call it again? *Friends with benefits.* And it would have to absolutely stay separate from whatever discussions they had over the truck names.

He was going to have to make sure Gabriel understood exactly and precisely what he wasn't going to be giving: maybe his body, but never his heart.

When he got to the Funky Cup, he stopped by the bar, but before he could order, Jackson glanced over at him. "Oh, Sean, it's you," he said. "Gabe said he'd meet you outside and that he already grabbed some drinks."

Sean was a little afraid that Gabriel had gotten him another manhattan. It might be easier to tell him about Milo if he had one of those in his hand, but tonight, he knew he wanted his edges sharp. When he walked outside, he saw that Gabriel had claimed a bench next to the smaller fire pit. It was a Wednesday, and a slower night at the bar, so other than a small trio laughing over by the other, much larger fire pit, they were alone.

"Hey," Gabriel said as he sat down. "I got you a beer."

Sean accepted it gratefully. As much as they'd argued over the last two years, they still knew each other pretty well. And maybe Gabriel had been paying better attention than he'd given him credit for.

"Thanks," Sean said. Noticed that Gabriel had another manhattan in his hand. He raised an eyebrow. "Need something stronger for yourself?"

Gabriel shrugged. "You gonna be telling me about a *he*, so yeah, probably."

"He was a lot more than just a *he*," Sean said, fingers tightening on the bottle. "He was my husband."

The shock written on Gabriel's features was obvious; he'd clearly had no idea. "He was your . . . *wait*, he . . . *was* your husband?" he asked.

"Yeah." Sean nodded. "His name was Milo and he died four and a half years ago, now."

"Oh god, I am so sorry," Gabriel said, and he sounded absolutely wretched. As sympathetic as anyone had ever sounded. If Sean had needed any additional evidence to prove that Gabriel wasn't a bad guy, this was it right here. But Sean discovered that he hadn't really needed it. He'd already known that Gabe was decent. He'd never have kissed him otherwise. No matter how much he wanted him.

"That was why I left Portland," Sean said. "We'd always talked about starting a food truck—I worked at this little cafe, I'd started there when I was getting my MBA, and I enjoyed it. A lot more than my business classes, actually. Milo hated his job, and we'd fantasize sometimes, about buying some run-down food truck and renovating it and building a business from the ground up." Sean sipped his beer, more to wet his suddenly dry throat than a need to drink. This was the hard part to talk about, even still. "A drunk driver plowed into him when he was on his bicycle heading home to me. I got a big settlement. Life insurance. Money from the man who'd killed Milo. I didn't touch it for awhile. Couldn't even imagine doing anything without him. Kept thinking that I wanted my guy back more than I wanted the money. But then . . . I guess, time happens, right? I started to live again, but I still felt so stuck in Portland. My therapist, he suggested I try somewhere new. That I use the money to fulfill the dream we'd always shared. So I did. I came to Los Angeles. I bought the food truck. And then I met you."

"Oh, god," Gabriel repeated, staring at him with wide eyes.

Sean's fingers picked at the edge of the label on his beer. "On a Roll was always what Milo wanted to call the truck. He thought it was funny. He loved stupid puns. And," he added with a wry smile, "it is pretty lame, if you think about it."

"That's why you didn't want to change the name," Gabriel said on a groan. He threw back the whole drink, and Sean watched his Adam's apple bob as he swallowed. "And I was such a fucking asshole about it. Especially that . . . that first day. Well, and *later*, too." Clearly he'd been thinking about the meatball missile too—but then how could he not, when Sean had gone out of his way to remind him about it?

"It's alright," Sean said, and discovered that . . . *yes,* it really was okay. He wasn't just saying the words; he meant them. "I just thought, you said you wanted to know, and I realized that you *should* know why. Not because it gives me any stronger right to the name, but because it was unfair of me to believe that you should just change your name because I thought you should."

"And because you have a dead husband," Gabriel said. His eyes widened and he slapped a hand over his mouth. "God, just . . . kill me now," he added. Then his eyes grew impossibly bigger.

Sean laughed. "No. And seriously, don't worry about it. Why do you think I don't tell people? Because of shit just like that. I don't want to be treated like I'm fragile, like I'm about to break at any moment."

"So . . . *nobody* knows?" Gabriel sounded like he couldn't quite believe it. "You didn't tell anyone?"

"No and that was probably also kind of selfish, too, now that I think about it," Sean said with a sigh. "But you get it, right?"

"Yeah, I do," Gabriel said, firmly. "For the record, I can't say I *get it*, because how could I?" He hesitated. "I've never been through something like that, and I'm certainly not going to judge you for what you had to do to get through it and stay strong. And for the record, you are. So goddamned strong."

Sean hadn't asked him for the praise, but he couldn't deny that the words felt sweet. "Thank you," he said. He reached out and put a hand on Gabriel's knee. He hadn't swallowed more than a few sips of beer, was as sober as a judge, but just touching Gabriel made his blood race and his head swim.

It had definitely been too long since he'd had sex.

"Thank you for telling me," Gabriel said. "You have to know that if you'd told me this story at any point in the last two years, I'd have caved like a terrible hand of cards." He breathed out, hard and fast. "Goddamn it, I'm halfway to doing it right now."

"No," Sean said, suddenly gripping Gabriel's knee. "No, that's not why I told you. I don't want you to give it to me just because I care about it for that reason. I told you because you wanted to know."

"I did want to know," Gabriel said wryly. "I honestly had no idea it was like that."

"You wouldn't. But that's okay. I want . . . I want this to be fair."

Gabriel shot him a look of sheer disbelief. "You want this to be fair now, after you've told me your dead husband named your truck?"

Sean had wondered if that was going to be a problem. He supposed if he'd ever really wanted their arguments to end permanently, all he'd had to do was tell Gabe the truth.

But he hadn't, hadn't ever even *considered* it, and told himself the entire time that it was because he wanted to keep Milo to himself. That he didn't want Gabriel's goddamned *pity*. But maybe it had been more than that.

"Yes," Sean said firmly. "I want it to be fair."

"I'm not sure that's even possible," Gabriel said. "We can't share it."

Sean sighed. "No, we can't. But maybe we can figure something else out."

"What?" Gabriel's gaze slid away, and Sean wanted to chase it. "I should have given in two years ago, and I should just do it now."

It was everything that Sean had wanted to hear, but he knew as soon as Gabriel said the words that he couldn't just let him do that.

It would ruin everything, tear them apart before Sean ever got to find out anything he really wanted to know. Like if his sex voice was gruff around the edges. If his naked shoulders were as broad as his t-shirts promised. If all that frustration and anger would boil over into something even hotter.

Sean had heard Ren tease his cousin on more than one occasion about his prowess, and yet, as long as Sean had known him, he'd never heard even a hint of Gabriel hooking up with anyone. Definitely not any relationships. Maybe he was picky? Maybe he . . .

No, Sean told himself firmly. *It has nothing to do with you.*

But, he added thoughtfully, maybe it could.

"I didn't tell you the truth to get you to give in," Sean said. "I told you the truth because it was the right thing to do, and also because you've asked about a thousand times."

"Alright." Gabriel set his empty glass on the brick edge of the fire pit. "So what do you want to do?"

Sean laughed nervously. "I mean, I think it's pretty obvious, right?"

Gabriel glanced over at him, and his eyes were dark and intense, pinning him to the spot. "Is it? I think I must've missed something."

"I . . . I . . ." Sean didn't remember if he'd ever just suggested to someone that they have sex. Not someone he didn't have strong feelings for, who returned them. He took a deep breath. He could do this. He'd kissed Gabriel last night, hadn't he? He'd always thought that would be the hard thing—kissing someone for the first time after Milo—but it had been so goddamn easy. Easier than breathing. He should be able to do this part of it, right?

"Well, if that's it," Gabriel said, "maybe I should go. I'm glad you told me, really. I'm . . ." He sighed. "I just wish this was easier. For both of us."

"What?" Sean found himself scrambling, reaching for Gabriel, but he shucked Sean's hand away. "No, you can't . . ."

Gabriel shot him a small smile. "I can't?"

"You were right," Sean said. "I can't stop thinking about it. Not about our stupid argument. Not about what Tony asked us to do. But *you*."

"I'm not sure what you're trying to tell me." Gabriel's expression morphed into something guarded. The wall had gone up, and Sean hadn't even realized it was rising.

"Neither do I," Sean lied. Why was this not easier? He felt like tearing his hair out. It had been *so* easy yesterday, to just lean in and kiss Gabriel. Why was it so hard to talk about it? Maybe he should just . . .

But before he could, Gabriel was standing up.

"No," Sean said with conviction, and when he reached for Gabriel, he didn't let go that easily. "No, you can't go. Not like this."

"Not like what?" Gabriel wondered. "I still haven't figured out what we're fucking talking about. You said you wanted to talk, and you did. You told me about your husband. Maybe you didn't intend to make me feel like an asshole, but I do anyway, and I just . . ."

"I want to kiss you again," Sean said it in a rush. Like he couldn't stop the words once he'd started.

"I thought that was something that happened that wasn't going to happen again?" Gabriel wondered. "I thought you weren't trying to lead me around by my dick."

"That's not what any of this is about," Sean said. "You said they could be separate and I didn't believe you, but maybe you were right."

Gabriel gazed down at him, at the hand that was still wrapped around his forearm. "You didn't believe that last night."

Yeah, last night, Sean had gone home and stared at the dark shadowed ceiling for hours, want pulsing through his blood, and he'd realized that maybe it *could* be separate. If he wanted Gabriel enough—and not only did he, but he was almost certain it was mutual—surely they could figure out how to make it work.

"I needed to think about it," Sean said. "And . . . it's time. A long time coming, I guess."

"Two years," Gabriel said, his gaze growing warmer, and suddenly he was crowding into Sean's space, making him breathless just by his nearness.

In some ways that was true. Maybe they had been building towards this during the two years they'd been bickering over the name. But he'd meant something else.

"Well," Sean hedged. "More than that, actually." He hadn't had an orgasm with another person since Milo. And that, along with the understanding that this was *just* sex, was something that he needed Gabriel to know.

"Oh?" Gabriel was leaning in, their lips were nearly brushing, and Sean knew he would be insane to stop him now, because he almost could taste him. Last night had been so good, unexpected but good, but now expectation was simmering inside him, and he knew it would be even better.

"Yeah," Sean said, hesitating. Surely, one kiss before he told Gabe everything would be okay? He didn't *technically* owe Gabriel anything, especially that kind of explanation, but he wasn't sure if he could live with himself otherwise.

He brushed a single kiss across Gabriel's mouth, and almost didn't pull back because even though they'd kissed only twenty-four hours ago, his body had forgotten how well they fit together. Like two halves of a puzzle.

"Wait," Sean said breathlessly, taking a step backwards, away from Gabriel. Before he got too carried away. "I need to tell you something first."

"Okay." Gabriel's expression was so warm. So pleased. Like he hadn't expected this, and the surprise of it was making him glow.

"What is it?" His eyes crinkled as he grinned. "You can tell me anything. Well, at least about this," he added.

Everyone said that Ren was the charming one. The one that nobody could resist. But Sean was having difficulty remembering when it was that he'd found Gabriel an annoying, clumsy oaf.

"I told you about Milo. When I said it'd been a long time . . ." Sean hesitated. "There's been nobody since him. Nobody that I really wanted like that. But I want you."

Gabriel stared at him. "Are you saying the last guy you had sex with was your dead husband?"

It was difficult to keep his wince inside, but Sean managed it. "Yes."

"Wow." Gabe scrubbed a hand over his face. "Wow."

"I thought you should know, and also . . ." Sean wanted to stop right there, because even that part of the confession seemed to have killed Gabriel's mood, but he owed it to both of them to keep going. "Also, I think I should be upfront about what I want out of this. Sex. That's what I want."

Gabriel's eyebrows shot up. "Well, I kinda assumed that was the endgame," he said. "I can't say I'm disappointed to hear it."

"No," Sean said, hating himself a little but *knowing* he needed to be honest. It was hard to believe that Gabriel could develop those kinds of feelings for him, but from seeing friends hook up, he knew honesty was the best policy. "No, I just want sex. No romance. No dating. Just . . . you, whenever you're willing."

If Gabriel had looked stunned before, when Sean had told him that he hadn't had sex in almost five years, he looked floored now. "You just want to hook up? No strings?"

"No strings. Just sex."

"Oh." Gabriel's expression had gone very, very flat. "I wasn't expecting that."

"I mean it makes sense, right? I don't want to give you any unfair expectation," Sean said, trying to still salvage this, but the look on Gabriel's face was freaking him the fuck out.

"Because of your husband."

Sean didn't think he'd ever heard Gabe's voice so flat. So emotionless. Yes, he had definitely fucked this up.

"Well, yeah, kind of." Sean didn't know if it would help or hurt the situation to tell Gabriel that when he thought of him, it was totally different from how he'd ever thought of Milo, even at the beginning. He had frustrated thoughts about Gabriel. And annoyed thoughts. And plenty of hot ones. But love and affection and caring? Yeah, that was not in the cards.

"You don't have to explain anymore," Gabriel said. "I get it."

"You do?" Sean felt hope begin to grow again. Maybe he hadn't ruined everything, after all.

"Yeah," Gabriel said. "You want to be my fuck buddy. Well, if you're interested in that, you should talk to Ren."

Sean's mouth dropped open. "Ren? But I don't . . ."

"I'm not going to be some kind of bizarre way for you to fuck your husband out of your system," Gabriel said. "Sorry." Except,

Sean thought, as he watched Gabriel walk away, that he didn't sound very sorry about it at all.

CHAPTER FOUR

THREE DAYS LATER, SEAN was still trying not to sulk about Gabriel's rejection.

In some ways, he understood *why* Gabe had walked away. But that didn't mean he was very happy about it, *and* he didn't think that Gabriel was being very reasonable about it, either. He hadn't asked Gabe to fuck away Milo's memory. He'd just wanted to make sure that Gabriel knew that he wasn't going to fall in love. If he was going to, he knew he would be feeling differently about Gabriel right now.

And what he felt for Gabe? Yeah, not even remotely similar.

Gabriel made him want to throw something at his head. Or punch a wall. Or push him up *against* a wall. He didn't make him feel warm or gooey or sentimental.

Sean didn't think he should apologize for that.

He also didn't think that Gabriel felt much differently than he did. But somehow, by trying to be honest, he'd insulted Gabriel's pride.

And Gabriel's pride, as they both knew, was a considerable thing.

"You're frowning again," Tate said, as they walked around the lot, making sure they'd picked up all the trash the night before.

"I'm just thinking," Sean said, leaning over and plucking a red plastic beer cup from the ground and tossing it into the trash bag he was carrying.

"Yeah, except you don't have resting bitch face normally," Tate said. "So what's going on? You and Gabriel still having some kind of deathmatch over who's going to keep the name?"

"Yes, and no," Sean said. He really didn't want to tell Tate about the rejection, even though he knew Tate wouldn't blab about it to everyone, like Tony might.

"Oh?" Tate asked. "What else is going on?"

"Ugh," Sean said as he uncovered a crushed plastic cup, holding the remnants of some of Gabe's meatballs and a bit of moldy sauce. "Gross." He picked it up with his glove-covered hand and shoved it in the bag. "I hate being on trash duty."

"Yeah, it's not a picnic," Tate agreed.

Sean glanced up. "Don't you dare say you're just happy to be here. You've earned your spot."

"Okay," Tate said with a sharp grin. "I won't, if you'll tell me what has you glowering at Gabe's trash."

"We just . . . well, we kind of kissed, the other night, after I'd had too much to drink."

Tate dropped the plastic bag he was holding. "What? Really? Oh my god," he said, sounding way more excited than Sean had expected. "This is *awesome*."

"It really isn't awesome," Sean complained.

"We've only been waiting for this for, *well*, a really long time," Tate said. "Wait until Tony finds out."

"Tony," Sean said, enunciating each word clearly so there could be *no* confusion, "is not going to find out."

"Alright, I get it. But why are you so pissy if you finally managed to stop fighting?"

Sean sighed. "I told him I just wanted to hook up," he said, because he wasn't quite ready to tell Tate his *other* secret yet. "And he got all offended."

"How do you know you just want to hook up?" Tate wondered.

"I just *know*," Sean said. "The man makes me hot. But that's it."

"Are you sure?" Tate asked. "Because Chase and I . . ."

"Yes, well, we're not a star-crossed love story that began in high school," Sean retorted. "So I'm not sure there's much to compare here. I want to get naked. Gabriel wants . . . I'm not sure what Gabriel wants actually, but apparently it's not *only* getting naked."

"You could always ask Ren," Tate suggested. "He's always down for a hookup."

"Yeah, I'm pretty sure that would make Gabe lose his fucking mind," Sean said. And then stopped abruptly. Right next to another few pieces of plasticware that had been hiding behind a bush. "You know, it really would, wouldn't it?"

"Are you attracted to Ren?" Tate asked.

Was he attracted to Ren? Not particularly. Other than the fact that he looked a little bit like Gabriel, he'd never really noticed the way Ren looked. At least not the way so many other people seemed to notice.

"Not really," Sean admitted. "But . . . it might be a good way to convince Gabriel that he's being stupid."

"Is he though?"

"Is he being stupid? Of course he's being stupid. He doesn't *like* me. He just got his pride hurt because I said I didn't want anything romantic. He doesn't want that either, I'm sure of it."

"You do seem pretty sure about it," Tate muttered.

"Well, has he *ever* seemed particularly interested in wooing me?" Sean demanded. "The man threw a meatball at me!"

"True, true," Tate acknowledged. "Well, maybe Ren would be willing to play along, like an experiment to see how pissed off Gabriel can get."

"He's so stubborn though," Sean said, pondering. The last thing he wanted to do was convince Gabriel further that getting naked was a bad idea. "But maybe . . . maybe if it was something he really wanted, and he got jealous . . ."

"You," Tate said, gesturing with a handful of plastic forks, "are playing with fire. And you might get burnt."

"As long as it's Gabriel doing the burning, I don't care," Sean said.

"I hate everything," Gabriel said.

"What is it now?" Ren asked as he finely diced an onion, his knife flashing so quickly in the morning sunlight that Gabriel could barely see it.

"What do you mean, what is it *now*?" Gabriel demanded.

Ren shot him a very unsympathetic look. "With you, it's always something. So, what totally unfair thing happened to you today?"

"For the record, it was the other night," Gabriel said, sulking because he couldn't quite help himself. "Sean . . . well, Sean wants to have sex."

Ren set his knife down. "Okay, I'm failing to see how this is ruining your life. Haven't you wanted him for, I don't know, *forever*?"

"Yeah," Gabriel admitted. And even admitting that wasn't easy for him. But it was true, and he could hardly deny it any longer.

"I'm failing to see the problem," Ren said very evenly. Too evenly. He had yet to pick his wickedly sharp knife back up, which probably boded well for Gabriel's balls.

"It's not cool for him to finally, *finally* get on the same goddamn page and then say, all brazen, that all he wants is sex. He wants to get naked, and that's it. I'm not even sure he *likes* me."

Ren cracked a smile. "I can kind of see where he's coming from, to be honest."

"What?" Gabriel couldn't help his outraged bellow.

"I mean, we're family. I'm sort of required to like you. But it can be a challenge, some days," Ren said, turning back to his rapidly growing pile of minced onion.

"It is not . . ." Gabriel spluttered. "But I have *feelings*."

That was not an easy thing to admit. He might not have even realized he did, until Sean had said so bluntly that he didn't. That he wouldn't, ever. That Gabriel could never expect him to.

Maybe it had been unfair to accuse Sean of asking him to fuck his dead husband out of his system, but that was what it amounted to, wasn't it? They'd have sex a few times, have a boiling hot hookup, and then Sean would push him out, and he'd end up dating someone he could actually *like*.

Leaving Gabriel to sulk. *Again.*

"I don't think anyone on this planet imagines that you don't have feelings," Ren said matter-of-factly. "You're kind of the King of Feelings."

"That is . . ."

"One hundred percent accurate. Yes, I know, you can thank Cousin Ren for being such an expert on your tortured psyche."

"I really hate you too, now," Gabriel grumbled. "You can't even spare an ounce of sympathy. I'm *dying* here."

"Like I said," Ren repeated, "the King of Feelings. Is it any wonder that Sean wanted to be honest about it being just sex? You're the kind of guy who's gonna be holding a boom box under his bedroom window two weeks in."

"I have *never* done that," Gabriel argued.

"But you *could*. You *would*."

Gabe hated that his cousin was right. He might. After all, he'd been obsessed with Sean since day one. It would have been so easy to just change the name on his truck, after all. He had it all ready to go. He'd just held off because . . . *well*, because that might change things. And as frustrating as the status quo could be sometimes, at least he knew what it was like.

At least it meant that Sean paid attention to him.

If they didn't have any reason to argue anymore, that would go right out the window.

He wasn't proud of his prevaricating, but it was working, wasn't it? Sean had finally been honest with him. Maybe it wasn't the kind of honesty he'd been expecting. Maybe he hadn't been expecting Sean to still be mourning the dead love of his life, but Gabriel was the first person he'd told.

Maybe over time he could wear Sean down. Make him see that they could be good for more than just sex.

"All I'm saying," Ren continued, "is that if the guy wants to get naked with you, what kind of idiot would you be to turn him down? He's *hot*, and honestly I've only kept my hands off, because well, you're all tangled up about him."

"That hasn't changed," Gabriel reminded his cousin pointedly.

"Yeah, I know," Ren retorted, throwing a wicked smile over this shoulder. "It's gotten *worse*."

"So you think I should just . . . let him fuck me and keep it just to fucking?"

"You don't do this very often," Ren said, "so I'm going to go gentle on you, but here's the thing . . . it's not *easy* to keep it just fucking. I have to work at it. I have all these rules to make sure that my hookups don't evolve into more."

"That's kind of fucked up," Gabriel said. "You realize that, right?"

Ren shrugged, clearly unconcerned that while Gabriel was the King of Feelings, he was the opposite. "It works for me. I prefer it that way, honestly. And while you're emoting all over the place, don't decide that you can *fix* me, okay? I'm not like Tony, I'm not going to meet the perfect guy for me and become a different person. Does a leopard change its spots?"

"No?" Gabriel hadn't even considered it. His own love life was enough of a disaster, why would he try to interfere in Ren's. "I'm not really worrying about you. You're . . . well, you're Ren. That's who you are."

"Exactly," Ren said with a sharp nod. "But you? You want more. And you want Sean to want more, too. Best way to go about changing his mind? Get naked with him."

"I'm really not sure that's true," Gabriel said. Ren was smart, and he was good at this, but he'd never tried to get someone to fall for him *ever*. In fact, he was unapologetic about the fact that he actively tried to do the opposite.

"Then don't listen to me," Ren said, throwing up his hands. "Keep arguing with him. Keep bickering and insulting him, that's definitely worked so well for you over the last two years."

"Hey, it got me a kiss. More than one kiss, even," Gabriel said.

Ren rolled his eyes. "We could call that an accident of chemistry. You want something, you actually have to *do* something. In this case, it's get naked, which really considering how attractive Sean is, shouldn't exactly be a hardship."

"It wouldn't be," Gabriel said. Just thinking about it made him tingle all over. "But should I really . . . *lie* about what I want?"

"You're gonna have to decide if you want to play fair and get nothing, or play unfair and get everything. For me, not a decision. But then I'm brutally, bluntly honest with every single hookup. You're gonna have to decide what's right here, for you, and for Sean."

"Right," Gabriel said uncertainly. It felt wrong for him, especially after Sean had been so honest about his husband, to enter into a sexual arrangement, and hide his true intentions. Even if Sean eventually fell for him, would it make it right? Gabriel didn't know.

He was going to have to think about it more. Figure out a way to resist if Sean showed up and tried to convince him again.

For better or for worse, Gabriel didn't have to wait very long to see how Sean was going to react.

It was a slow lunch day, and an even slower afternoon.

Days like today, when they could take as many long breaks as they wanted, lounging in the sunshine and catching up on their reading or their podcasts, made up for the weekend days when even having an extra person didn't make the endless lines any less crazy.

Ren was sitting on the picnic table just outside the food truck, browsing something on his phone. His shirt was off, and he was working on his tan. Between infrequent customers, Gabriel had amused himself by observing all the visitors to the lot do a double take at the sight of him.

Maybe Gabriel should go to the gym with Ren and Lucas more. If he took his shirt off, he definitely wouldn't be getting that many admiring looks.

He was thinking of sending Lucas a text about when his training hours were, when a figure approaching out of the corner caught all his attention.

It was Sean. At first, Gabriel was sure that he'd come over to talk to *him*, but he didn't spare even a single glance for Gabe, up in the truck, clearly outlined in the big window. Instead, he'd stopped by Ren, and Gabriel had expected Sean to say a few words and move on. He wasn't . . . moving on, that was. He was standing there, laughing with Ren like Ren had been his primary objective the whole time.

And that was . . . Gabriel couldn't handle that.

Before he'd not really ever considered Ren a threat when it came to Sean, but now that Gabriel knew that he was only looking for sex? And his cousin was rather infamous for only providing sex?

It was a terrible, rather perfect combination, and Gabriel felt a chill right down his spine at the thought that Sean had figured that out. That he'd try to replace Gabriel with his cousin.

Gabriel didn't even remember yanking his apron off and running down the back stairs of the truck but he felt his feet hit the ground and that was when he realized he could *hear* them.

"So you go twice a week, then?" Sean said, and *yeah*, Gabriel thought with anguish, that was undeniably admiration in his voice. For *Ren's* undeniably gorgeous physique.

Gabriel felt like throwing up.

"Sometimes three times," Ren said, and yeah, Gabriel would have to be deaf not to hear the flirtatious edge to Ren's voice. That was the same tone he used every single time he was setting up for a hookup.

He wouldn't do that to Gabriel. Would he?

Gabriel didn't want to discover the hard way that he *might*.

"Wow. Well, I can definitely tell," Sean sounded very impressed. Gabriel rolled his eyes. He considered walking around the truck and interrupting them, but . . . he also felt stuck in place. Mesmerized by the horrible possibilities blooming right in front of him.

So instead, he kept listening.

"Maybe I could stop by sometime," Sean continued. "Get you to help me out."

It truly was bad enough that Ren was considering doing this at all. It was even worse that Sean was initiating it.

"Oh, maybe. I usually go on Mondays, Wednesdays, and Fridays," Ren said very casually and normally, Gabriel might not feel a surge of righteous indignation—but he knew exactly what Ren was doing. This was what he *did*. And he'd clearly decided that if Gabriel wasn't going to take Sean up on his very obvious offer, then he might as well.

But that was *not* okay, Gabriel decided in a huff. Ren knew how he felt! He had *feelings*, and even though Ren might think that was silly, they still mattered.

He marched right out from behind the truck and over to where they were sitting. All cozied up together on the picnic table. Ren still had his shirt off and he looked tan, and if he hadn't been Gabriel's cousin and he also hadn't hated every molecule in his body right now, he might have been tempted too.

It was more than a person could goddamn bear.

"What are you doing?" he asked, glaring at both of them, and refusing to specify who the question was actually for.

"I'm sorry, were we bothering you?" Ren asked in a silky tone. "I thought you were up in the truck, keeping yourself busy."

"Well, I *was*," Gabriel said, "but I couldn't help but hear your little . . . *conversation*."

"Oh, you were eavesdropping," Sean said. He shot Ren a look. "Don't you ever get really, really tired of his bullshit?"

"All the time," Ren said airily. Gabriel had a sudden realization that his cousin was actually . . . *enjoying* this. Anger surged inside him again.

"That explains it, then," Sean said.

"Explains what?" Gabriel demanded to know between clenched teeth. If he'd thought this situation was unfair before, finding Ren flirting, *shirtless*, with Sean, was on a whole new level.

"Explains why Ren is so cool," Sean said. "He's got to balance you out, man."

Gabriel was half a breath away from retorting that his general Gabriel-ness had not bothered Sean last night, when he'd propositioned him, or the night before that, when he'd kissed him. *Twice*.

"Ren is not . . ." Gabriel felt his temper begin to short-circuit.

"Right, of course not. Ren's not anything," Sean said, unconvincingly. "I was just asking how he got so ripped. Wondered what gym he went to."

Gabriel's temper frayed the rest of the way. "And I'm sure he wasn't out here so you'd come by and coo over his muscles either."

Ren shot him a look. "I'm working on my tan. You know that."

"Yeah," Gabriel said. "You're working on something, that's for fucking sure. When you're done 'working' on that, maybe you could get your ass back in the truck and actually do something I pay you for."

"You're being an asshole," Ren said in precise, careful words. "But alright. I guess my break's over." He turned to Sean. "Sorry about that. But then you know how he is."

"That I do." Sean shot Ren a blindingly beautiful smile. Gabriel realized with a sinking, pathetic heart, that Sean had *never* looked at him like that.

What was he even doing? He wasn't going to win the guy over with gruff words and accusations and arguments. He'd learned that much over the last two years. But he couldn't seem to help it. He saw Sean and he saw red—but also green and blue and purple and a whole rainbow of colors. He saw a *future*. But Sean? All he saw was that annoying asshole he wouldn't mind fucking.

It was enough to bring a grown man to his goddamn knees. Enough to make a guy *cry*.

Sean turned to go, and Gabriel realized, not only had he handled that in completely the wrong way, he was everything that Ren claimed he was. He was the King of Feelings.

How did someone like that fuck with *no* feelings? He didn't know—but he should at least *try*, shouldn't he? Or could he give Sean up, to Ren, and then to the unknown guy who *would* win him over? Convince him that there was love and life and happiness after pain?

"Hey, wait," Gabriel said, getting his voice back. "Don't . . . I'm sorry."

Sean turned, a wry expression on his face. "What are you sorry for?"

What was he sorry for? God, a whole laundry list of things. So many it was impossible to get into now.

But mostly, right at this moment, he was sorry for wanting to be a caveman, and wanting to throw Sean over his shoulder and cart him back to his food truck for a lot of hot, messy sex.

And then after, cuddling and hopefully sharing all their feelings.

"I'm sorry I was a jerk." That seemed like a better option than the caveman idea.

"You should apologize to your cousin, too," Sean said reproachfully.

"Why?" Gabriel said. "We express our love through insults."

"Maybe everyone isn't like you," Sean said.

"Well, that's a pity," Gabriel said.

Sean rolled his eyes. "Actually, it's not."

"That's not what you were saying the other night," Gabriel said, lowering his voice. "Because I remember that too. I can't forget about it."

"You said you weren't interested in . . . what was it? Fucking away the memory of my dead husband."

Ouch, he *had* said that. Definitely not his best moment.

"So, I thought that maybe your cousin might be," Sean said.

"He's not," Gabriel said, even though he worried that Ren *might*. Normally, knowing Ren, he'd have been all over it, but considering Gabe's feelings, he sure hoped that Ren wasn't interested.

Or if he was, that he hid it well.

"You seem pretty sure about that," Sean said, smiling. "Maybe you didn't see him flirting with me just now."

"Ren flirts with anything with a pulse. I once saw him wink at a labradoodle."

"You don't want me, so I'm not sure why you care," Sean said casually.

The problem was, Gabriel could think of a million ways to prove to Sean that he wanted him a whole hell of a lot more than Ren possibly could, but none of those ways were casual.

"I . . ." Gabriel stuttered. He couldn't bring himself to say, *no, I do, and I'm willing to do it any way you want it.* Maybe because the future felt so full of unknowns. If they got in deeper, if Gabriel gave him exactly what he wanted, he'd want to give him everything. And he was not sure Sean was even interested in any of it.

"That's what I thought," Sean said, and turned and walked away.

Gabriel watched him go, and wished he was not quite so familiar with Sean's back—or his ass in those cute denim cutoffs. Or that he wasn't so goddamned hot in them Gabriel wanted to melt through the floor.

"Wow, you really suck at this."

Gabriel turned and groaned. Ren was standing there, leaning against the side of the truck, a knowing grin on his face.

"I do not," Gabe grumbled, even though he was willing to accept Ren's assessment. After all, he'd just let Sean walk away *again*. How many times could that happen before Sean stopped showing up?

He wasn't sure he wanted to find out.

"Take him up on it, before I do," Ren said.

"You wouldn't," Gabriel said, as he stomped to the back stairs and climbed into the truck. Surely there was something he could do, could put his hands on, so he wouldn't go insane with boredom and frustration.

"I don't know," Ren said, following behind him. "I might. The guy's practically gagging for it."

Ren didn't know because Sean wouldn't have told him. He couldn't have any idea that Sean had spent the last four and a half years being celibate. By this point, he probably *was* gagging for it.

"I'm just saying," Ren continued, because the guy *never* knew when to shut up, even if it was good for him, "if you don't do it, I will. It'd practically be a public service at this point."

"It would be a public fucking service if you quit talking about it," Gabriel grumbled.

"Fine, fine," Ren said. "But at some point, he's gonna meet someone who isn't as nice and charitable as I am. And you're going to lose him."

"Let's prep for tomorrow," Gabriel said, pulling a bag of onions out of one of their storage bins. "It's slow, and we can get a head start, and maybe even sleep in."

"Message received," Ren said. "You don't want to talk about it."

He didn't. He didn't want to *think* about it either. Sean with another guy . . . it was just wrong. It felt wrong. But at the same time, calling whatever they had between them just sex felt wrong, too. Like Gabe had already accepted that he could never live up to the man that Sean had loved and lost.

Maybe he couldn't. But a Moretti never gave up without a fight.

CHAPTER FIVE

"I can't believe we made it six months," Tony said as he balanced precariously on a ladder and attached another strand of lights to the pole that sat at the north end of the lot.

Sean had been prepping for the day, roasting chicken off in his tiny oven, and setting up for the lunch crowd, when he'd watched Tony lug out the ladder. He had firsthand experience with how terribly Tony and ladders mixed, so he'd come, ostensibly to chat, but really to make sure that Tony didn't maim himself.

"You didn't think we'd make it here?" Sean asked, surprised. Tony always seemed so confident, so sure in what he was doing—in what *they* were doing.

"Nope," Tony said, beginning to descend the ladder, which shook precariously. Sean reached out and held on. "I kinda thought we might all kill each other first."

"You mean, you thought Gabe and I would kill each other," Sean said.

Tony shot him a grin as he reached the ground. "Kind of, yeah." He tucked a piece of dark hair behind one ear. "So . . ."

"No," Sean said. He didn't want to talk about it. Definitely not with Tony. "We're working on it. That's all you need to know."

"Do you both still have all your vital organs?" Tony asked, pulling out his phone and turning on the new strand of lights with the Bluetooth adapter he'd installed first. The strand shone brightly, even in the Los Angeles morning sunshine.

Yes, Sean wanted to say, *but some of them are feeling mighty unfulfilled right now.* But even worse than Tony interfering with the name problem would be Tony interfering with their potential hookup.

"Yeah," Sean said. "It's cool."

"Good," Tony said, drawing him into a quick side hug. "You know I love both you guys. I want you to stick around."

"Yeah." Sean couldn't imagine going anywhere else. Ever since Milo had died, he'd felt rootless and aimless, but coming to LA and meeting Tony and the other guys had given him a purpose. Given him a *home*.

As much as he wanted to throttle Gabriel sometimes, he was part of that feeling, and Sean didn't want to look too closely at how much of it was about Gabe. Why hadn't he just accepted Sean's offer and enjoyed a bout of hot, stringless sex before it could mean anything?

"You're coming tonight, right?" Tony asked, referring to the big party they were throwing for the friends and family of everyone in the lot. When Sean nodded, he added with a sudden sly grin, "Bringing anyone?"

"No," Sean said. Gabe would be there, of course, and Ren, if he wanted to keep driving Gabriel nuts by flirting with his cousin. Pushing his buttons wasn't nearly as fun as getting a hand on his dick, but it passed the time.

"You know, you can bring a guy around, if you wanted to," Tony said. "Even if it's not a thing. You know, Lucas and I started out pretty casual."

Sean rolled his eyes. "That's a lie, and you know it. You and Lucas were gaga for each other from practically the first moment. I saw you two together, remember? Making out outside the Funky Cup? That isn't 'just hanging out' and you know it."

"Well," Tony drawled. "*He* thought it was pretty casual, any-way."

Sean laughed. "Yeah, okay."

"The point is, you can bring someone, even if it's not serious. I know Lucas and I are like couple goals, and Tate has Chase now, but it doesn't have to be some lifelong commitment for you to bring someone to the party."

"Yeah," Sean said. "Well, honestly . . . I think Ren and I might be hooking up, soon."

Tony's jaw dropped open. "*What?*"

"Yeah," Sean said, suddenly wishing that he hadn't said anything. He had no intention of actually hooking up with Ren—and he was pretty sure Ren knew it too—but he'd imagined that the first thing Tony would do was run to Gabriel and tell him everything.

"You're not serious," Tony said, voice dropping as he took a few steps closer. "You wouldn't, really?"

"Why shouldn't I?" Sean said.

"Well, I don't know, maybe because Gabriel is fucking obsessed with you," Tony said. "And sleeping with Ren, well, that's a big fuck you, if you really wanted it to be. But . . ." He hesitated. "I'm not really sure you want it to be."

Tony was right; he didn't want it to be. All he'd ever wanted to do was push Gabriel's buttons, and the Ren thing had worked him up more than he'd been in *months*.

Actually, Sean realized, that wasn't true. The thing that had worked him up the most? Those kisses they'd shared.

"Well, suffice it to say, I'm not bringing a date," Sean said. "If that's okay with you."

"Hey," Tony said, "however you want to run your personal life, fine by me."

"Good," Sean said, and watched as Tony grabbed the ladder, but instead of heading off to hang the next strand of lights, walked straight over to Gabriel's truck.

He sighed. He'd done this—he'd known exactly what Tony was going to do. So why did he feel so guilty about it?

Eight hours later, Sean was still feeling guilty—and not happy about his sudden attack of conscience, either.

He hadn't seen Gabriel all day, and lately, that was unusual. Usually, one of them could manufacture a reason to have to pop over to the other side of the lot. But today? He'd stayed in his own truck, embarrassed and a little ashamed that he'd used Tony like that. Why had he thought that was a good idea? Pushing Gabriel's buttons had always been a fun way to pass the time. When had he started *caring* what the fallout was?

He didn't know, but he cared *now*.

After the trucks closed—an hour early, for the anniversary celebration—Sean spent all his cleanup time vacillating on whether he should actually go to the party.

Gabriel would be there. And so would Ren.

Two people who'd know, in detail, how Sean kept throwing himself at guys who didn't really want him.

He sighed, leaning against the counter. He thought it'd be so easy; he knew Gabriel wanted him. He'd known that before Tony had said so. He'd known since they'd kissed.

Nobody could kiss you like that and *not* want you.

It had been a long time for Sean, but not *that* long.

He stared out the window at the twinkling lights, the big fire pit that Lucas was building one log at a time, Tony and Jackson standing next to him.

Ash and Tate were lugging in a huge cooler, the one that Tony usually kept his fresh catch in for the most famous fish tacos in the

LA area, and laughing—probably at the smell of fish emanating from the plastic.

He really *should* go. He was part of this. These guys were his family, now, and it would be stupid to stay away for some silly reason like embarrassment.

And if he just happened to proposition Ren—maybe for *real* this time—then he would. Ren was hot. He didn't feel the same tingly sensation he had every single time he looked at Gabriel—but that wasn't required, was it? He was horny, goddamn it, and Ren was *right there*. And looked enough like Gabriel that . . . *well*, maybe he could settle for that.

Sean pulled his apron off, and then the navy blue t-shirt he'd worn under it. It was still really warm even though it was almost nine, and he grabbed a white tank, tugging it over his head.

He should wear something else. He spent so much time inside his food truck, his skin didn't have that delicious golden sheen that Ren's did. That *Gabriel's* did. Sean had spent so many nights around the fire pit, watching the light catch Gabe's exposed skin.

Wanting to put his mouth all over it.

He hadn't even understood back then that was what he wanted, he'd only known that he couldn't ever tear his eyes away.

But now he knew, and he couldn't ever pretend otherwise.

His own skin was pale and milky, and maybe not the best contrast with the white of his tank, but he decided he didn't give a fuck.

If Gabriel decided he didn't like *his* skin, then Sean wasn't going to cry about it.

He pushed his hair back, took a deep breath and exited the back of the truck, locking the door behind him.

"Hey," Ash said as he joined the circle around the fire pit. Someone had hooked up some speakers, and upbeat music started playing. "Beer's in the cooler over there. And I think Jackson brought some shit from the bar, if you want something harder."

Sean glanced over at where Gabriel and Ren were standing, beer bottles in hand, way over on the other side of the fire pit. Were they avoiding him? Sean couldn't say for sure, one way or the other, but he wasn't going to stand for that shit.

"I'll find Jackson, thanks," Sean said. Hesitated. Ash was the other single guy who was part of the lot, and he couldn't help but think of what Tony had offered today. "Did Tony go out of his way to tell you that you could bring a date?" he wondered.

Ash laughed. "Not this time, because I told him next time he asked, I was going to use his balls for earrings."

"Really?" Ash was even shorter than Sean—and even blonder, too. He looked like an angel, but took absolutely no shit from anyone, and often Sean wished he could be a little more like Ash.

Ash nodded. "Last time Tony asked me if I had a date. I date plenty, but they sure fucking don't need to come around here, not until I'm sure."

"And you haven't been that sure," Sean said hesitantly.

"Not yet." Ash's voice was cheerful, like it was totally alright that he hadn't had a serious boyfriend since Sean had known him. And maybe two years wasn't quite almost *five*, and maybe Ash didn't have a dead husband he wasn't trying to get over, but *still*.

Sean wasn't made of fucking glass. He had *needs*. And if Gabriel wasn't going to satisfy them, then he was going to find someone who would.

"But," Ash continued, "I'm always optimistic. You know that military guy, the one who keeps showing up?"

"Lennox? Yeah, he's cute," Sean said. More accurately he'd thought Lennox was cute, but not nearly as cute as Gabriel.

"He is," Ash said. Dropped his voice. "Tony's gonna freak out, but I invited him here, tonight."

"You did?"

Ash shot him a sympathetic look, and Sean wondered just how many of their friends had been wondering and waiting if he and Gabriel would hook up. "Sometimes," he said, "you've got to take matters into your own hands. You want something? You fucking make it happen."

"Yeah," Sean said. "*Yeah*."

Ash patted him on the back. "Go get 'em, tiger," he said.

First thing, Sean went and found Jackson, who'd set up a makeshift bar on a picnic table. Alexis, his boyfriend, and the guy who made the best fucking hummus Sean had ever been lucky enough to eat, had his hand tucked into the back pocket of Jackson's shorts, and they were laughing about something.

"Hey," Sean said. "I heard a rumor you had something harder than beer over here."

Jackson turned and smiled. "Looking for a little Dutch courage?"

Sean rolled his eyes. "Why would I want that?" Apparently everyone knew what was going on. That, he reminded himself, was because you had to open your big fucking mouth and tell Tony. Nobody gossiped like Tony did.

"Something a little birdy told me," Jackson said, pouring him a shot of vodka in a little plastic cup. "Here you go, champ, just don't go overboard."

Sean threw back the shot in one burning gulp. He didn't love vodka, but Jackson was annoyingly right; if he was going to be as audacious as he wanted to be, he was going to need it.

Jackson poured him a second shot when he held his cup out. "That's all you get," Jackson said. "You're a fucking lightweight, and I don't want your drunk ass on my conscience."

"This is fine," Sean said, sipping this shot instead of taking it all at once. "I'll be fine."

Jackson raised an eyebrow. "Guess we'll see about that."

"Guess we will," Sean said, and took off to get his guy.

Sean decided there was no reason to be subtle. That ship had sailed, long ago.

"So," he said, as he walked up to where Gabriel and Ren were standing. "Which one of you is going to fuck me?"

Gabriel choked on his beer, and Ren just smiled, like the cat who'd just won the cream.

"Um," Gabriel said, trying to clear his throat. "Uh. Are you okay? Are you drunk?"

"I'm not drunk," Sean said, trying to be casual, even though his fingers were clamped tightly around the plastic cup he was holding. He wanted, more than he'd ever imagined, more than he'd anticipated, Gabriel to be the one to stand up and say, *me, it has to be me. It was only ever going to be me.*

"We're not doing this," Gabriel said in a hard voice. Not the tender, intimate one he'd spoken in when Sean had confessed to him all about Milo. Maybe he never should have told Gabriel the truth. Maybe he'd created shoes that were too big to fill. Too much pressure. Too much tension. Too much *something.*

"Then," Sean said, turning to Ren. "How about you? You wanna get out of here?" He hoped that none of his disappointment—the *hurt*—showed on his face.

Ren sighed. "Sweetheart," he said, "you really don't want me. You want *him.*" He pointed to Gabriel. "And I'm not stupid enough to get in the way. Besides, sex is only really fun if the feeling's mutual."

"But . . ."

"No," Ren said gently. "No."

Sean downed the rest of his vodka. He couldn't look at Gabriel. It ached too much, the rejection seeping deep inside him. Flirting with Ren—or with someone else—wasn't going to help now. Even finishing the vodka, burning low in his belly, didn't make it feel any better.

The fire danced in front of his eyelids, and he felt so fucking *stupid*.

Of course Ren didn't really want him. And Gabriel? Sean swallowed hard. He couldn't think about him *at all*.

"My cousin isn't stupid."

Sean's gaze flicked to Gabriel, who was still standing there, uncertainly. Ren was gone, Sean didn't even know where. Probably to find someone who actually wanted to have sex with him. Out of the corner of his eye, Sean saw him across the lot, talking to Ash and that new guy, the tense one, the one that Ash had invited. Lennox? Yeah, that was his name.

Why couldn't he be more like Ash? Easy come and easy go? Never worried or anxious about how a relationship would turn out?

He *wanted* to be that way. Specifically he wanted to be that way about Gabriel.

"No, he's not," Sean said wretchedly.

If he was insane, he would go over to where Ash was standing, with the new guy, and maybe keep throwing himself at people who didn't want him. But he felt rooted in place. It was impossible to tell where Gabriel was going with his train of thought—he was unpredictable, even at the best of times—but Sean discovered he really didn't care.

In a minute, he'd go back to Jackson's makeshift bar and tolerate how loved up he and his boyfriend were just so he could grab another shot of vodka. Maybe it would dull . . . *everything*.

"Ren's not stupid enough to fuck with you, because he knows I'd kill him. Slowly."

Sean glanced up, and realized that Gabriel had walked closer, and was only an arm's length away. His jaw was clenched, his dark gaze intense.

"Why would you even bother doing that?" Sean wondered.

"You know why," Gabriel said, his voice still annoyingly steady. "You weren't even serious about hooking up with Ren; you just wanted to push my buttons." He hesitated. Sean looked up at him, again. He couldn't seem to tear his eyes away. A problem he'd never been able to solve, not in two long years of frustrated bickering. "Consider them pushed."

Before Sean could stop him, Gabriel plucked the empty plastic cup from his hand. "You won't need this any more," he said.

"That's mine," Sean said. It wasn't easy to make his voice hard and frosty—before, it had been *so* easy, as easy as breathing, but something had changed when they'd kissed. An inevitability, sliding right into its given place, and changing everything.

"Do you really want to get drunk?" Gabriel asked, and suddenly he was even closer, and his voice was hushed and reverent.

That was an easy enough question.

There'd been a period right after Milo, when he'd used alcohol as a crutch. He'd been unable to face the reality of his new life, and it had been easier with the cushion of a shot of booze in his coffee every morning. Then it had been easier with a beer at lunch. And it had spiraled from there. With the help of his therapist, he'd pulled himself out of that spiral, but he'd been cautious around alcohol ever since.

"No," Sean said. And meant it.

"Good. Because I try to avoid having sex with drunk people," Gabriel said.

"What?" Sean wasn't sure he'd heard him correctly.

Gabe sighed. "You want to do this, except it's kind of a disaster waiting to happen. We have so much . . . crap . . . between us. But I can't deny that this is probably inevitable."

"Are you saying that throwing a meatball at me was a kind of come-on?" Sean wondered.

"I don't know what it was," Gabriel admitted. "But there's a part of me that's very glad I did it."

"Because it meant we spent the next two years fighting?" Sean asked. He could still feel the weight of it, as it had hit his chest. At the time, he'd thought that was the end of his new beginning. That he'd never make any friends because that guy that everyone already seemed to like had decided to hate him.

But it hadn't been the end at all.

Maybe he wasn't quite as mad about it as he had been, all those years ago.

Because not only had Gabriel's friends become his own friends—he'd gotten *Gabriel*.

"No," Gabe said. "Because it meant that someday, I was gonna get to do this." He leaned in, and for a second, Sean tensed, remembering they were surrounded by those friends, and they were probably all watching. But then just because they'd agreed it would be a no-strings hookup didn't mean they had to hide it, like they were ashamed of it, right?

That would be silly.

Sean didn't want to keep any more secrets. Especially not from people he cared about.

He reached up, tangling his fingers in the soft hair, right at the base of Gabriel's neck. "I'm glad, too," he said, and pressed his lips to Gabe's.

There was only the barest impression of a hot, needy mouth on his—the taste addicting and Sean wondered, briefly, if he would ever get enough of it—and then it was gone.

"Hey," Gabriel said, their breath still mingling together. His arm was a firm hot line against Sean's back, and he felt something he hadn't in so long. It was support, both physical and metaphysical. Maybe this was a terrible idea. Maybe he'd end up changing Milo's name for their food truck, and he couldn't help but feel a pang of hurt at that, but what would he gain, instead? Sean didn't know. He felt the world opening up in a way that it hadn't in a very long time.

And *god*, more than that, he was feeling his blood heat up just from that brief kiss and from having Gabe touch him. "Hey," Sean repeated with a grin, "we should get out of here."

"Nope," Gabriel said firmly. "We made it six goddamn months here, and we deserve to celebrate."

"What's a better celebration than getting naked?" Sean teased.

"Oh, that's happening, but just a little bit later," Gabriel promised. He leaned down and kissed him again—another one of those all-too-brief moments where it ended practically before it began. Sean had been hungry for it before, but now he felt ravenous.

"Haven't we waited long enough?" Sean wondered.

"Yeah," Gabriel said. His arm slid down Sean's back and rested right at the curve of it, right above his ass. The heat of it burned into his skin, through the thin cotton of his tank. "But I think we can wait a little longer."

"Can you though?" Sean trailed a finger down Gabriel's bare arm. It seemed wild and impossible that they'd never touched like this before, because it felt like they'd been in each other's space for so damn long, but he knew that this was all new because it *felt* new.

He watched as Gabe swallowed hard, his Adam's apple bobbing. "I guess we'll see," Gabriel admitted. "Trust me, there's nothing I want to do more than drag you behind my truck and pin you down and make you scream. Give you everything you've wanted." His tone was rough and strained, and the look in his eyes was so intense, Sean felt like he could fall in and be perfectly happy staying there.

"Yes." Sean didn't even recognize his own voice. "Yes, let's do that. Right now."

Gabriel threw his head back and laughed, deep and slow. "You could tempt a saint, you know?"

"Good thing you're not a saint," Sean said.

"Yeah, but I'm serious. Tony went to a lot of trouble for this party. He'd be disappointed if we ducked out early."

"You don't think he'd be excited?"

Gabriel laughed again, and his fingertips dug into Sean's skin. His breath came a little harder. "Let's grab another beer and make the necessary rounds, okay?"

"Fine," Sean said, trying not to sulk.

He'd waited years, a few more hours shouldn't be the end of the world. But it felt like it. Like he'd been strung too tight and he might just explode.

Gabe nudged him. "Should I tell Ren that he should find another place to sleep tonight?"

"Does he do that?" Sean wondered, which was really a stupid question—of course Ren did—but it felt like all his brain cells had been reduced to ash. What would he feel like after Gabriel took him apart and put him together again? Destroyed, probably, in the best possible way.

Gabriel chuckled. "If I ask, I'm sure it won't exactly be a hardship for him to figure it out."

"We could always go to my place." Milo had never set foot in his townhouse, so it didn't feel wrong to suggest that Gabriel come over.

"You're sure about that?" Gabriel asked.

Sean hadn't even noticed they were moving, but they'd ended up in front of the cooler. He'd been too absorbed in Gabriel, probably. He watched as Gabriel grabbed them two beers, taking the tops off with a quick flick of his wrist. He took the one Gabe handed him, taking a long sip. "I'm sure," he said.

Gabriel smiled again, deeper and sweeter. More private, like it was just for Sean. "Okay, that's decided, then."

"I guess we really have to go socialize, don't we?" Sean said. He glanced around. The number of people milling around the fire pit had grown. Tate's sister had shown up, and his boyfriend, too, who'd brought along a few of his friends, all members of the Los Angeles Riptide.

They weren't the only professional athletes either—Ryan Flores, the co-owner of the lot, had invited some of his team-mates, from the Dodgers organization.

Sean saw Lennox, the gruff guy that Ash had invited over by the bar, chatting with Jackson and Alexis.

"You know, this might be even better than the Funky Cup," Gabriel said, his own gaze following Sean's, as he took in the crowd that was slowly growing. So many people who'd been there for them during the last six months.

"Don't let Jackson hear you," Sean said. "And you know what, it *is* better, because it's *ours.*"

"Yeah," Gabe said, and Sean could feel his gaze on him, hot and possessive, and his hand settled again on his back, the heat of it soaking through his shirt. Sean thought for the fiftieth time in the last ten minutes, why were they waiting? They could leave *right now.*

Nobody would even notice if they left.

The only person he needed to convince was someone who was beyond stubborn; who wouldn't leave just because he'd decided they shouldn't.

But really, it wouldn't be that hard to convince him. All Sean had to do was tap into that dark, hot, passionate streak that he *knew* Gabriel had. He was all fire and heat and impulsiveness.

Sean tipped his head up towards Gabe. "Hey," he said quietly, "I need to grab something from my truck. You wanna come with me?"

"What a stupid question," Gabe said. "I'm not letting you out of my sight."

They were halfway across the lot, when they were stopped by Tony.

His eyes were glued to where Gabe had a hand on Sean's back still. "Hey, guys," he said, his casual tone nothing like the intense interest in his expression. "What's going on? You bugging out already?"

"Nope," Sean said. "I'm just grabbing something from my truck." *Gabe's dick, that's what I'm gonna be grabbing, and it's gonna be good, so you'd better leave us alone. Same way we left you alone when you and Lucas were all up in each other's business.*

"Oh, good," Tony said. He clearly was dying to ask what was going on. He shifted his weight from one foot to the other once, and then again. "You still know that you've got to figure out the name change thing, right? *That,*" he said, gesturing to where Gabe's hand was settled on Sean's back, "doesn't change anything."

"We know," Gabe said, the edge of his voice distinctly annoyed. "We got the memo, okay?"

"Okay," Tony said awkwardly. "Well, I'll let you get to . . . whatever you need to do in your truck . . . when we're closed . . ."

He took off, heading towards the fire pit, and Gabe and Sean both burst into laughter. "Oh, god," Gabe gasped, between deep gales of laughter, "I thought his head was gonna explode."

"It might still," Sean said. "Look at him, he's telling Lucas all about it."

And yeah, he was. The way Tony's hands were gesturing in their direction as he relayed what had just happened to his boyfriend were unmistakable.

"I really was worried for a second," Gabe confessed as they walked the last few feet to Sean's truck. "Tony brought up the name, and I thought, this is it. This is the cold water I've been dreading."

"Cold water?" Sean questioned as he made a big show of digging in his pocket for his keys. Though he had no intention of actually unlocking anything. He'd just wanted to get Gabe alone, and behind the truck, where nobody could see them.

"Yeah, make you decide that this was all a bad idea," Gabe said with a self-conscious shrug. "Change your mind, or something."

Sean stared at him intently, at the concern shadowing his handsome face. At the need in his dark eyes. "I'm not going to change my mind," he said. Didn't Gabriel understand what he was going through? It felt like he was waking up after being numb for almost five years. Every inch of his skin felt like he was on fire, burning for the man in front of him. He'd never felt desire that threatened to bring him to his knees, metaphorically and literally, but he was feeling it now. He'd never expected to feel it for Gabriel, but it was undeniable and once he'd stopped fighting it, he'd realized just how impossible it was to resist.

"Oh good." Gabriel not only sounded embarrassed, he *looked* embarrassed.

Sean might not be as big or as broad as Gabriel, but he didn't fight when Sean took his arm and pushed him up against the side of the truck. "I want you," he said, their lips nearly brushing. He could feel Gabriel's whole body tense against his, and Sean pressed into him even more forcefully. "I want you so bad. I'm not going to change my mind about that. I don't think I could, even if I wanted to."

"I think . . ." Gabriel cleared his throat, his arms sliding around Sean's back, tugging him in even closer. "I think you really mean that."

Sean didn't even bother answering, he reached up and kissed Gabriel. Each and every time they kissed, it felt more natural, more right, like instead of spending the last two years fighting with their words, they should've been using their mouths for a very different purpose.

Gabe's hands slid up his body and cupped his head, tilting it so he could delve deeper into Sean's mouth. Maybe Sean had started the kiss, but Gabe clearly intended to finish it. And that, Sean thought with satisfaction, was exactly what he'd hoped. He'd wanted Gabe to quit holding back. To forget entirely about the leash he'd put them on.

All he'd need was a little extra encouragement, Sean knew, and he'd give in. He slid a thigh in between Gabe's, panting into his mouth as they kissed and kissed, his hardening cock rubbing against Gabe's. He'd just decided that it would be okay to reach down, to feel Gabriel's huge hard-on for himself, when a voice interrupted them.

"Well, this isn't what I expected to find back here."

Gabe tore his mouth from Sean's, and they sprang apart.

It wasn't Tony. Or Lucas. Or Tate. Or even Ash.

It was that guy that Ash had invited; the one who'd been hanging around the lot so much in the last month.

The one who wore that hard, unrelenting expression most of the time.

Lennox, Tony had said his name was. But nobody knew if that was his first name or his last name, or anything else about the guy. He wouldn't share any other tidbits about himself.

And now he'd just discovered them practically dry humping against Sean's food truck.

Sean sold this guy a chicken caesar salad wrap at least once a week. His face flared with the bright red of embarrassment. They might be more casual about things than most restaurants, but they were still supposed to be professionals.

"Uh," Sean said, "I'm sorry. I . . . we . . ."

"Were obviously preoccupied," Lennox said in that stiff voice of his. Sean didn't think he'd ever seen him relax. Not once.

"A little," Gabriel said apologetically. "Sorry about that."

Lennox didn't acknowledge the apology. His expression didn't soften even a fraction. It was still as stiff as the leather jacket he was wearing. A leather jacket in *summer* in Los Angeles. Sean wasn't sure he understood what the fuck the guy's problem was. But even if he was cute, he wasn't sure Ash knew quite what he was getting into.

"I'd heard things were wild down here after hours," Lennox finally said. Still refusing to crack a smile. "I guess some rumors are true."

"We . . . uh . . ." Gabe shrugged uncomfortably. "It's not always like this."

Except, it kind of was. There was Tony and Lucas, who had never met a vertical or horizontal surface they didn't want to fuck against, and then there was Tate and Chase, who were always looking for some kind of dark corner. And Sean wasn't even counting the single guys, specifically Ren.

They were kind of a hotbed of gay sex, now that Sean thought about it.

Maybe . . . what if this guy was a homophobe? Surely, he'd figured out that everyone here was queer in some way, shape, or form, but maybe he hadn't? Maybe he was just discovering this now.

Sean tensed, but all Lennox said next was, "Tony asked me to check the lighting, to make sure things were bright enough. I guess we've found a spot where the lighting could be improved."

"Tony asked you to do that tonight?" Gabe sounded surprised, and Sean was too. It was a party; didn't Lennox know how to party? But then, considering the tense way he was always holding himself, maybe he didn't. Maybe he'd never had a chance.

Well, if he kept hanging around here, he'd have to figure it out.

"No," Lennox said. "But he mentioned it the other day, and I was here and . . ."

"I'm pretty sure Tony didn't mean *tonight*," Gabe said, reaching out and patting him awkwardly on the shoulder. "Come on, let's go back to the party."

"I don't know. I'm here now," Lennox said, and Sean looked closer and realized that he wasn't just tense—he was *awkward*. He really didn't know what to do with them, living in all their queer messiness.

"Seriously," Sean said. "This is a party. Not a security check." He reached out and didn't miss how Lennox's face flinched at the casual contact when Sean wrapped a loose hand around his forearm. "And if you want to take that hot jacket off, we can always stow it in my truck," he added.

"No, thanks," Lennox said. "I'm good."

"Alright, well, it's your loss, 'cause there's gonna be dancing later, and you're gonna be boiling in all that leather," Sean said, and Gabriel nodded with him.

"I'll be fine," Lennox said.

Sean wasn't sure that was true, but he wasn't going to argue with such a statue anymore. Did the man ever give anything away? He hadn't seen more than a hint of any kind of personality. Maybe Ash got off on all that mystery, but Sean preferred something a lot more obvious.

Like how shamelessly Gabriel had been humping his leg only a few minutes earlier. Internally, he sighed reluctantly. He guessed they *wouldn't* be leaving the party early, after all. He'd just have to figure out how to cool down, and learn to wait.

CHAPTER SIX

GABRIEL KNEW THAT SEAN thought he'd been being very sly, with the whole *let's go grab something in my truck* charade, but he'd seen through it in a hot second.

But what was he going to do? Reject Sean's attempts to seduce him? When they felt so sweet and Gabriel knew how good they could be together? He might be an asshole, but he wasn't a *stupid* asshole.

"Hey, sorry we got . . . interrupted." Sean glanced up at him, all coy eyes, tongue flicking out to lick his lips, and Gabe thought if he wanted to drag him back behind the truck again, he'd be down for that.

But they'd just left, pulling Lennox along with them, and there was something so odd about that guy, how mixed up he was, so awkward and cold and yet the way he kept staring at the crowd around the fire pit? There was a yearning there, a wanting to belong. Maybe even a belief he couldn't ever.

And Gabriel might be an asshole, but this guy had bought a lot of meatball sandwiches off him in the last few months, and he also hated to see anyone who wanted something he couldn't have.

It cut a little too close to home, because even though he was definitely, undeniably, getting Sean naked tonight, he still wasn't getting what he really wanted, was he?

"It's alright," Gabriel said. "Will you have any unexpected visitors at your place?"

Sean's forehead crinkled adorably, and he shot him the look that had made him want to kiss him, basically from the first time he'd ever directed it in Gabriel's direction. The one that screamed, in neon flashing letters, *what the fuck are you even talking about, buddy?*

Maybe it shouldn't have been so freaking cute, but it was. Every single damn time since the first time. That alone should have clued Gabriel in to his single-minded obsession with Sean, but he'd been in denial. How could two people who argued so much actually want each other enough to nearly rip their clothes off? It was a mystery, but it was one that Gabriel was one hundred and ten percent into exploring.

"No, nobody at my place. Just us," Sean said.

"Then we won't be interrupted later. That's all I care about," Gabriel said. "Because once I get you naked, there's no going back."

"I already knew that," Sean said with a sniff, but Gabe could feel him trembling under his shirt. And Gabriel? He was trembling at the exact same frequency.

"Just making sure we're on the same page," Gabriel said as he steered them over to the bar where Jackson and Alexis had abandoned the bottles for cuddling on the same bench.

"You want a beer?" Sean said, turning to Lennox, who was trailing a few feet behind them. "I think there's some other booze here, too, if you want something else."

"I'm good with beer," Lennox said stiffly.

"Three beers coming up," Gabe said, pulling open the cooler, which still smelled vaguely like fish. Considering all the fresh catch that Wyatt and Tony stored in it, the fish smell would probably end up lingering forever.

"So, what do you do for work?" Sean said, turning towards Lennox. He'd obviously decided to adopt the guy, his feelings clearly similar to Gabe's, and he'd have to be a lot colder to not find it sweet. Sean could be a super thoughtful, caring guy, and that was a part of his personality that Gabe had hoped he could explore more fully when they finally started hooking up.

But considering that Sean had claimed that it could *only* be sex and nothing else, Gabriel wasn't sure that was going to happen anymore. He was trying to manage his expectations and not be disappointed by impossibilities.

"Me?" Lennox asked, putting a hand up to his chest, a little self-consciously. "Uh, well, I own a business. A security business." He hesitated, clearly uncomfortable talking about himself. "We opened a new office a few blocks away from the lot, and that's when I started coming here."

"Oh, that must be why Tony asked you to check out the security lighting," Sean said, laughing. "I feel dumb now."

"No, Tony didn't know, I didn't tell him, I . . ."

"Don't like sharing much about yourself?" Gabriel chimed in. "Yeah, I kinda got that impression. Well, a warning, that's not going to last long around here. We're a fairly open group."

"Yeah, I got that impression, too," Lennox said dryly.

"Impression of what?" Ash appeared at his elbow, a beer in one hand, and one of those plastic shot glasses in the other. His tanned face was flushed, and when he looked up at Lennox, the flush deepened.

"That everyone's fine fucking around," Lennox said.

Sean frowned because *yes*, he'd discovered them doing that exact thing, but it was still a little harsh. Because they *did* run a successful business here. Six successful businesses, actually. They'd never be able to do that if they were actually fucking around all the time.

"That's not true," Ash said righteously.

Lennox regarded him steadily, without even a whiff of guilt. "I just know what I've seen."

"You certainly have no issue coming around buying meals from us," Tony said.

For the first time, Sean saw the beginning of a crack in Lennox's steely composure.

"I don't have any issues," Lennox said firmly. "I apologize if you think I did. You're free to live your lives however you see fit."

But now that Sean had seen the uncertainty hiding in his eyes, it was impossible not to see it.

He didn't think Lennox disagreed with their lifestyle choices. Instead, he was fairly certain that was envy in his voice.

"We certainly will," Ash said.

"I guess I'll see you around," Lennox said, and with a single, opaque glance towards Ash, walked off. Nobody stopped him.

"Well, he was a major buzzkill," Tony said as soon as he was out of hearing distance. "Why'd you invite him, anyway?" he asked, turning towards Ash.

"He seemed like a nice enough guy. Could use some friends," Ash said.

"I think he probably still could," Tate said, speaking up for the first time. Sean knew then that his quietly observant friend had seen the same thing he had.

"Yeah, I think so too," Sean agreed.

"Don't expect *me* to be the one inviting him next time," Ash said. "I've learned my lesson."

Except, Sean knew how promises like that went. He'd started out that way too, sure that he was going to hate Gabriel for all time. So painfully certain that he'd never forget that meatball, rocketing towards him. And what was he doing now? Finding dark corners so he could try to seduce him.

"I like to think nobody's hopeless," Sean said.

"Yeah, you *would*," Ash teased him, a smile suddenly lighting up his face. "I don't suppose you'd want to go on record and tell us what's going on between you and Gabe?"

"Nope," Sean said, exchanging a smile of his own with Gabriel. "We're good, thanks."

"Just how good?" Tony wondered.

"Ask me tomorrow," Gabriel said, and Sean tried very hard not to flush just as red as Ash had. He glanced down at him, a knowing look in his eyes. "You ready to get out of here?"

He'd been ready for hours, ever since Gabriel had finally seen the light and agreed to Sean's plan.

"Yeah, definitely," Sean said, reaching out to take Gabe's hand. "Hey, guys, thanks for a great six months," he said. "And here's to a hell of a lot more."

"Cheers to that," Lucas said, raising his glass. "Have fun, and be safe, you two crazy kids."

It wasn't until they were walking through the warm night air towards Sean's townhouse that Gabriel began to get nervous.

He was excited. He was turned on. And, he discovered, he was also terrified.

"Hey," he said, giving Sean's hand a little squeeze. "Has it . . ." He cleared his throat. "Has it really been almost five years for you?

Nothing else, not since your . . ." He hesitated. He'd been more than a little insensitive before, about Sean's dead husband, and he didn't want to fuck everything up by doing it again.

"Husband? Milo?" Sean supplied with a quick grin. "You can say it, you know, I'm not made of glass. I'm not going to shatter."

"I know," Gabriel said. Couldn't help but think that Sean might be the strongest person he knew. If he ever fell in love the way Sean had with his husband, and then he died, he didn't think he'd ever get out of bed again. But not only had Sean pulled himself up, he'd come here to LA and created a new life for himself. That was strength personified.

"But no, nothing. No one since him." Sean's gaze was so trusting, it sent another wave of apprehension washing through Gabriel. "I didn't want anyone else, and that was okay. But now I do, and that's okay, too."

Gabriel wasn't quite as confident as Sean was. It was one of the reasons he'd hesitated to agree to his friends-with-benefits plan. The other was that he definitely felt more than just friendly towards Sean—he wasn't sure he could precisely identify his feelings, but he knew it wasn't just platonic lust. But between watching Sean try to hit on anything with a dick and learning to live with what morsels Sean was willing to give him? In the end, the decision was a no-brainer.

"I just don't want this to be a mistake," Gabriel said, more honestly than he'd intended.

Sean gazed up at him. "It won't be," he said, his voice still so certain.

"Alright," Gabriel said. Maybe the trust in Sean's eyes didn't solve every problem, but he'd be lying if he tried to claim that it didn't make any difference.

Sean had chosen him. He hadn't wanted anyone, not after Milo, but now he did, and Gabriel still couldn't quite believe that it was *him*.

After their conversation, Gabriel felt his jitters calm, and his blood begin to race. In a few minutes, he'd have Sean exactly where he'd wanted him for so long.

And if he knew one thing, he knew that he could make it good for him. Just the thought of it—Sean naked beneath him, cock hard and leaking just for him—made his heart race and his own dick begin to harden. He didn't know how he was possibly going to resist just pinning him against the door and taking him.

"This is a nice place," Gabriel said, hating how inane he sounded as he watched Sean type in the code to unlock the door.

Sean laughed. "You don't have to do any of that. It's . . . well, it's a place to sleep, you know?"

Gabriel knew what Sean meant the second the door swung open. He'd left a lamp on in the tiny living room, but the couch, coffee table, and TV stand were all very plain and basic, no personal touches to them at all. It was like when he'd moved here, Sean had picked out everything online and had it delivered, not really giving a shit what it looked like or how it fit together. Or if it reflected who he was, at all.

And, Gabriel realized with a sudden jolt it was very likely that was exactly how it had happened. When Sean had moved here, he'd been starting over.

"Hey," Sean said, and there was that edge of uncertainty that Gabriel had been dreading to hear.

That was all it took. He crowded the guy against the front door just as it closed behind them, and—because he finally could, because he was finally *allowed*—he shoved his hands into Sean's hair and captured his mouth.

He was learning quickly how restrained and unsure Sean had been during that first kiss, and a little bit less so during the second, and even less when they'd made out earlier tonight against the back of Sean's truck. But now? It was like Sean had flung away the last of his concerns, and he was *in* this, kissing Gabriel back like he was starving and he hadn't had a proper meal in ages.

Years, Gabriel realized dimly as Sean's foot wound its way up his leg. *He hadn't had anything in years.*

"God, please, *yes*." Sean's pleading was echoing in his ears as he pushed Sean harder against the door. He could feel Sean's cock, rock hard, under his thigh, and when his eyes flicked open, he could see Sean's head was tipped against the door, his mouth open, red and wet. And he knew, without any doubt in his mind, what he needed to do.

Gabe went to his knees, his fingers reaching up to tug on the button on Sean's jean shorts.

His teeth sunk into his lower lip, deep enough to leave a mark. "Wait," he panted. "Wait, I won't . . ."

"Won't last?" Gabriel nodded. "I know. It's been so long for you, but that's okay. We've got all night."

"I wanted . . ." Sean said, a crinkle appearing between his brows. "I wanted . . ."

"Yeah, I've got you, don't worry about anything," Gabriel reassured him. He'd finally wrenched the button open, and was tugging the shorts down, only to be surprised to see Sean's rock-hard cock, precome smeared over the bright red tip. Gabe gave in to his best instincts, running his thumb over the wetness, enjoying the throaty moan Sean gave him in response.

"Feels good, huh?" Gabriel said, closing his hand around his dick, and stroking it, quick and a little rough. Giving him as much pleasure as he could handle, hoping to tip him over the edge nice and easy.

"So good," Sean said, his gaze searing as it met Gabriel's. "So fucking good. I just don't know . . ."

Gabriel worked him through it, the way Sean's eyes glazed over, the back of his head thumping rhythmically against the door. He could tell Sean was close, and could tell he was holding on. Trying to eke out every single bit of pleasure?

What Gabriel really wanted was for him to let go, to stop holding back. "Come on, baby," he cooed as he stroked Sean's dick. It was just as pretty as the rest of him, and he still intended to get him totally naked by the end of the night, begging to be fucked by his cock. But he needed to let the orgasm take him if he had any chance of that happening.

Every muscle in Sean's body tensed, and then he was coming in long, stuttering pulses, and it went on forever, dripping onto the hardwood floor in front of the door. Gabriel already knew he'd never be able to look at Sean again and not automatically think of Sean turning into mush, all for him.

"Fuck, you shouldn't have . . ." Sean mumbled as Gabe rose up. There was a tissue box on the coffee table and he grabbed a few, cleaning up his hand, and settling back at Sean's feet so he could clean up the floor.

"Yes, I should. It was what you wanted, wasn't it? What you needed," Gabriel reminded him. He'd been so worked up, horny and desperate, and that wasn't really such a surprise considering how long he'd denied his body's basic needs.

"Yeah, but . . ."

"Oh," Gabriel said, rising up again. His cock was uncomfortably hard in his jeans. But he'd given Sean what he'd needed and that was a beautiful kind of pleasure on its own. "Did you think we were done? We're not done by a long shot."

A smile broke over Sean's face. "How did you know?"

"That this was what you needed?" Gabriel shrugged. "It wasn't that hard to guess."

Sean swayed towards him, loose-limbed and sleepy-eyed and so fucking gorgeous that Gabriel felt his heart clench.

"I want to get my hands all over you," Sean said, "but first . . ." He leaned in, and Gabe could get behind more kissing. The more kissing they did, the less this felt like one of those hookup situations and more like . . . something bigger and brighter and sweeter.

Something that Gabe was craving and he couldn't even put a name to.

The kiss spun out, all tongue and hot, insistent mouths, and Gabriel thought for a second, *this is what going insane must feel like.* But then Sean was kissing up his neck and mouthing insistently at his earlobe. "Bedroom," he said, and started tugging Gabriel—he assumed in that particular direction. A few stumbles later, Sean was pushing him down on a soft, fluffy surface. *The bed*, he realized.

But then that was hardly something to be embarrassed about, considering how little blood was still left in his brain.

"I wanna give you something," Sean said softly, intimately, and then he was on *his* knees, and he was pulling Gabe's shirt off, and his fingers were on his belt, tugging down his jeans and then his boxers, until it was just Sean and his dick, face to face for the first time.

He'd had so many fantasies about this. Every time Sean had opened his mouth to be difficult or rude or snarky, Gabe had thought about shoving his dick into it.

But the reality was so much sweeter. Sean was certainly eager enough for it, and he hadn't been in any of those faraway fantasies. Then Sean's tongue flicked out, curling around the tip and Gabriel swore. He'd worried about Sean not being able to last, but his own needs had risen precariously close to the breaking point.

"Wait," Gabriel said, digging his fingers into the bedding on either side of him. But Sean wasn't waiting for anything—his mouth slid right down his dick like it was born to take it, and Gabe shook as the pleasure rose through him.

But if he let himself be overwhelmed by it, he'd never be able to fuck Sean like he'd asked him to. Of course, the chance of being able to do that now, anyway, after he was this close to the goddamn edge was laughable. He should just let the wave take him. Enjoy Sean's mouth the way Sean seemed to be enjoying his cock.

He kept making these hungry little noises around it, as his tongue dipped lower and lower, tracing the most irresistible pattern until Gabe didn't think he could even *think* any longer. All that was keeping him anchored to the earth were his hands clinging to the blankets, and Sean's hot palm on his bare thigh.

"Wait," Gabe gasped out, but Sean just pushed him harder and higher until maybe he wasn't on solid ground anymore—instead he was flying, shuddering through his release.

He only realized when he heard Sean cough into his hand that he probably hadn't prepared him well enough, and *god,* he was a fucking idiot. How long had it been since Sean had given a blowjob? And he'd just blasted right through good blowjob eti-quette by not warning him first.

"Shit," Gabriel said, leaning down and cupping Sean's face. He didn't look too rough, a little dribble of come on his cheek, but honestly, the only thing that Gabriel noticed was that he'd never seen his eyes so peaceful and relaxed, like a calm blue ocean.

"It's alright, seriously," Sean said, wiping his mouth with the back of his hand. "I guess it's not quite like riding a bike, after all."

"I'm so sorry, I should have been more . . ."

But before Gabriel could finish his apology, Sean was rising up, interrupting him. "No," he said firmly. "You were incredible. So worried about me and my pleasure and my control." He looked dreamy, almost, as he thought about what they'd just done to-gether. "It was all amazing. I'm so glad; I was a little bit worried, but I shouldn't have been."

Gabe didn't know whether to be relieved or offended. "Oh?"

"I guess it was probably inevitable," Sean admitted, flopping down next to him on the bed. Still, half-clothed. Gabe reached over and tugged that white tank over his head, so he was just as naked as Gabriel was. "But I didn't want you to know it."

"I knew it," Gabriel said.

"Oh," Sean said, chuckling under his breath, "I guess I didn't hide it very well."

He had, actually. Gabriel had just gotten very good at reading him. Plus, how could he *not* be nervous? It'd been a long time since he'd had sex. And it had been even longer since he'd had sex with someone that he wasn't married to. Once Gabe had guessed, it had been easy enough to watch Sean carefully and see the hesitancy and the nerves in his eyes.

"You're good now, though?" Gabriel asked. Held his breath. Sean didn't *seem* disappointed, but what if, deep down, he wished that he hadn't picked Gabriel to end his celibacy with? What if it hadn't been worth it?

"I'm good," Sean said, and his smile was like the brightest sunrise after a late-night storm. He straight-up *giggled*. "I'm so good."

"That," Gabriel said, "means you obviously waited too long."

"Too long?" Sean laughed again. "I was *trying,* but you kept putting me off."

"For a week!" Gabriel heard his voice go high and squeaky. He'd have been embarrassed but Sean looked so amused, so charmed, that he let it go, putting his arm around Sean's shoulders, and tugging him closer. "I meant . . . maybe you should have thought about it before last week."

Gabriel wasn't stupid. He wanted Sean to say something like, *oh, big awesome man who gives great orgasms, I've been waiting for you.* But he knew that Sean hadn't been; it was all about the timing.

"I just wasn't ready," Sean said simply. "And then I was."

"Well, I'm glad I was hanging around and happened to be standing there the moment you decided you were ready," Gabriel said flippantly.

"Me too," Sean said with an earnest smile. So earnest, it made Gabe's heart twist in his chest—even as he reminded himself that none of this meant anything. Sean had been as straightforward as possible, and in taking him up on his offer, Gabe had agreed to abide by that rule. They were just going to have sex. That was all.

It was the last thing he wanted to do, but Gabriel pushed himself upright. Away from Sean. Cuddling after sex? Probably not something friends with benefits did. He couldn't imagine Ren doing that with any of his hookups. And that, he realized, as much as he loathed the idea, was going to have to be his litmus test: *what would Ren do?*

"Where are you going?" Sean wondered.

Suddenly Gabriel wasn't sure. He wanted to do the *right* thing, whatever that was, but even though he'd promised Sean a second round, it was way too early for that. Would it be weird to say he was hanging around until that was possible?

"Um," Gabriel said. "I wasn't . . . I don't know what you want to do."

Ren had told him to be confident. To set the parameters. To not give too much. To not take too much.

The problem was that Gabe wanted it all.

"What I want is a quesadilla," Sean announced, sitting up too. "You want a quesadilla?"

It was definitely not what Gabriel had expected him to say, but food was always a good answer to unsolvable problems. "Uh, sure?"

"Good," Sean said. He stood up, unapologetically, gloriously naked. Gabriel had wanted to get him naked more than he'd wanted to take his next breath, and now he wanted to *keep* getting him naked. He glanced around. "Where's my briefs?"

Gabriel grinned. "You weren't wearing any, which, let me just say, was a *very* nice surprise for me."

"I figured, why waste time?" Sean said with a laugh. He opened a drawer on the big, turquoise dresser in the corner, and pulled out a pair, tugging them on.

"I'm glad we were on the same page," Gabriel said. He reached down, finding his own boxers in the tangle of his clothes on the floor.

"Let's go make a quesadilla," Sean said, and sounded so goddamn excited about the concept that Gabriel didn't even argue, just followed him like a lovesick idiot back through the living room and into the kitchen.

Sean flipped on the light and it glinted off the golden strands in his hair, tucked between the lighter brown. Gabriel reached over and ruffled it. "I didn't realize how blond you were."

"Just in the summer," Sean said, his voice muffled as he was deep in the fridge, pulling out ingredients haphazardly and setting them on the counter. "All that sun, you know. Especially since I moved to LA."

"Why *did* you move to LA?" Gabriel asked as he watched Sean grab a frying pan from the rack hanging above the stove. For a small townhouse, Sean's kitchen was surprisingly bright and well laid out. His own kitchen at the loft he shared with Ren was not nearly as nice as this one.

"Well, like I said the other night, I wanted a fresh start. I wanted to stay on the West Coast, and let's face it," Sean said, shooting him a lopsided grin, "Seattle wasn't really an option. Plus, second best place for food trucks, other than Portland, is Los Angeles."

"Why not Seattle?"

"More rain than Portland? No, thank you," Sean said. "Don't get me wrong, it's a great city, at least to visit. But to live? I wanted a little more sun in my life."

"Nobody could blame you for wanting that." Gabriel could only imagine how gray and dismal the years after Milo's death must have seemed to Sean. He couldn't blame him for chasing the sun. "You need any help?"

"If you can find the salsa, I think I forgot to grab it," Sean said as he drizzled oil into the skillet and slid a tortilla in, covering it liberally with cheese.

"Cheese? Salsa?" Gabriel teased as he pulled open the fridge door and poked around, finally unearthing a tub of pico de gallo. "What would Health Food Nut and Wrap God Sean say to that?"

"I serve things that aren't healthy," Sean protested.

"No," Gabe said. "You serve salad dressed up in a shell that resembles salad more than it does any kind of delicious carb-like item."

Sean flipped the quesadilla with so much confidence Gabriel knew he'd done it a hundred times. A thousand. He'd clearly won the jackpot and was lucky enough to be privy to a very common post-work routine for Sean.

"I know you like my wraps," Sean said, and he was still smiling. "You can pretend all you want. Sometimes you can't eat another garlic butter-slathered roll loaded with cheese."

"Sometimes," Gabriel admitted with a laugh. "You know," he added, patting his (mostly) flat belly, "I gotta stay hot for the guys who are desperate to get me naked."

"And who are these guys?" Sean asked, arching an eyebrow as he slid the beautifully crisp and browned tortilla, melty cheese leaking out of the sides, onto a plate. "I wasn't aware that there was a queue. Unless we're counting Ren's queue as your own."

"We're not," Gabriel said, taking the plate from Sean. He dumped a good spoonful of pico on the quesadilla, and then drizzled it with another squeeze bottle he'd found in the fridge.

"What is that?" Sean exclaimed as he started the next quesadilla cooking. "Did you just ruin my beautiful meal by pouring *ranch* all over it?"

"Fun story: ranch is delicious with tortillas and cheese," Gabriel proclaimed.

Sean just shook his head. "And here I thought you were some kind of purist."

"I'm Italian, baby, not *Mexican*," he reminded him.

Sean rolled his eyes, but the corners of his mouth were still upturned in a smile. Like he couldn't quite help himself. "You're ridiculous," he said.

"Ridiculously brilliant," Gabe said. He sat down on one of the barstools across from the stove, and dug into the quesadilla. It was the perfect salty-crunchy combination. Why had he never considered quesadillas as the ideal post-coital snack?

Probably because he was Italian.

"But hey," Gabe said, after he chewed and swallowed, "you're pretty goddamned brilliant too, it turns out."

"Thanks," Sean said, and grabbing his own plate, sat down next to Gabe. As they ate, his foot was swinging, and more than once, it tapped Gabriel's. He was pretty sure that he was trying to play footsy with him, but *why* would he? They were just supposed to be having sex. Their feet weren't necessarily involved in that—unless Sean was into shit that he hadn't told Gabriel about yet.

"That was fucking delicious," Gabriel said, after they both finished. "If the wrap thing doesn't ever work out, you can always branch into Mexican food."

"I kind of thought about diversifying a bit," Sean said thoughtfully. "Quesadillas aren't that much different from wraps, you know? And I thought I could do some really fun stuff with the fillings."

"Cheese is where it's at, baby," Gabriel teased him. "Stick to the classics. Look at Tate, and what he's done to the grilled cheese sandwich."

"He's got all kinds of different variations, though," Sean pointed out. "He's got the classic, yeah, but he's got other kinds too.

Just like I have the chicken caesar salad wrap, and that's always a bestseller, but the peanut butter tofu wrap? It's a dark horse."

"I find that hard to believe," Gabriel said. "But then this is LA, right? People like tofu here."

"People like tofu a lot of different places," Sean pointed out.

"I'll have to take your word for that."

"Yes, you will," Sean said. "Have you thought about trying some meat alternatives for your meatballs? There's a vegetarian and health-conscious crowd that hangs out at the lot, and I know Tony's done really well attracting them, and Lucas' new vegan truck is killing it."

"And you," Gabriel said. "You've been courting them too." He sighed. "I'm not . . . it's not my kind of thing. That's all."

Sean elbowed him sharply. "Why? Because you're Italian? Don't be silly."

It wasn't about that at all. Gabriel just . . . *well*, he did what he knew. He'd always done what he knew, and what his family knew was meatballs and sauce and garlic bread and the best goddamn baked ziti and carbonara that anyone had ever tasted. He didn't know how to adapt. The only way he'd ever figured out how to break out was to put the same ingredients into one easy-to-carry roll.

That was it.

He hadn't built a business from scratch the way that Sean had. He'd had his family's backing, and his nonna's recipes. It was practically a no-fail venture.

He shifted uncomfortably in his seat. "That's not really why."

"Then why?" Sean sounded like he really wanted to know. His blue eyes gleamed with genuine interest. "You're a great cook."

He'd fooled Sean, too, like he'd fooled everyone else. "I'm not, really," he admitted. "I'm good at following a recipe, that's all."

"I find that hard to believe," Sean said, forehead creasing, like he couldn't quite envision a world in which Gabriel wasn't his normal overly confident self.

But Sean had confessed about Milo. He could tell Sean about his nonna.

"You know my family's in restaurants, right?"

Sean nodded. "Yeah, up in Napa, right?"

"Yeah," Gabriel said. "My parents run the restaurants still, though my brother, Luca, he's taken over now that they've retired to Florida."

"Restaurants? I didn't realize there was more than one."

"Five, actually," Gabriel said. "I could have worked in one of them. Everyone else does, and they're happy to do it."

"But you weren't," Sean stated, rather than asked. Like he'd already seen deep into Gabriel—knew how he ticked and how he hadn't wanted to just be another Moretti, making ziti and lasagna and throwing pizzas for the lunch crowd.

"I wanted some space," Gabe admitted. "I *needed* some space. And then Ren came with me, and that helped too, but I took all the family recipes with me. Even took the name, at least before I changed it." Sean made a face, and maybe before a week ago, that would have led to another round of bickering, but tonight he just let it slide. "So no, I'm not some great chef. I'm just . . . a guy with a really talented nonna."

"But you could be," Sean said.

"Hardly," Gabriel scoffed.

"I just think you should at least think about it. I'm always trying new stuff. I know a lot of the other trucks are, too, and sometimes it really pays off for them. Look at Tony. He was all about meat and now he's helping Lucas with his vegan truck. And he's totally on board."

"He's also totally in love," Gabriel pointed out.

"Yeah, but I don't think that's why." Sean stood and picked up their plates, heading towards the sink. "Just because it's something you've done forever doesn't mean it's something you have to *keep* doing. I learned that, when Milo died. I stayed in this horrible gray rut of misery for months and months. *Years*, actually, and I didn't need to. Milo wouldn't have wanted me to stay there. He'd have been just as upset as I was that I was only just existing."

"So you came here," Gabriel said.

"Yeah." Sean turned on the faucet and began to rinse the plates. "But it's not just about living with grief. You can do something different. You just have to make it happen. You already did it once."

"Yeah, I took Luca's loan and came down here with Ren. That . . ." Gabriel swallowed hard. "That wasn't exactly going out on a limb."

"Doesn't matter," Sean said matter-of-factly. "You still did it."

Gabe didn't want to tell Sean that he was wrong, but he was pretty sure he was. Instead, he stood. "I think . . . I think maybe I should go now."

Sean looked over, surprise in his eyes. "Okay," he said. "I thought . . . thought you might want to . . ."

"I want to," Gabriel said.

What he wanted was to stay. To sleep next to Sean and watch the way the morning light shone in his hair. But that was not going to happen anytime soon.

Sean wrapped his arms around him and then they were kissing again.

Gabriel knew he'd promised a second round, had hoped it would happen, but he'd never imagined that Sean would be so eager. Or that he'd be the one tugging him towards the bedroom again.

They were kind-of friends. And they were having sex. *Again*.

If Gabe kept reminding himself of these two facts, maybe he'd figure out how to keep his heart out of it. He knew that his heart was already in it. His heart had always been in it. As Sean wrapped his hand around Gabriel's cock and he reciprocated, he swore he could feel it skip a beat.

No matter how good the sex was, Gabriel was always going to want more.

CHAPTER SEVEN

SEAN TOLD HIMSELF THAT he was not disappointed that Gabriel hadn't stayed.

After all, he was the one who'd set the expectations. They were going to have sex, and scratch a mutual itch, and that was it.

He just hadn't expected to *like* spending non-naked time—*and* naked time—with Gabriel so much. He'd known him for two years now, and it was not exactly a mystery that they hadn't really liked each other. The guy had thrown a *meatball* at Sean. He'd been floored when he'd discovered how much he wanted to have sex with him. But discovering that he actually enjoyed spending time with him? That was a discovery that was throwing him a hell of a lot more.

"You're frowning at that kale mix like it did something to you," Tate said, as they sat in the shade, eating a late lunch together. "Does it need to apologize?"

"What?" Sean's head jerked up. He'd been lost in his thoughts. He'd had too many questions recently. Like, why had it been three days since Gabriel had been over and he hadn't asked if Sean wanted to get together again?

Sean was thinking he might have to ask him himself, and that thought made him both hot and cold all over.

With nerves, and with undeniable anticipation.

It had been so good the first—and the second—time. How good would it be the third?

"Does your salad need to apologize?" Tate asked again, still patient. Always so patient. He deserved a better friend than Sean was being.

"No, no, I'm just . . . thinking," Sean said. *About Gabriel.*

"About Gabe?" Tate asked, so casually that for a split second, Sean was terrified that he'd actually said that part out loud.

"No!" Sean said quickly. "No, of course not. Why would I be thinking about him?"

Tate chewed his wrap thoughtfully. "Maybe because you had sex with him?"

"I . . . we . . ." Sean spluttered, and Tate rolled his eyes.

"You were all over each other at the party and then you left together. You definitely had sex."

"Oh, yeah, *that*," Sean said weakly. "Um, yeah, we did. But no, I am definitely not thinking about him. No way. It's just . . . a sex thing. That's it."

"That's it?" Tate repeated with disbelief.

Okay, so Sean was a terrible liar. If he hadn't been so convinced he couldn't possibly have any feelings—he'd *know*, because he'd been deeply in love before and it would be impossible for him to mistake it for lust—he wouldn't have even convinced himself.

"It's just a sex thing," he said. "No big deal, right?"

The look Tate shot his direction made it clear that it was *very much* a big deal, but that was why Sean hadn't gone around sharing any details of what they'd done. It was nobody's business but their own.

Especially since it wasn't going anywhere.

"Right," Tate said, clearly not convinced.

Sean decided it was time to change the subject. "Have you ever met any of Gabriel's family?" he asked. Okay, so it was technically *not* a change of subject, but Sean was really curious after their conversation the other day.

"Only a few of them," Tate said, "There's like a million of them. Did Gabe tell you he's the middle child? Like *literal* middle child? Of seven kids?"

No, he had not. Sean told himself again that he had no right to feel disappointed.

"Wow," Sean said. No wonder Gabriel had left the family restaurant business to branch out.

"I met Luca once—he's the oldest," Tate said. "He comes down once a year, to make sure Gabe isn't fucking up or something." Tate rolled his eyes. "He's a little ridiculous. Imagine Gabriel times about a hundred. And talk about anal retentive. Geez."

"I bet Gabriel can't stand it," Sean said. Not surprised that he'd never met Luca; back then, he'd have wanted to keep Sean away from any vulnerable spots.

But things between them had changed. Maybe they would never see eye to eye about who should change their name, but they weren't constantly at each other's throats any more.

"Oh, he does," Tate said. "And last year, he brought Dario, who I think is a year younger than Gabriel."

"What's he like? Are he and Gabriel friends?"

"Well, anything looks good compared to Luca," Tate said. "But yeah, they seemed to be." He hesitated. "You sure seem interested in Gabriel, considering all you have is a sex thing."

Tate was not wrong. He rarely was.

"Oh, well, just gathering info, you know. I've got to convince Gabriel to change his name, and well, why not go back to the original? That's the family restaurant name, right?"

Even as he said it, Sean *knew* Gabriel wouldn't want to go back to that. He'd changed it for a reason *and* he'd already told Sean that he didn't feel like he could take any credit for anything he did. Changing the name would only make that worse.

"Yeah," Tate said. "But I wouldn't hold my breath."

"I'm not," Sean reassured him. "Just exploring some options."

Tate did not look totally convinced. "You could both change it, you know, and that would be a solution where neither of you feels like you lost," he suggested. "Maybe you could even be friends afterwards."

Tate was sweet; he really did mean well. But he didn't have all the facts. He didn't know about Milo. He didn't know that Sean was *never* going to give in.

Gabriel would just have to figure out a way to reconcile himself to a new name, or the old one.

"Speak of the devil," Tate said, gathering together his trash and standing to dump it into the bin a few feet away. "Looks like Gabe's coming over this way."

Sean squinted against the bright sun, wishing he'd brought his sunglasses, but Tate was right, Gabriel was on his way over, a determined expression on his handsome face.

"I'll let you two . . . well"—Tate paused—"do whatever it is you two do together."

Sean opened his mouth to argue, but snapped it shut again. "See you later," he finally said. They'd been stupid enough to be all over each other at the party; it was inevitable they were going to get some shit for hooking up.

Maybe they should just own it.

Gabriel wandered over, all casual, like he hadn't been clearly walking this direction for the last sixty seconds.

"Hey," he said. "What's going on?"

"Nothing," Sean said.

Gabriel shifted his weight from one foot to the other. "Busy day," he said. "You finally get a break?"

It was almost three now. Gabe was right, it had been a crazy day, if he was only just eating lunch mid-afternoon.

"Yeah," Sean said. "Lunch was busy for you guys, too?"

Gabriel nodded. "Super busy."

You should just ask him now. It'd be so easy. Just say: hey, do you want to come over after work and fuck me?

They should be easy to say. He *knew* Gabriel wanted him. They'd already had a really good time together once. They'd clearly left it open-ended—like it *could* happen again.

Who was he kidding? They both desperately wanted it to happen again. That was why Gabriel was over here, eying him like there was something he wanted to say—*needed* to say—but couldn't quite spit it out. And Sean? Well, he was just as pathetic. If Gabriel hadn't come over, he'd have gone over to Gabe's truck after his break and done just about the same goddamn thing.

"Are you busy later?" Gabriel finally asked.

"Like this afternoon?" Sean wondered.

"No," Gabriel said, and he shoved his hands into his pockets. "Like way later. Like after we close, later."

"Oh." *Duh.* "Well, yeah, I'm free." Gabriel had come part of the way, Sean reasoned, he could at least go the rest. "Did you want to come over again?"

"Yeah, I would," Gabriel said, a sudden smile breaking across his face. "That would be great."

Sean found himself smiling right back, so wide his face literally hurt. "Yeah, it really would."

"Alright. So . . . meet you after close?" Gabriel said hopefully.

"Yeah, sounds good," Sean said, rising and throwing away his mostly uneaten salad. He hated to waste food, but between the midday heat and the sudden excitement pumping through his veins, he wasn't hungry at all.

Well, that wasn't quite true, Sean thought as he and Gabriel just stared at each other. Like neither of them knew quite what to say. He *was* hungry. Just not for food.

"Alright, I should get back to the truck; give Ren a break," Gabriel said, but didn't move.

"Yeah," Sean said. Not moving either. "I should re-open."

The air between them was practically crackling with the tension—it was somewhat similar to how they'd always been, Sean realized, but different now too. Because he knew how Gabriel tasted and he smelled and the noises he made when he came.

Everything between them, which had always felt so impersonal before, felt intensely personal now.

Gabriel knew about Milo. He'd told Sean about his family and a little about his insecurities.

Nothing, Sean realized, was going to be the same after that.

And suddenly, he really did not know what they were going to do about the name. He couldn't change it, but knowing what he did now, about Gabriel and his family, could he legitimately ask him, even as a friend, to change it *back*?

He didn't know.

Maybe Tate had the right idea after all, and they should both change it.

But that tiny sore spot inside of Sean, the one that still occasionally thought that Milo might pop his head through the door and shoot Sean that big smile of his, the one that he continued to remember and to grieve, it rebelled. He couldn't give in; if he did, what kind of a person would that make him?

"Maybe you could make me one of those quesadillas again," Gabriel said hopefully.

"I'd love to," Sean said, and discovered he meant it.

Wasn't that weird? He could have sex with Gabriel and make him a quesadilla and it was fine, but the thought of changing the food truck's name made him panic.

"Good." Gabriel still hadn't walked away.

Sean really needed to re-open his truck, though if he was a few minutes late, who would know? Maybe he could sneak Gabriel back there for a quick make-out session. Just something to ease the tension a bit.

But would it? He didn't really think it would. Kissing Gabe would only make him want him more.

"I . . ." Sean hesitated. "I guess I'll see you later?"

"Yeah," Gabriel said.

There was finally nothing left to do but to turn and walk back to his truck. And Sean was left feeling the whole time that he'd just left something behind. He just couldn't figure out what it was.

The afternoon and evening both crawled and sped by, all at the same time. It was just as busy for the dinner rush as lunch had been, and even though Sean was busy, taking orders, assembling wraps, and feeding hungry people, he found for the first time in a long time that he couldn't lose himself in his work.

Instead, he was thinking about what was going to happen when he flipped his sign from *Open* to *Closed* and he met up with Gabriel.

What would they do?

The thoughts kept racing through Sean's head, until he was overwhelmed by the possibilities.

Would he let Gabriel take control again and let him make the decisions about how things would unfold the moment they walked into his house?

Or would Sean put his foot down and demand the thing he'd wanted last time? The idea of being fucked again, of *Gabe* doing the fucking? It made his fingertips tremble as he rolled up a wrap. It had been something he'd wanted before they'd ever touched each other, but now that he knew what Gabriel sounded like when he was just about to lose control, the thought was inevitable.

How would he sound when he was deep inside Sean?

"You look distracted," Ren said when he came by to grab a late dinner.

"I'm not distracted," Sean lied. "Not even remotely."

"Okay, good, well, you should know that Gabriel's barely been able to put one foot in front of the other the last three days. So please go fuck him so he's useful to me again."

Sean couldn't stop his cheeks from flaming bright red. "Oh, uh, I don't . . ."

Ren held up a hand, shooting Sean a wry smile. "It's alright. I know what's going on. It's not hard to read, when you know what you're looking for. And you've got flashing neon lights."

Sean hoped it was flashing neon lights that advertised that he was only here for sex. The last thing he wanted was to give Gabriel the idea that he could *feel* something. That was why he'd been so clear upfront.

"We were hardly hiding it the other night," Sean said slowly. Tried to steady his still-trembling fingers as he finished folding Ren's chicken caesar salad wrap.

In the last two years, he'd done this approximately a million times, but his hands felt clumsy and unsure as he wrapped it up in paper and sliced neatly through the center with one of his sharp knives.

"No, but now you're all shy," Ren said and Sean instantly felt his hackles rise. He wasn't *shy*. He was . . . well, it was a big thing to have sex again. It was an even bigger thing to have *regular* sex again. Especially with someone that, before the last week, he hadn't been sure he even *liked*.

"If you really want to know, we're meeting up tonight," Sean said, determined *not* to be shy. Especially determined that Ren wouldn't find him shy and awkward. Because Ren was clearly the expert on hookups, and if he was speaking with so much disdain about shyness, then that was something Sean *needed* to overcome. He'd done it the other night, hadn't he?

"I'm glad to hear it," Ren said with a wink. "Maybe Gabe'll be less of a bear."

"I'll see what I can do," Sean promised, sliding Ren's wrap through the window.

Ren took it but didn't leave. Dusk had fallen, and the lot had emptied out, only a few stragglers behind. He could probably theoretically close *now*, which might even be something Gabriel was considering too, especially if Ren was eating his late dinner.

"You know," Ren said slowly, "Gabriel isn't really like me. We might look a little bit alike, but we're not really similar underneath."

"Oh, you're much hotter than Gabe," Sean said, which was another lie. A lie he hoped, desperately, would not make it back to the man in question.

Ren smiled softly. "I'm just saying we're not very similar. I don't think I've ever gotten hurt in my entire life—not from a hookup. It's neat and easy, and there's a lot to be said for that. But Gabe? He likes it messy."

"Messy?" Sean wasn't sure what Ren was getting at exactly.

"Yeah. Just . . . remember that, okay?"

"Alright." Sean frowned as he watched Ren walk off.

He puzzled through Ren's words all through his cleanup, but he still wasn't quite sure what he'd meant. Was Ren trying to warn him away from Gabe? Warn him that he could get hurt? Tell him that he shouldn't get involved? Sean thought that if that was the case, then Ren wouldn't have encouraged them in the first place.

And he most definitely had.

When he met up with Gabe half an hour later, he still wasn't sure what Ren had meant, but the moment he saw Gabriel, all the doubts and all his confusion just melted away. This was why he'd wanted Gabriel; no matter what Ren claimed about his cousin liking things messy, this was as easy and as natural as breathing.

"Hey," Gabriel said, breaking into a huge grin when he saw Sean approaching where he was sitting on one of the picnic table-tops, flicking through something on his phone.

"Hey," Sean said. "Sorry if you were waiting."

"Not for long," Gabriel said, jumping down. Without even discussing it, they headed out of the lot the same way they had the other night. Towards Sean's townhouse. "Ren was insufferable today, so I let him take most of the cleanup."

"You should be nicer to him, you know," Sean chided him, thinking of how earlier, Ren had possibly tried to protect Gabriel.

"Why?" Gabriel asked. "He's a pain in my ass."

"He means well," Sean said. Though he wasn't sure that was quite true. On the surface, Ren was a very straightforward person, but now that he thought about it, there were almost certainly mysterious depths to him.

"He fucking does not," Gabriel said with a chuckle. "He practically started a fist fight in line today, during lunch."

"Seriously?"

"His flirting is lethal. You know that," Gabriel added, the edge of his voice going a little darker. "Anyway, I told him to cut that shit out. I don't need two people throwing down for the chance at his fucking phone number."

"Do you think he'll ever settle down?" Sean wondered. Thinking he wasn't just asking about Ren, who'd made free and easy his trademark, but himself, too. Would he be happy like this, just hooking up, with no strings, forever? Would he ever find what he'd shared with Milo again?

For a very long time, he'd been sure that was impossible. Milo had been one of a kind, and there was no way he could ever fall for someone that easily ever again.

"Naw," Gabriel said. "He's a free spirit. I think he actually likes the hookup thing. Free and easy, you know?"

Sean knew, because Ren had just told him, and he'd also just told him that Gabriel didn't like things free and easy. He liked it *messy*. And Sean didn't think that Ren was talking about getting down and dirty during sex.

Maybe Sean liked it a little messy too; if he didn't, he wouldn't have picked Gabe to be his hookup. Of course, he hadn't really deliberately *picked* Gabriel; if he thought about it, it was his cock that had done all the picking.

"Yeah, I can see that," Sean said.

They were quiet on the last block before Sean's townhouse.

He was wondering the whole time, with every step closer they took, if Gabriel would be on him the second the door closed, if it would be like last time or if it would be different. If Gabriel would change it up.

He did.

Sean unlocked the door, and even though he felt the warmth of the man beside him, hovering close, he didn't touch him. Didn't even touch him when they were inside. Just stood there, looking at Sean like he was some kind of mystery he wanted to unravel.

He'd been so relieved that last time things hadn't been awkward. That Gabriel had just seamlessly taken over, and made him feel good, and hadn't let him think too much or too hard about it.

But now, he couldn't *stop* thinking.

"I wasn't sure we were going to do this again," was what Gabriel finally said, and Sean wanted, despite that he *knew* better, to scream at him.

"Why?" he asked, instead. Because if he did scream, then this definitely *wouldn't* be happening again.

"I don't know." Gabriel shifted his weight again, looking just as uneasy as he had earlier today. "You didn't say you wanted me again."

Sean rolled his eyes. Was that what this was really about? That he hadn't, the very next day, gone up to Gabriel, and confessed how life-changing the sex had been? The man was smart, but he could be pretty damn stupid, too.

"Get over here," Sean said gruffly, and Gabriel *came*, melting into him like it was just the invitation he'd been waiting for.

Sean's fingers tangled in his hair, and he tilted him just the way he wanted, kissing him deeply. It was incredible how Gabriel shivered in response just with a kiss, his cock a hard, hot line against his thigh.

He pulled away for a second, sliding his fingertips down Gabriel's exposed arms, feeling the goose bumps rise on his skin as he touched him. "Let's go to the bedroom," he said.

Gabriel's eyes were dark. Intense. Sean sometimes felt like he could lose himself in them, if he didn't keep one foot on solid ground. "What do you want?" he murmured. His hand, hot and certain, trailed down Sean's spine, resting right above the curve of his ass. "Do you still want what you did last time?"

Did he still want it? He was *desperate* for it.

"Yes," Sean said.

Maybe he should be embarrassed at how crazy he was for it, especially considering that he'd gone this long without. But suddenly, it was unacceptable that Gabriel wasn't inside him *right now*.

"Okay," Gabriel said. "We'll see what we can do about that."

Sean didn't realize what he'd *really* meant by those words until they'd gotten to the bedroom, and were trading kisses of increasing fervor, between pulling their shirts off. He nibbled Gabriel's bottom lip, and he groaned, pulling back.

"Hey, you'd better be careful with that, or you've got no chance in hell of eventually getting what you want."

"What?" Sean asked impudently. "Don't like a little nibbling?" He leaned in, nibbling again, and was rewarded with an even louder groan. "I think you *really* like a little nibbling," he said.

"Probably too much," Gabriel admitted, his cheeks flushing. "I'm gonna come before I even get a finger in you."

"What about your cock?" Sean pouted. He knew he'd need prep. It had been a *long* time, and Gabriel's dick wasn't exactly small.

"Eventually," Gabriel said, and Sean knew he was being deliberately evasive.

Sean frowned, his fingers stilling on the button of Gabriel's khaki shorts. "I'm not made of glass, you know. I'm not going to fucking break."

"It's just . . . it's been a long time for you."

Before it had all been hot passion, but now Sean could see the care in Gabriel's eyes. But he didn't *want* to see it. He'd asked Gabriel here for one purpose and one purpose only. To *fuck* him.

He almost thought, *if he won't, I'll find someone who will.* But he didn't, because it was a lie. He didn't want Ren, or just any random guy. He wanted *Gabriel*.

"So what, you're going to give me a finger or two and hope that's enough?" Sean said, crossing his arms over his chest. "I said I wanted to get *fucked,* not finger fucked, thank you very much."

"I . . ." Gabriel tried to say but Sean wasn't done, and interrupted him.

"And if I can't handle something, I'll tell you. We'll deal with it. But you don't get to make my choices for me. We're fucking, that's all."

Gabriel's gaze narrowed. "If fucking is what you want, fucking is what you're gonna get."

"Oh?" Sean decided he liked this determined version of Gabriel. It reminded him of how pissed off he'd been right before the meatball had gone sailing through the air.

Maybe if they'd just decided to fuck then, they could've saved two years of bickering.

Gabe's hand was firm and so, *so* sure as he reached out and grabbed Sean's ass, gripping it hard.

He and Milo had always been so careful with each other. Careful in the way that Gabe kept wanting to be, but Sean discovered that this was really good, too. It worked him up, made his blood race as he thought about Gabriel manhandling him, fingers digging into his hips as he worked his cock in.

And then he *did* manhandle him onto the bed, pushing him up onto it, using his larger size and unexpected strength and then he was stripping the rest of Sean's clothes off with a single-mindedness that left him dizzy.

"This what you wanted?" Gabriel said, all casual intensity as he leaned down, his mouth a breath away from Sean's.

"Yes, yes," Sean said breathlessly.

"Just wanted to get me worked up, didn't you?" Gabriel asked, raising an eyebrow.

Had he? Sean hadn't really thought about it, but he'd liked it when Gabe had taken control the other night, taken away the decisions from him, the *thinking*, and he'd also liked the idea of finally getting what he wanted.

This was the best of both worlds, wasn't it?

"Yes," Sean repeated, and Gabriel grinned wildly.

"Well, baby, you're gonna get it now."

"Is that a promise?" Sean asked. "Because from here, it looks like you're all talk so far."

Gabriel's smile went wicked at the edges and Sean couldn't help the moan that escaped him as his fingers wrapped around his cock, tugging insistently.

"Guess I'm not," Gabriel said. He nodded towards the bedside table and its drawer. "You got everything I'm going to need in there?"

Lube. A condom. Sean licked his suddenly dry lips. There was no reason to be nervous. Even if he hadn't done this in awhile. He'd made sure he was stocked, with brand-new products.

"Yeah," Sean said, watching as Gabriel leaned over, pulling open the drawer, and finding what he'd stashed there. A new tube of lubricant, and a fresh box of condoms. Anything he'd owned before had been thrown out when he'd moved to LA.

Back then he hadn't been sure he'd ever be ready to take this step again.

But the morning after Gabe had been here last, Sean had stopped by the drugstore and made sure he was prepared.

It was one thing to ask for this, though, and it was another to guarantee it happening. But over the last three days, nerves had melted into a heady anticipation, and now, though he felt adrenaline sparking in him, it wasn't because he was scared.

He knew what he wanted now, and Gabriel was going to give it to him.

"Look at you, all prepared," Gabriel cooed, and the dark edge to his voice made Sean shiver. "I like this side of you."

"Which side?" Sean gasped as Gabriel stroked his cock again, then slipped his fingers lower, pushing his thighs open.

"The side that's all prepared to be bad," Gabriel said, his tone and the look in his eyes hypnotizing. "That knows what it wants and is gonna get it."

"I want you," Sean said, even though they both knew that.

Gabriel hesitated, and leaned down, his kiss gentle and sweet at first and then turning surprisingly dirty and hot, tongue stroking over Sean's. He wasn't proud of it, but between Gabe's hand on his dick and his tongue in his mouth, it was hard to even focus, and when it ended, Gabriel pulling away, he almost cried out with frustration. He was so goddamn horny, didn't Gabe see that?

Couldn't he feel him pulsing in his hand, twitching with every touch? Couldn't he feel how hard he was? How wet, precome bubbling out of his slit?

"Come on," Gabe ground out, "I wanna get a finger in you."

Sean swallowed hard, suddenly afraid that after all his insistence that the fucking happen *tonight*, that he'd lose it the moment Gabriel started.

How had he gotten to the edge so quickly?

Five years without this, was the easy answer.

He squeezed his eyes shut, trying to shut out all the things that were driving him there—Gabriel's big body caging his, how good he smelled still, even after a whole day working in the heat, how insanely bitable the ridge of muscle on his shoulder was, the intensity in his gaze, like he could eat Sean alive, and still not have fed all his hunger. But even with his eyes closed, he could hear the bottle open and then close and then he could *feel*.

Sean and Milo had figured this out together—they'd both been sheltered, new to any kind of gay scene, and there'd been plenty of mistakes. But Gabriel knew exactly what he was doing, brushing the pad of his finger over his hole, smoothing the lube around.

He gasped when that thumb slid in, and cried out when he went so slow, so *goddamned* slow. He wanted more. Might even be craving the inevitable stretch of it.

"Oh, yeah, you fucking love this," Gabe ground out, like the fact that he did was the sexiest thing he'd ever heard. And he *did*, he was pushing against that thumb, wanting it deeper, wanting more, wanting to be filled up and by *Gabriel*.

"Another, please," Sean gasped out, still worried he wasn't going to be able to make it last. The moment he felt Gabe's cock sinking in, he was probably going to lose it. He was so close now, like the handjob that Gabriel had given him the other day hadn't even happened. It was like he was fresh and new again, a teenager just experimenting with this stuff for the first time.

"Oh, yeah, you fucking love it." Gabe's voice was gruff, guttural. And Sean realized, with a shiver up his spine, that this was his sex voice. All this time they'd known each other and he'd never wondered what Gabriel's sex voice would sound like.

The truth was, it sounded really fucking good. Sean wanted to get lost in it. Wanted Gabe to talk him through fucking him, tell him how incredible he felt, how tight and hot, how insane he drove him, as Gabriel drove him insane right back.

The pain hit when Gabriel's second finger was halfway in, the burning stretch of it, but Sean forced himself to relax. He'd done this for the first time before, he knew how to deal with it. It was just like riding a bicycle.

"That's it, baby, take it," Gabriel cooed, working him through it, until the discomfort melted into pure pleasure, making him feel perfect and whole and *alive*.

"Come on, come on," Sean chanted through clenched teeth. He was so turned on, walking along that razor-thin edge for so long that it felt like anything might just tip him over. And he wanted it to be Gabriel's cock. *Needed* it to be Gabriel's cock.

"Alright, bossy," Gabriel said, and Sean gasped as his fingers pulled out, leaving him feeling so empty. "Just a goddamned second."

Sean heard the condom wrapper rip and glanced down, watching as Gabriel rolled the rubber on. His cock was as hard as it had been the other night, when he'd sucked him dry, and seemed to look even impossibly bigger than it had then. But he could do this. He *wanted* to do this. More than he wanted anything else.

How long had it been since he took anything for himself? So goddamn long.

He *deserved* this cock. He deserved to come his fucking brains out on it.

"Oh yeah," Gabriel groaned as he began to push in. It was overwhelming. So much more sensation than his fingers, spearing him open, and he felt every inch of it.

"Fuck, fuck," Sean breathed out, as Gabriel continued to slide in. How was it that there was so goddamn much? He felt so full already and Gabe was still moving, still pushing in.

"You good?" Gabriel asked, tipping his forehead against Sean's. "I can . . ."

"No," Sean said, wild for it. The pain was already beginning to slip away, and *god*, that was the end of it, wasn't it? The blunt tip resting, it felt like, right against his prostate. "Oh my god, oh my god." It was so much, almost *too* much, and he needed it to end, before he imploded with how much he was feeling. He began to reach down for his own cock, because that was what he needed—a few good hard strokes and he'd be coming and it would . . .

"Hell no," Gabriel said, nimbly catching his hand and then pulling the other one to join it, his palm steadily pressing Sean's wrists into the pillow. "You wanted fucked, you're gonna get fucked. None of this coming early shit," he said. Panted a little. "'Cause maybe now I really want to fuck this tight ass."

"Do you?" Sean felt a little out of his mind with the pressure at his wrists, and the pressure everywhere else.

"Fuck yes I do," Gabriel said, and thrust a little, and then a little more, still being gentle, but Sean had the sudden thought of how fucking good it would be when he wasn't holding back anymore. What would it be like when Gabe lost control?

Fucking amazing, that's what it would be like.

"Oh god," Sean moaned as his hips sped up and even his very good imagination hadn't been able to conjure how good this would feel. He was going out of his fucking mind, needing to just get a hand on his own cock, to relieve the pressure, but Gabe wouldn't let up and wouldn't stop.

"You are so fucking perfect just like this," Gabriel said with a groan. "I could do this forever."

Sean reared up and bit him on his shoulder, because he was beyond words, beyond anything really, and he needed something, *anything*, to push him over the edge, and the taste of Gabriel's skin in his mouth felt like as good a method as any.

"Fuck," Gabriel shouted, and Sean realized he hadn't been lying. The nibbling—and apparently the biting, too—really got him going because he was screwing his eyes shut, hips thrusting erratically, and Sean realized with desperation that he was about to come, and Sean *still* hadn't.

He pushed up even further, sliding his drippy cock right up against Gabriel's firm stomach and that was all it took, he was catapulting past anything he thought he could bear, pleasure roaring through him in a dizzying wave.

"Oh my god," Sean wailed as he clenched around Gabriel's cock. "Oh my god."

Gabriel's head fell to his shoulder, and he shuddered out his own orgasm, filling the condom.

Finally, his hips stilled and Sean could only lie there, feeling everything still. His wrists, caught up in Gabriel's hand. His huge cock, continuing to touch all the oversensitive spots inside him.

"That was . . ." Gabriel let out a guttural sigh.

"Something else," Sean finished for him with a semi-hysterical laugh.

"Yeah," Gabriel agreed, his smile so warm.

"We could do it again," Sean said.

Gabriel's smile morphed into faux shock. "Right now? I hate to break it to you, but I'm not eighteen still."

"No, no," Sean giggled. "Not right now. Like . . . tomorrow. I just . . . realized I didn't want us to get too up in our own heads like we had last time. So I thought it'd be a good idea to establish that *yes*, I want to do it again. As soon as possible."

Gabriel raised a questioning eyebrow. "You think you're going to get any arguments out of me?"

Sean laughed. "For once, *no*."

CHAPTER EIGHT

THE ONLY GOOD PART of the weekly staff meeting was that Tony held it at the Funky Cup.

If Gabriel was going to have to listen to his friends bitch and whine and complain about all the injustices that had been delivered upon them during the last week, he wanted to be able to drink a few beers while doing it.

In their defense, they did a whole lot more than whining, typically, but by the end, that was usually what it devolved to. Tate told a story about how a customer wanted a grilled cheese, no cheese. Lucas joked about a vegetarian who'd ordered the fish tacos and then complained he couldn't eat them.

Gabriel had just finished up his second beer, and was eyeing Sean from across the room, wondering if it was too soon or if he would look too desperate to suggest they go back to his place. But before he could decide one way or the other, Tony threw a wrench in.

It *was* Tony, so he shouldn't have been surprised.

"So, we've been open six months now," Tony announced casually, "and I want to start implementing some of my bigger ideas for the lot."

"Like what?" Tate asked.

"I'm so glad you asked," Tony said with a mischievous grin that almost never boded well for anyone. "I thought it would be so cool if we paired up two trucks and had them develop a dish that they could both serve, kind of a mashup of their two specialties."

Later, Gabriel would look back and *know* that Tony was absolutely, definitely fucking with them. But stupidly, at the moment, he actually nodded and said, "I think that's a really great idea."

"It is," Lucas chimed in, because of course he did. He had to live with Tony, didn't he?

"It could be cool," Ash said, and he was the most hesitant voice so far. "What do you think, Alexis?"

Alexis was not usually a very vocal member of the meeting. Mostly he just smiled and nodded along, keeping his own counsel. Of course, Gabe was secretly convinced he had the best sales of any of them, and didn't want them to know it.

"Uh, I think it's good," Alexis said, speaking up. "I'd be happy to do it. Would we both serve the dish?"

"Yeah, that'd be the idea. A collaborative effort, that both trucks get to benefit from. We'll do some special signage around the lot, try to drum up some extra business."

"Are you thinking we'll do this all at once? All of us?" Sean wondered, sounding suspicious.

If Gabriel had ever needed evidence that Sean was smarter than he was, it was right then. But he still didn't see it.

"Nope, we'll do one pairing a month I think," Tony said. "And the idea is that it'll just be for that month. Something special to get people coming to the lot, and then hopefully coming back for more."

"Alright," Ash said. "I'm in."

"Great," Tony said with a lot of enthusiasm.

Too much enthusiasm.

"Who's going first?" Lucas wondered.

"Oh, I was thinking we'd start with . . ." Tony grinned. "Gabe and Sean."

It took Gabriel a minute to realize that Tony had said his name and Sean's together for a purpose other than giving him shit. Was he suggesting . . .? Oh yes, he was. Oh, that motherfucking interfering asshole.

Sean's deepening frown made it *very* obvious that he'd already figured out that Tony had been planning this from the moment he'd brought it up.

Ash laughed nervously. "Do you really think that's a good idea?"

"Why wouldn't it be?" But Tony couldn't pull off that faux innocent tone even if he'd had a thousand years to practice it. He was clearly feeling this idea and also the major explosive device he'd just thrown in their path.

"I mean," Ash said hesitatingly. "I love Gabe and Sean, but they don't always . . . well, they don't always get along, you know?"

"Oh, they seemed to be getting along plenty fine the other night," Tony said with a knowing chuckle. "I think it'll work out just fine. I've got no concerns at all."

Not everyone looked convinced of this, but Tony moved on before there could be any more arguments voiced. "Next on the agenda," he said, "is that huge City of Food festival that Los Angeles is holding in Santa Anita Park. They're expanding from a weekend to a whole week. I know a lot of you want to participate, so I was considering closing the lot for that week. Thoughts?"

Gabriel had considered participating, but the agreement he'd signed with Tony and Wyatt, promising to be at the lot and open for six days out of the seven, did make it a problem. It seemed a lot of the other guys had discovered the same issue.

"I don't have an issue," Lucas said. "It's big visibility. The vegan truck is already signed up. I know Wyatt is trying to get Nana's Desserts in, too."

"It would be great for us to have a big presence at the festival," Tate said. Gabriel knew he was one of the people who'd mentioned wanting to go, but hadn't been sure how to go about doing it.

"I agree," Tony said. "So we'll just close that whole week. Post announcements ahead of time, and signs directing anyone to the festival. Santa Anita Park isn't that far from the lot."

"It's not," Alexis agreed. "I will definitely be applying."

Gabe still didn't know if he wanted to. The weekend alone had always been nuts and had drained him and Ren for weeks after. To spend a whole seven days there? He wasn't sure, visibility or not, that he wanted to commit to it.

Maybe he could actually take a vacation.

"Speaking of the lot closing," Tony continued, "let's talk about security."

"Security?" Sean wondered.

"Yeah, Wyatt and I have been discussing the possibility of adding more trucks this fall, and well, I'm concerned about the security. We have the lights, but that's only going to keep problems at bay for so long. I think we need to install a security system. You know," he said with a wave of his hand. "Cameras and all that shit."

"Really?" Tate sounded dubious. "Have we had any problems?"

"A few," Tony admitted. "You know Alexis had his door scratched up a month or so back, like someone was trying to pick the lock. And there's been some reports of some suspicious people lurking around. The lights won't scare them away forever."

"With more trucks, it's going to become a bigger enticement," Lucas pointed out. "There's a lot of expensive equipment we're leaving with just a weak lock to protect it. I don't think it'd hurt to not only have cameras but a security patrol at night."

"Wait a minute, a security patrol . . ." Ash stood up abruptly, the chair legs clattering on the concrete floor. "You are fucking *out of line*, Tony."

"What do you mean?" But Tony had that suspicious tone again—the one that everyone knew meant that Tony thought he'd put one over on everyone, but was actually transparent as fuck.

"You are going to hire Lennox," Ash said. "I know you are."

"He's already a customer, which makes him an obvious choice," Tony argued.

"I don't want that guy hanging around," Ash argued bitterly. "I don't like him."

Clearly Ash had moved on from *this guy might be cute and could be interested* to *I don't like him*. Didn't bode well for Lennox getting into Ash's pants—or the other way around.

"Well, unfortunately he's a highly recommended professional who already knows how our business works," Tony said, not sounding sorry at all.

Ash glanced at Gabriel, the look full of mutual commiseration, as Tony continued prattling on and on about how qualified Lennox was.

Yeah, Tony had definitely managed to screw both of them over, that was for sure.

A few minutes later, the meeting broke up and Gabriel guzzled the rest of his beer, wondering if he might have time to grab another before he had his inevitable confrontation with Tony.

But before he could make a break for it, Tony appeared at his right elbow, steering him towards the bar.

"Hey," Tony said in a low voice. A quick glance around told Gabriel that Sean had already left. Before Gabriel could even proposition him for another night of hot sex. Yet *another* thing that Tony had screwed him on.

"What do you want?" Gabriel asked, leaning against the bar, gesturing to Shaw that he wanted another beer. "You got any other bright and wonderful ideas designed to ruin my life?"

"That wasn't . . ." Tony started to say but Gabriel held up a hand.

"Don't even try it," Gabe said. "I know what you're about. Well, what *someone* is about. This plan is too smart for you. Who came up with it?"

"What do you mean?" Tony asked.

"I mean," Gabriel said, taking a drink of his beer, "that this is a little subtle for you, dude."

"Hey, you know, I told you guys to fix the name shit, and instead of doing it, you started fucking. So I figure, you're getting along so great, might as well work together some more."

"That is . . ." Gabriel groaned. "That is not the point."

"Well, it kind of fucking is," Tony said pleasantly. "I expect to see your collaboration up on both of your menus next week."

"I really hate you, you know," Gabriel said, equally pleasantly. "You are determined to make this impossible for me. For *us*."

He'd been depending on the fact that they didn't really *work* together to keep this new harmony continuing. But forcing them into the same truck? To develop a recipe? Well, their professional relationship had been a disaster from the first moment, and Gabriel was afraid this was just going to be more of the same.

"I am, huh? Then why did I have to find out from *Ren* that you already have a new name all picked out, with a logo and everything?"

"I don't . . . it's just a mockup," Gabriel said hurriedly. Why had Ren sold him out that way? Why would he? He was not *ready*, goddamn it. Sean wasn't ready. Not even remotely. They were still trying to figure out how to hook up without awkwardness.

If it fell apart now, it would *fall apart*.

And Gabriel hadn't figured out a way to fix it yet, or even tougher, to come to terms with it.

"Really," Tony drawled. "Okay, then, you have a mockup all ready to go. So, *go*."

"It's complicated," Gabriel said defensively. "Did anyone interfere when you and Lucas were figuring your shit out? When you didn't fucking listen to anyone about that asshole Jeremy who was stealing from you?"

"No," Tony said. "Though maybe in retrospect, you maybe should have been more forceful about it. I really fucked that up good." He took a deep breath. "Kinda like you might fuck this up with Sean, if you're not careful."

"I've got it under control," Gabriel insisted. Even though he definitely did not. Not even by a long shot. "Though if you keep fucking interfering, I definitely won't anymore."

"Hey, I haven't heard you guys snap at each other for two weeks now. That's practically a honeymoon period."

"Tony," Gabriel warned.

Tony threw up his hands. "Okay, okay, I'll back off. But the collab plan? It's still on. And for the record, the whole thing was *originally* my idea."

"Really?" Gabriel was not convinced.

"Well," Tony corrected, "the collaboration might have originally been my idea, but I wasn't going to implement it this quickly."

"I thought so." Gabriel stared at his bottle of beer. "I'm gonna have to fix this mess you just created."

"Or you and Sean could fix it *together*, which is the whole fucking point, you know? I told you to take care of it, and I thought you would. If you had, we wouldn't be having this conversation right now."

Yeah, and Sean and I wouldn't be fucking right now.

"Maybe. Maybe not."

"Fix this," Tony said, stealing his beer and taking a huge gulp of it. "I mean it."

An hour and two beers later, Gabriel was listening to Ash bitch about Tony and about Lennox, when he got a text. When he glanced at his phone, his pulse increased. It was from Sean.

Maybe he was inviting him over anyway. It was late, maybe, but as far as Gabriel was concerned, it was never going to be *too* late.

But when he opened the text, instead of a late-night booty call, Sean was asking when he would have free time in the next few days to start their collaboration.

Even worse, his words felt formal and strained. Like the last thing Sean *wanted* to do was collaborate with Gabriel, but he was doing it because he *had* to.

He hadn't intended to actually groan out loud, but he must have because Ash finally stopped talking and stared at him. "You okay?" he asked.

"No," Gabriel said, rubbing a hand across his face. "No. Tony is determined to hack this all up."

"I'm hardly a fan of his at the moment," Ash said precisely, swirling his bourbon in the squat glass, "but I'm wondering if you didn't get at least halfway there, all on your own."

"What do you mean?" Gabriel wondered, even though he had his suspicions.

"I mean, just *fucking change your name*," Ash said. "It can't be that hard, can it? You've already done it once."

"Yeah, which means I shouldn't have to do it *twice*," Gabriel said.

"This isn't like Ross with his three divorces," Ash teased him, referring to the character from *Friends*. "It's not like there's some kind of concrete limit you've got to stick to."

"If it was that easy," Gabriel said, "don't you think I'd have already done it?" He thought about that packet he'd gathered together. The new name, the new logo, everything ready to go—but he'd never been able to bear pulling the trigger.

He still couldn't bear it.

"Yeah, actually I do," Ash said, leaning back in his chair. "You must have some kind of master plan. How to get out of this with the name *and* the guy."

He didn't have any kind of fucking plan. "That'd be great," Gabriel muttered. Even though it seemed impossible now.

His fingers hovered over his phone's keyboard, unsure of what he should say. *How* he should say it. Finally, he just typed out a message that hopefully didn't look like he was trying too goddamn hard.

I could do tomorrow morning. How about you?

"Hey, maybe this whole thing will be a blessing in disguise," Ash offered. "Maybe Sean will realize how great you work together . . . and not just in bed."

Gabriel rolled his eyes. "That doesn't seem very likely."

He felt the buzz of his phone vibrating, with Sean's return text.

Works for me. Eight AM, was all it said.

Ash shot him another one of those annoying commiserating glances. He hated that he felt like he deserved them. "You deserve another beer."

He did. He really did. But now he had to get up early, and if he had another, tomorrow was going to be miserable in more ways than one.

"Actually, I think I'm going to take off," Gabriel said, draining the last of his beer and standing up.

"Well," Ash said, shooting him a grin, "I hope you don't kill each other."

Gabriel hoped for that too, but truthfully, his expectations were low.

It turned out that Gabriel's expectations were not *quite* low enough.

He slept badly, tossing and turning, worrying about what would happen the next day. It didn't help that he'd had four beers, along with very little dinner, and he was more hungover than he wanted to admit when he woke up far earlier than he usually did.

It didn't help when he stumbled out of his bedroom and into the rest of the living space he and Ren shared, and found a strange pair of shoes next to the couch, and a coat he didn't recognize hanging on one of the wall hooks.

If all had gone to plan, he'd been hoping that he too could sleep over. The last two times they'd hooked up, Sean had seemed disappointed that he'd left instead of staying the night. Gabriel had hoped that he could change the pattern last night. But instead of hooking up, he'd ended up alone in his cold bed, while Ren had sex *again*.

He wasn't jealous, exactly, because he had no interest in doing what Ren did, but he did feel like Sean was slipping through his fingers.

Then he pulled open the cabinet and realized they were out of coffee.

Sure enough, *coffee* was written on the little notepad Ren had put on the side of their fridge, but with the craziness of the summer, it seemed neither of them had had time to go to the store.

"Ugh," Gabriel groaned out loud. "No fucking coffee."

He could stop on the way to the lot, but he was already running behind, and he'd intended to be *early*, because Sean was unfailingly on time. He'd be pissed if Gabe was late, and that was definitely not the right way to start out this whole collaboration thing.

But there was nothing he could do about it now, Gabriel thought with frustration as he took the quickest shower he could, throwing clothes on and racing down the stairs of their building.

The line at the coffee shop was longer than usual, and by the time Gabe set foot on the lot, it was 8:09. And sure enough, Sean was standing by his truck, sipping his coffee from a Starbucks cup, a disgruntled expression on his face.

"You're late," Sean said as a greeting as Gabriel approached.

"I . . ." Gabe thought about giving all the excuses he'd thought up. He was tired. He'd gone to bed late, and *alone.* They'd been out of coffee, and everyone at the coffee shop had been taking their sweet-ass time. But he snapped his mouth shut. Sean hated excuses as much as he hated people not respecting his schedule. "Sorry."

"I bet you are," Sean said.

It was useless to try to prove that he actually was. Especially when Sean was in such a clearly prickly mood. Gabriel set his coffee down and unlocked the door of his truck. "Have you thought about what you'd like to do?" He had, during his sleepless night. Hoped that he could convince Sean that the path of least resistance was the best route for them to take.

But considering the set of Sean's firm jaw, and the stubborn glint in his eyes, he had a feeling that was already out of the question.

"I have a few ideas," Sean said as they climbed into his truck. Everything was clean and sparkling, from Ren's deep cleaning the night before. Not that Gabriel had expected less, but it felt good that Sean wouldn't be able to complain or say something snarky about Gabe's truck.

"I thought we could just do something simple," Gabriel said. "Like a meatball wrap, or something."

"You don't think that's a little obvious?" Sean said, raising an eyebrow.

"Maybe it should be." *Maybe it should be easy. Because nothing else is fucking easy.*

Sean crossed his arms over his chest.

Gabriel knew that movement—had spent the last two years alternately hoping for and dreading the moment it showed up. It *always* meant that Sean was bound and determined to get his way. And usually that meant an argument, because Gabriel almost never agreed.

"Don't you want to do something interesting and exciting?" Sean questioned. "Maybe Tony is fucking with us, but just because he is, doesn't mean we should just phone it in, and do something shitty and expected."

"Maybe." Gabriel wasn't really sure he gave a fuck, honestly—but he wasn't surprised that Sean did. That was what Sean *did*, and if he was being painfully blunt about it with himself, that was part of why he goddamned *liked* Sean so much. He fucking cared. Always, and with a passion that Gabriel had always envied.

Gabriel was set in his ways because he was stubborn to the point of insanity, and for a handful of reasons that probably all originated from him being the middle child in a huge family that had always expected him to be a little Moretti clone.

But Sean? He not only had passion for doing things the *right* way, he had principles. He wanted to be the best, and not just for himself. Because he felt an intrinsic obligation to Tony, even when he was screwing him over, for inviting him to participate, and for including him in his food truck family. And, Gabriel thought darkly, because Sean also had a memory of someone he'd loved, that he was trying to live for.

No, he was totally not jealous of Milo. Not at all.

"Well, *I'm* not going to do something shitty and expected," Sean announced. "You can do whatever you want, but that's not something I'm participating it."

"Except I *can't*," Gabriel argued. "We're supposed to work together. This stupid thing is supposed to be a representation of *both* of us."

"Yes, well," Sean said snippily, "if that was what Tony really wanted, maybe he should have started with a different pairing."

"What, so we can only work together when we're fucking?" Gabriel asked, even though he was afraid to hear the answer—because of everything, that was the thing he feared the most.

Sean glanced away. "That's not what I meant."

"Then what did you mean?" Gabriel told himself that it didn't matter what Sean said, but that was such a blatant lie.

"I just mean that we approach things so differently," Sean said. "You see that, don't you?"

"Maybe instead of thinking about all the ways we're different, we should think about what we do that's similar." Gabriel wasn't stupid enough to think that would work; it was a pipe dream, born of too many fantasies where they could be more to each other than just enemies and fuck buddies.

"What is that?" Sean asked.

Gabe had not really been expecting that question. Right or wrong, he'd thought that Sean would keep arguing with him. And he was left grasping for straws. What ways were they similar? He didn't even know.

"We both really care about our food," he said. Which *was* true. "As long as what we make is delicious, what does it matter if it's innovative or not? The point is feeding people and bringing joy to their lives, right?"

"Right," Sean said suspiciously. "So you really want to do this meatball wrap."

"I mean, it would be the easiest way to accomplish the goal," Gabe said. But Sean still didn't look convinced.

"I guess we could give it a try," Sean said. "I'll go grab a few wraps from my truck."

Gabriel nodded, beginning to pull a few tubs and bins out of the under-counter fridges where they stored their leftover prepped ingredients. "I'll heat up some stuff," he said. "Meatballs and sauce."

He also grabbed a tub of their famous roasted garlic butter, which got slathered all over the roll before it was dressed with meatballs and sauce and then a healthy helping of cheese—provolone *and* mozzarella.

He was just heating a pan on the stove when Sean showed back up. He was carrying a whole bunch of stuff—bins and bins and not just the plastic package of oversized tortillas he used for his wraps.

"I brought two kinds," Sean said, setting everything down on one of the shiny stainless steel counters. "Tomato basil and spinach."

"Tomato basil might be too much tomato," Gabriel said, after thinking for a second. "Why don't we try the spinach?"

"Works for me," Sean said, opening the package. "I'm just surprised you'd allow a vegetable this close to your workspace."

"Hey, I have vegetables," Gabriel argued. "I freaking import tomatoes from Italy."

"Tomatoes are a fruit," Sean pointed out.

"And there's some ground onion in the meatballs," Gabriel said, ignoring the fruit jab.

"Oh wow, *onions*. Next you're going to be claiming garlic is a vegetable," Sean said, as he pulled a spinach wrap out of the package.

"I'm Italian, aren't I?" Gabe said. "Garlic is practically our national vegetable."

"Exactly," Sean said with an exaggerated eye roll. "Where do you want to heat this up? On the flat-top grill?"

"Yeah, sure," Gabriel said absently, as he spooned sauce into his sauté pan, enjoying the sound and smell of the tomatoes hitting the heat. His stomach growled, and Sean glanced up, laughing.

"Was that *you*?" he asked.

"Yeah," Gabe said, trying not to be embarrassed. "It was coffee or food, and well, unsurprisingly, coffee won. Hands down."

"Of course it did," Sean said. "Well, good news. You're gonna get something to eat soon."

"Yeah," Gabriel said, as he tossed three meatballs into the sauce, and then added another for good measure. He wasn't sure it was all going to fit, but he didn't want Sean to accuse him of being stingy.

Shaking the pan, letting the sauce continue to sizzle and the meatballs heat through, he grabbed the cheese. The mozzarella, of course, and the provolone slices, and even a little dusting of parmesan for good measure, he thought.

"Three kinds of cheese?" Sean asked, raising an eyebrow, as he flipped the tortilla on the flat top. "Should we try to melt them now, when this is heating up?"

"Yeah, good idea," Gabe said, and passed the three bins to Sean.

He watched as Sean placed the bare minimum of cheese on the tortilla. "Really?" he asked. "Cheese is glue. You should know that."

"Cheese is also full of fat," Sean argued.

"Well, I've eaten my weight in cheese over the years," Gabe retorted, "and it's not like you were complaining the other night."

Sean didn't say a word to that, but did, Gabriel notice, surreptitiously add another handful of mozzarella shreds.

When he glanced up and saw that Gabe was watching, he just shrugged. "You're right, it's like glue. And I have no idea how this is going to work with all that sauce."

Gabriel thought, *that was what you said about my cock and your body, and it worked better than either of us could've imagined.* "It'll be fine," he said. Even though it was stupid to assume that Sean would believe a relationship might be possible if this mashup of their two most famous dishes worked out.

"It's just going to be a little wet, that's all," Gabriel said. "Messy, maybe. But nothing a few extra napkins won't fix."

Sean looked skeptical at this, and the skepticism in his expression only deepened as he slid the tortilla onto a plate, and watched as Gabriel attempted to spoon the meatballs over the cheese. They wouldn't stay contained, and rolled everywhere they weren't supposed to.

"Funny," Gabriel ground out, "we don't have this problem with the roll. Because they're nestled in all nice and easylike."

"Well, we're not using a roll today," Sean shot back. "Here, let me help you."

Gabriel had noticed that he'd kept his distance this morning, but now Sean crowded in close, and Gabe's fingers trembled as he tried to help him roll up the tortilla. But Sean was right. It was wet from the sauce he'd drizzled over the meatballs, which had taken a detour around the wrap, and now everything was covered in it.

"This isn't going to work," Sean finally said.

"What if I cut the meatballs in half," Gabe offered. "Might keep them in place better."

"Alright, that's a good idea," Sean agreed, his tone begrudging. "Let me heat another tortilla."

Gabe slid the meatballs and all the sauce he could salvage back into his sauté pan.

"You should get one of those smaller flat tops, and put it in your truck," Gabriel said as he watched him competently flip the tortilla and then load it with cheese. "It'd be a lot easier than that heat press you're using."

He realized a second too late that he shouldn't have said it. They were already prickly with each other this morning, and always before, Gabriel trying to be helpful and share his knowledge after spending his entire lifetime in professional kitchens, would have resulted in Sean getting even pricklier, and probably a big argument.

But to Gabriel's surprise, Sean just glanced up at him. "I've actually been thinking of that," Sean admitted. "Upgrading in general. I could use some help, actually, and some more space and well . . ."

"Your truck is barely big enough for you?"

"Barely," Sean admitted with a quick grin. "And you know, I've got plans. I'd need something like this if I wanted to add the quesadillas to the menu."

Gabriel did *not* mention that upgrading his truck and his kitchen would be a great opportunity to change the name of it. Why? because he wasn't *stupid*. He could hear Ren in his head, telling him that if he actually *liked* Sean, then he shouldn't do everything in his power to antagonize him.

"I know some great secondhand kitchen supply stores," Gabriel offered casually. "We could make an afternoon of it next Sunday."

"You really think we could find something that would make it work?" Sean sounded skeptical as he slid the warmed tortilla onto a plate and handed it to Gabriel. He'd roughly cut up the meatballs with the side of his spatula, and it definitely helped to get them in the right spot this time around.

"Yeah, you know they've got portable ones. We'd just have to find one of the smaller ones," Gabe said. "But if you took out that press and rearranged a few other things, I think you could make it work. Maybe keep your truck for a few months longer. Maybe even til the off-season."

Gabriel finished scooping the meatballs in and this time only layered in a little bit of sauce—which went against everything he was as an Italian—but he didn't want to end up with another soggy mess.

They needed something to prove to Tony that they could work together. Because that, despite all of Tony's posturing and ideas about bringing new customers into the food truck lot, was really what this was about.

"Here, let me," Sean said, but instead of sounding patronizing, like he couldn't believe that Gabriel couldn't fold up the wrap with the same terrifyingly quick efficiency, he sounded like he genuinely wanted to help. He leaned over, and with a few motions, had the sides overlapped and then tucked in, in a very loose interpretation of a wrap.

Sean took a step back and looked at the lumpy mass critically. "It looks terrible," he said. It kind of did.

"Maybe it'll look better if we brush it with garlic butter."

Sean raised an eyebrow.

"Okay, or that could make it impossible to hold," Gabriel amended. "But maybe if we cut it in half?"

"Why not," Sean said. "I'm not sure we can make it look worse."

Gabriel had argued with Sean's assessments on everything from food to lighting to kitchen supplies to whether or not paper straws were an abomination. He really wished that he could argue with him now, but he really couldn't.

Because he wasn't sure it *could* look worse.

He grabbed a knife, and carefully sliced the wrap in half.

Immediately sauce and cheese started oozing out of the middle, and half a meatball plopped onto the plate.

"Maybe it tastes good?" Gabriel said, and reached in, picking up one of the halves and juggling it awkwardly as it began to drip sauce. The tortilla, while plenty sturdy enough for Sean's fillings, clearly couldn't handle anything this saucy, and it began to split down the middle. Gabriel barely managed to shovel half of it into his mouth before it totally began to disintegrate, sauce landing with a plop on his chin and then the floor.

The flavors he expected exploded on his tongue. The ripeness of the tomato, the rich unctuousness of the meatball, the sharp bite of the provolone and the mild creaminess of the mozzarella.

It was delicious. But even though it tasted great, Gabriel knew that construction issues notwithstanding, they couldn't sell this. It was basically a *worse* copy of his most popular menu item.

He watched as Sean juggled his own half, narrowly maneuvering it to his mouth before it fell apart on his fingers, leaving them smeared with red sauce and melted cheese.

"Well," Sean said after he'd chewed and swallowed, "that was an epic fail."

Gabriel nodded, and Sean actually had the nerve to look surprised. Like he'd thought Gabe was going to try to argue that this was still a good idea.

Half of the wrap was currently dripping down his previously pristine stainless steel cabinet and the other half was on his chin. He was hardly in a position to argue.

Grabbing a handful of paper towels by the small sink, he wiped down, and then handed a fresh one to Sean, who shot him a grateful smile.

It was nothing. It should have meant nothing. But it meant *everything*.

Gabe cursed the day Sean had showed up in Los Angeles and had, without even trying, tied him up into so many knots he wasn't sure he could ever untangle himself.

CHAPTER NINE

"So," Sean asked, hesitating because Gabe could be so . . . well, *Gabe-ish* and difficult about things that shouldn't be so difficult, "what are we going to try now?"

Gabriel shrugged. "I don't know," he said. "That was my one and only idea, and let's face it, it sucked."

"It . . ." Sean hesitated again. "It kind of did."

But to his surprise, Gabe chuckled. "Don't hold back or anything."

"It was really good, if it makes you feel any better, but I think sticking to rolls as a delivery mechanism is a smart choice."

"Best idea I ever came up with," Gabriel said with a nod. "Though, I do think serving them in the cup, for those who don't eat gluten or carbs . . . that was also a pretty genius invention."

Sean did not know what he'd expected when Tony had announced that he and Gabe were going to be working together—and not in bed. In the *kitchen*. The one place they'd never agreed on a single fucking thing. It had been easy enough to let all that crap that lay between them go, when they were at his townhouse, and in his bed. It felt like a different part of his life, and he'd been working hard at compartmentalizing.

But this? This gentle teasing—this *flirting* without any acrimony at all—was new, and it was different, and it was kind of freaking him out.

Could they have had this before? Or had they needed to get all that shit out of their system first? Sean didn't know.

The one thing he did not let himself consider was what would have happened between them if they'd never shared the same name.

"Confession," Sean said, before he could stop himself, "I've ordered plenty of meatball cups over the years. They're great."

Gabriel's face screwed up, his nose crinkling adorably. "What?"

"Just . . ." Sean swallowed hard. "Just not usually from you."

"You're ordering them from Ren?" Gabe said with what sure sounded like mock outrage. "Waiting til I leave and *then* coming over here? That's a low blow."

"You make a great meatball, Moretti," Sean said, which was really something he probably should have told him ages ago, but their relationship had been so sour at points, he hadn't wanted Gabriel to know how he felt.

He hadn't felt particularly guilty about that before, but he felt guilty about it now.

"Thanks," Gabe said, and he smiled, bright and surprised.

And suddenly, unexpectedly, Sean had an idea.

"What if we . . . what if we take one of my ideas that I've been working on," Sean said, "and we use meatballs as the protein."

"What do you mean, one of *your* ideas?" Gabriel asked.

Sean told himself that the vaguely suspicious edge to his tone was to be expected. Hadn't he been unsure of Gabriel's idea? Of course, he'd been sure it would fail for exactly the reasons why it had failed. Sean told himself it was different, but had it been, really? Or was that just an excuse he was telling himself?

He pulled his phone out of his pocket. He kept a running list of possible wrap ideas and recipe notes in an app and he pulled it up now, browsing through the list.

"I collect ideas all the time," Sean said by way of explanation. "And there's plenty I haven't implemented yet, that we could use your meatballs in. What about this Thai crunch wrap idea? We could do like a ginger sesame meatball, with like some kind of sticky glaze."

"Thai?" Gabriel sounded dubious. Sean supposed that was to be expected.

"Thai," Sean said. "Like really, it's just a bunch of fresh veggies, with some crunch from some sweet and spicy candied peanuts." This was one of his best unused ideas that he'd been thinking about and making notes on for months now. There was part of him that thought it might be a mistake to waste the idea on this temporary project, but maybe if it was a runaway success—the way that it could be, if the chips fell right—then Tony would let them keep it on their menus.

"Vegetables," Gabriel stated, shaking his head. "I . . . I can't believe you're going to talk me into this."

Sean had barely gotten started. But he knew, more than anything else, that the flavors he thought they could create together would be more than evidence enough. Gabriel might be the most stubborn asshole on the planet, but he knew his food, and if it turned out even remotely as good as Sean envisioned, he'd never be able to say no. "Do you have some meatballs that aren't in any sauce?" he asked.

"Yes," Gabriel said, pointing to one of the containers. "But they're not . . . ginger sesame or whatever."

"What's in them?" Sean asked. Thinking that maybe they might not need to even make a new kind of meatball for this. If the flavor was generic enough, the glaze would do all the heavy lifting, imparting all that Asian flavor without actually changing what was essentially an Italian recipe.

Gabriel shot him an alarmed look.

"I really, really don't want to steal your recipe," Sean said hurriedly, remembering what Gabe had told him about his nonna and her recipes. "I was just thinking . . . maybe we don't need to change the meatballs at all. Just add the glaze."

"Alright," Gabriel said cautiously. "They are pretty simple. Beef, pork, lamb, egg, and breadcrumb mixed together—since we started promoting the gluten-free meatball cups, I've actually swapped the breadcrumbs out for this cracker meal that's gluten-free. Then there's your basic seasonings. Garlic, salt, and pepper. I try to keep them simple, let the sauce shine through."

"And it does," Sean said, doing an internal fist pump. They wouldn't have to change them at all. They could use them, and then glaze them, and then slide them right into the bed of crunchy veggies that Sean had envisioned and they'd be *perfect*.

"You really think this is going to work?" Gabriel asked.

"I think it's worth a try," Sean said. "But we can't do it here. We need to move to my truck. That's where I've got what we need."

"What should I bring?" Gabriel sounded suddenly self-conscious. "Just the meatballs?"

"Yeah," Sean said, shooting him a quick grin. And before he could help himself, he added, "Just your meat, baby."

Sean *knew* just how tiny his little food truck was. When he'd first bought it, he'd envisioned that he'd never really need more space than he had. That room for one person to work was plenty.

When he'd been planning his truck, he'd never imagined that one day he might need to share it with one big, tall, excited Italian.

There was barely room for the both of them in the truck, and that was with their hips pressed together, and their hands essentially sharing the same space.

Before, it would have been impossible, because Sean hadn't been so comfortable with Gabe back then. But now? Being so close made him think of one thing and one thing only.

So much for being able to separate their professional and their personal lives.

Of course, if Sean had been counting on that, suggesting they share basically one person's worth of space was a terrible idea.

"Well, I think I'm going to put a vote in for a bigger truck," Gabe said with a low, intimate chuckle that made the hairs on Sean's neck stand up.

"I'm shocked," Sean retorted but it had no heat behind it. Nope—all that heat was pooling in his belly.

He wanted so badly to turn and let his body fit into Gabriel's, the way he knew it did so perfectly. They'd only had sex a handful of times but it didn't feel like even nearly enough.

Not that they could do it now. The rest of the food truck lot was beginning to come to life as owners and employees showed up to prep for the lunch hour. They'd seen Tate walk in, and then Ren, from across the way, as he slunk in and opened up Gabriel's truck.

Sean dragged his attention back to the pan on the little burner in front of him. He was reducing some soy sauce, garlic, and sesame oil, with a little extra brown sugar that Gabe had begged from the bakery truck down the street, in an attempt to make their first version of glaze.

"Smells good," Gabe said, leaning down and taking a big sniff. "I'm just not sure it's gonna get sticky enough."

Sean was worried about that too. He'd consulted a few recipes online, trying to find the right proportions, but so far it didn't seem to be coming together to be quite as thick as he'd hoped.

And frankly, the longer they stayed cooped up here together, the more likely it was that he was going to lean in and kiss Gabe.

It would hardly be the end of the world; but he'd been trying *so hard* to keep their hookups away from regular business hours, in what was probably a very stupid attempt to make the whole name thing easier.

But it was never going to be *easy*. Sean had come to realize at least that much. They were too intertwined, and now because of Tony's stupid plan, there were even more threads that were holding them together.

"I have an idea," Gabe said. "What about some balsamic vinegar?"

"What?" Sean refrained from explaining, in very small words, that this was supposed to be an *Asian* dish. He might have, a few weeks ago. But now he waited for Gabriel to clarify what he meant.

"We need it to be thicker, right?" Gabriel said. "And we talked about needing some kind of acid to offset the sweetness. I know this is supposed to be Thai . . ."

"I'd say it's a very loose interpretation," Sean admitted. He was hardly an expert. And unfortunately, he couldn't really call up Jet Tila and ask him.

"So you want me to grab some?" Gabriel asked. He was clearly trying to be casual about it, but Sean could hear the excitement in his tone. "We do that caprese salad special sometimes, so I've got some in the truck."

"Sure, why not," Sean said. Theoretically it sounded like a decent idea, and it would give Gabriel more representation in the final dish.

"I'll be right back," Gabriel said, and when he turned and climbed down the little stairs to the ground, Sean was embarrassed to realize that he actually *missed* the heat of him after he left.

A minute later though, Gabriel was back, like he'd actually raced across the lot so he could grab the vinegar. "Here you go," he said, breathlessly, setting it on the countertop next to Sean's burner. "I think maybe a tablespoon or two?"

"That sounds like a good place to start," Sean agreed. He drizzled it in, and then kept stirring, incorporating it into the mixture.

Out of the corner of his eye, Sean saw Gabe's hand reach out towards the pan and at the last second, he slapped it away.

"What are you doing?" he demanded.

Gabe's expression was sheepish. "Trying it?"

"Then get a spoon, you heathen," he said. "Also, this is *hot*, and it has sugar in it, and you'd probably have burned the hell out of your fingers."

"I've burned them so many times, I think I've got permanent callouses on the tips," Gabriel admitted.

Sean knew; he'd felt them, when Gabriel had touched him all over. Just the idea of those soft-rough fingers touching him now made him shiver.

"Maybe," he said, dropping his voice, because while they might be in his truck, the window was open and people could overhear them, "maybe I want to make sure your fingers are in excellent condition for later."

"Later, huh?" Gabriel raised an eyebrow, his dark eyes sparkling. "I like the sound of that."

"I'd thought about inviting you over last night . . ." Sean said, trailing off. But after Tony's announcement, it had felt weird, like the two worlds he was desperately trying to keep separate had collided. Maybe they were still colliding, but he'd talked himself off that cliff last night. He'd been *so* clear before this whole thing started. It was just sex. And this, Sean reminded himself, wasn't even a date! This was for work. They'd been assigned this task by Tony, and while they were both technically independent and could've told him to fuck off, Tony would make them regret it.

"I *wanted* to come over last night," Gabriel said.

Sean liked his bluntness. Liked that they weren't dancing around this as much. It was easier, clearer, way less complicated to just state outright what they both wanted. And it reassured him because it felt nothing like dating.

They were working together. They were fucking. That was all.

"Well, you can tonight, if you want," Sean said.

"I do want." Gabriel's voice had gone very low and there was an intensity in his expression—not just a want, but a need—and Sean felt himself go very hot and then very cold, all over.

He really loved his job. Had loved it for the two years he'd done it. But suddenly, he wished that he could just take a day off.

Turn off the burner and lock the door behind them and drag Gabriel back to his house *now*.

Sean glanced up at him, their gazes locking, and his fingers trembled on the spatula. "I wish . . ."

"I know," Gabriel said.

It had been a long time since he'd dated, but he swore that friends with only benefits didn't look at each other like that. Didn't *yearn* for each other the way he was yearning now. *You're just fucking,* Sean reminded himself, *that's what you asked for, and that's what you're getting.*

Instead of holding Gabriel's gaze, Sean glanced down at the pan and gave it another half-hearted stir. The good news is that if things were intense now, right in this moment, they'd definitely be calmer by the end of the night, when Gabriel walked home with him. He knew they would be.

As for right now, he could focus on the task at hand. Fulfill Tony's request, and do it, to everyone's likely shock, without killing each other.

"Can you grab me that spoon over there?" Sean asked, gesturing to the organizer full of utensils. "I think this is about ready."

Gabe slapped the spoon into Sean's waiting palm. "You think so?" he said.

Sean stirred the mixture with the spoon and then let it slowly drizzle out. It seemed thick and also sticky enough. The only question was, did it taste good? He lifted the spoon to his mouth and this time it was Gabe's hand that shot out and held his elbow, preventing him from actually tasting it.

"You're gonna burn your mouth," Gabe said, "and I'm definitely going to need it later."

Sean laughed. "Fine, fine, fine," he said, carefully blowing on the hot liquid on the spoon, waiting another second until it was probably not nuclear. "I'll save my tongue for you," he said.

"Damn straight you will," Gabriel said with an amused chuckle.

This time when Sean raised the spoon to his lips, he was more careful, flicking his tongue out, just to taste the tiniest bit, because Gabe was annoyingly right, he *didn't* want to burn his tongue.

Flavor exploded across it. Garlic and sesame and the umami of the soy sauce, balanced by the sweetness of the brown sugar, and then the slightest hint of tang from the balsamic vinegar.

"It's really good," Sean said, offering the spoon to Gabriel, who *didn't* carefully lick it, he stuck the whole thing in his mouth and smiled widely as he tasted it.

"That is really fucking good," Gabe agreed. "And don't get all pissy, but it's the balsamic that makes it."

Sean had been thinking the same thing, and hoping that Gabriel wouldn't notice, but of course he had. Despite what he thought—that all he did was make his nonna's recipes—Gabriel was a great cook and a very talented chef.

"It works," Sean said noncommittally. He liked Gabriel now, though the truth was, he wasn't exactly sure when that had begun, but they weren't getting all buddy buddy. Just in bed, that was all. He didn't need to fix Gabriel's crisis of confidence.

"Yeah, it does," Gabriel said, sounding very pleased with himself.

And maybe he didn't need to, anyway. After all, Sean had never had even an inkling that Gabriel wasn't confident until his confession the other night. There were even times he'd believed Gabriel was annoyingly *overconfident*.

Maybe it was an act, but Sean decided that it wasn't his business. He was just here for the fucking, thank you very much.

"Let's get the meatballs in there," Sean said, and Gabriel nodded, popping the lid on the container. He grabbed a knife from the bin and casually cut them in his hand as he dropped them one by one into the glaze.

"Four, yeah?" Gabriel asked.

"I think so," Sean said, frowning. He'd grabbed another tortilla—spinach, again, because he liked the bright green color of it so much—and stuck it in the press, warming it up enough that it'd be pliable enough to fold.

When it was done, he pulled it out, and let it cool just for a second, so his veggies wouldn't wilt. Then, he pulled off the plastic covers of the fresh veggie bins that he'd stocked early this morning, before Gabriel had even arrived.

Matchstick length carrots and cucumbers and pickled red onions, and shredded cabbage and lettuce went on, followed by a dusting of fresh cilantro and mint, and then the peanuts.

"These," Sean explained as he sprinkled them on, "aren't candied the way I want them to be, but I thought I'd experiment some after hours, maybe at home, with getting them just the way I want them. But it'll give you some idea of the crunch aspect."

"Alright," Gabriel said. He was staring intently at the wrap as Sean built the base, and then began to layer on the meatballs, sticky and sweet. "That's a lot of vegetables."

"Yeah, well, it's *supposed* to be," Sean said. "That's kind of my signature."

"It's not mine," Gabriel retorted, that stubborn glint returning to his eye.

"And?" Sean said. "This is supposed to be about compromise. We're compromising. Do you need a definition of what that means?"

"No," Gabriel said. "But . . . *cabbage*. On my meatballs."

"Technically," Sean said with a grin, "the cabbage is *under* your meatballs."

"Oh, is that supposed to make it better?"

Sean shrugged. "Maybe? But I think this is gonna be good." He finished wrapping it up, and without all the extra red sauce, and with the added stickiness of the glaze, it was much easier. He sliced it in half with a knife, and then picked up the side closest to him. "Cheers," he said, tilting his head.

Gabriel rolled his eyes but picked up the other half.

Sean had been working on various kinds of wraps for years now. Long before he'd ever dreamed of owning his own food truck. But there was always something special about the first bite of something he knew could be extraordinary. And this definitely had that possibility.

He could see from the look on Gabriel's face as he took one bite and chewed, and then another, his expression carefully blank. But it was *never* blank, almost ever, and that alone was enough to tell Sean everything he needed to know.

Gabriel liked it, and didn't *want* to like it.

"Well, I think this is a solid first pass," Sean said. "This is our dish."

"You think so?"

Sean shot him a look. Only Gabriel would try to claim something wasn't delicious when it so clearly was. "I do. I guess the only question is . . . do *you*?"

It was almost fun to watch him try to hedge. "It's fine," he said. "You know, the cabbage notwithstanding."

"I almost think," Sean said, after chewing a third bite and swallowing, "that the veg could use like a really light dressing. Like lime, some really neutral oil maybe."

"Is that going to change the cabbage to be *not* cabbage?" Gabriel wondered.

Sean elbowed him in the side. "What is with you and the cabbage?" he asked.

"I guess I should be grateful you didn't put kale on it," he said.

"So I suppose the kale chip idea is out, then," Sean teased him back.

"Kale *chips*?" Gabriel sounded aghast at the idea. "Chips are potatoes, thank you very much, and I wouldn't want to put them with so many vegetables. Might get the wrong idea."

"That what? They're both vegetables?"

"No," Gabriel said, "that they're *healthy*."

"Ugh," Sean said. "It's amazing *you're* healthy."

"It's these good Italian genes. And the olive oil." Gabriel finished the wrap in another two bites. "I guess," he finally conceded, "that you were right."

"And you were wrong?" It was a bit like playing with fire to antagonize Gabe this way. But Sean had been dipping his toes in it for two years now, and it could be quite fun. The way Gabe's eyes darkened today, that was *definitely* fun.

"I wouldn't go that far," Gabriel said.

"Of course not," Sean said, rolling his eyes. "Because that might dent your belief in your complete superiority."

"Hey," Gabe said, leaning down, and suddenly, he was *so* close. Close enough that all Sean would have to do to lick that tiny speck of glaze off his upper lip was flick his tongue out. And he *wanted* to. The craving was practically staggering him. "You weren't exactly complaining last time about my *complete superiority.*"

He hadn't been. He'd been so overwhelmed by the pleasure of it that for a split second, he'd forgotten about everything.

And that, Sean discovered, was kind of a nice thing.

He wanted Gabriel to do it again.

"And maybe I won't this time, either," he teased, and before he could help himself, reached up and licked that speck right off Gabriel's lip.

His stunned expression was going to be worth the blue balls he'd be forced to endure *all freaking day.*

It was a struggle to pretend that he wasn't right on the edge of desperation.

It was hard to force his stride to match Gabriel's casual, *clearly not in any big hurry* pace as they walked back to his townhouse after a day in which Sean thought, more than once, that he was just going to give up and admit defeat and walk right over to Gabriel's food truck and demand that he come with him *right now.*

It was even harder when they reached the house, and Sean felt like he was nearly going out of his skin, but Gabriel was apparently unconcerned, relaying a seemingly endless story about Ren and one of their customers.

"And then he said that . . ." was all Gabriel got out before the door closed and Sean could think of no other way to put it, but he *pounced*.

The first night they'd spent together, Gabriel had taken over, had pressed him to the door, all sweet, hot drugging kisses that had made him lose it so much faster than he'd intended. But this was all white-hot flashing heat, a day's worth of agonizing want condensed into one single moment.

He had Gabriel pushed against the door in a second, and then they were kissing, wildly, breaking apart only so Gabe could gasp out, "What . . . uh . . ."

"Shut up," Sean said, and then forcibly dragged him towards the bedroom.

"Were you like this all day?" Gabe wondered as he watched Sean pull his shirt off, and toe off his sneakers. So much for *shut up*. "All . . . ready to go?"

Gabe might be into all this talking, and Sean wasn't necessarily *not* into it, but right now, what he was into was getting naked and getting off.

How had he gone all those years without anything? He didn't know, because now it was like a tsunami had been unleashed and he was just letting the wave carry him.

Sean reached for Gabe's hand and took it, pressing it against his hard-on, as he wiggled out of his shorts. "Get me off," he said, "*now*."

Gabriel raised an eyebrow. "By the way," he said, conversationally, like he wasn't already driving Sean crazy with the way his fingers were tracing his cock in his briefs, "I really like this."

"Me being bossy?"

"You being so worked up," Gabriel said, grinning. He pushed Sean onto the bed, and lowered himself to his knees. "Just look at this," he said, as he pulled down his briefs and his cock bobbed out, hard and so red at the tip. "You're so worked up. And it's all for me."

Sean wanted to disagree, to tell him he was just horny *in general*, thank you very much, but then Gabriel leaned forward and his tongue was stroking the head of his cock and it felt so goddamned good that all Sean could do was moan.

Thankfully, sucking his cock was the one thing that actually seemed to shut Gabe up—though Sean was sure he wouldn't have noticed anyway. He was too far gone, his fingers clenching the sheets on the bed, already having to resist the urge to just thrust into Gabriel's mouth, to let the overwhelming pleasure overtake him. But he'd wanted it too long to let it go so quickly. He wanted to *enjoy* it.

Gabe made a guttural groan deep in his throat as he sucked more of him down, and it was intoxicating, that he loved it as much as Sean did.

When he glanced down, the sight of Gabe on his knees, sucking his cock, was almost enough, pushing him right to the edge, and then he saw Gabe rocking against his own hand, shoved down his pants, like he couldn't wait either, and that was enough to completely unravel him.

"Oh my god, yes," Sean cried out as his hips thrust, almost involuntarily, and when Gabe groaned again, he couldn't help himself. He did it again. And again, the pleasure roaring through him was not some meek little thing, but a beast, with *claws*. It tore at him, and he barely had a second to warn Gabriel before he was coming, long, shuddering pulses.

"Fuck," Gabriel said, wiping his face with the back of his hand. "Fuck, that was so goddamn hot."

"Was it?" Sean said, sleepily, opening his eyes to see that Gabe had left a mess of his own, right there on the hardwood floor. He smiled. "I guess it was."

"I couldn't help it," Gabriel said, almost apologetically. "You should . . . we should . . ."

"Yeah," Sean agreed, because he knew what he was saying. They should do that every single goddamn day.

Gabriel nodded, taking the tissues that Sean handed him and cleaning up. After he'd tossed them in the trash, he climbed on the bed, putting too much weight on him, but Sean decided he didn't mind. Decided he almost kind of liked it.

Milo had been about his size, maybe even a bit thinner. The weight and heft of Gabriel was reassuring, almost.

"I should . . ."

Sean knew what he was going to say. He should leave. But it was clear from his voice that he didn't want to, and Sean already knew he didn't want him to. Maybe it was poor hookup etiquette, maybe Ren would be horrified, but Sean felt safe because he'd made the parameters so clear early on. Surely staying the night wouldn't mean anything, not when he'd been so cut and dry about the way this arrangement was going to work.

"You should stay," Sean said with finality. "If you want to, that is."

"I should stay?" Gabriel sounded very surprised. So surprised that Sean freaked out at the last moment, digging into his orgasm-fuzzy brain for a good excuse.

"Yeah, well, I was going to make those nuts. You could help me," he said. "And then, you know, we could do that again."

"That sounds like a really great plan," Gabe said, putting an arm around Sean and tugging him even closer. He was quiet for a minute, and Sean couldn't help but enjoy the closeness. It had been so long since he'd been able to just cuddle with someone. He hugged the other guys sometimes—sometimes when things went very right or sometimes when he was having a bad day and he needed one—but cuddling? That hadn't happened in four years.

Maybe he hadn't just been sex-starved, he'd been *touch*-starved.

"This is nice," Sean said softly. He hadn't moved yet, and he wasn't sure he could.

"Yeah, it is," Gabriel agreed. He shifted around, until Sean was pressed up against his side. He was still partially dressed. Sean still had his socks on. He wiggled his toes inside of them, wondering if he should try to take them off without moving.

Or, he could soak this up for a moment longer, and then slide out of bed and start the nuts. He thought he had everything in the kitchen that he needed.

He was just running down a list of ingredients he'd need when he heard something next to him. A quiet, rumbling noise.

Not obtrusive, but somehow, comforting.

Sean opened his eyes and smiled as Gabriel slept away next to him.

Maybe the nuts could wait for the next day. Tonight? He was going to get all the touch he needed.

CHAPTER TEN

"So you just . . . *stayed* . . ." Ren gaped at Gabriel as he poured coffee into his travel mug.

"Yeah," Gabriel said. "Is that a problem?"

"Well, *yeah*," Ren said as he grabbed his favorite jean jacket from the chair by the door. "I thought you were trying to follow the hookup guidelines I gave you."

"It was his idea," Gabriel said, rolling his eyes. "Not even mine."

Technically, of course, Sean hadn't suggested outright that he stay the night, but he'd kept him from leaving, and he'd hardly kicked him out of bed when he'd fallen asleep in it.

"You are playing with fire," Ren muttered darkly. "And it might not turn out very well."

"I don't know what you're talking about," Gabriel said, taking a big gulp of coffee. Except he totally did.

Usually he slept like crap in beds that weren't his own, but cuddled up next to Sean? He'd slept like a goddamned baby, and he wasn't stupid enough to deny why that was.

He had real feelings for Sean. Real, deepening feelings. Sometimes he still wanted to smack him, sometimes he still made him halfway to crazy with his deliberate obtuseness or his stubbornness, but the truth was, when it came down to it, none of that mattered.

He might even love him.

"Yes, you do," Ren said as he closed and locked the door behind them. "You know exactly what I'm talking about. And it's going to end up in a huge fucking mess. You thought the meatball missile was bad? The war to come is gonna make that look like child's play."

"That's your opinion," Gabriel said as they took the stairs down to the ground floor.

"No," Ren said, "that's my *experience*."

"It's . . . he's a little screwed up about relationships," Gabe said. He pushed open the front door to their building. It was a gorgeous morning. A fucking *amazing* morning, no matter how much crap Ren kept giving him.

"No, he told you that he didn't want a relationship. That's not being screwed up about relationships," Ren said, like he knew exactly what Sean meant. He didn't, because he didn't know the whole story, but it did make Gabriel wonder what it was that happened to Ren to screw *him* up about relationships. He'd always assumed that Ren didn't have some big sob story in his background, making him always stick to hookups, but just because he'd never heard about it didn't mean it hadn't happened.

He knew Sean's story, but he didn't think that when Sean had told him, that it gave him permission to tell anyone else.

Still, he could at least *try,* without any of the details, to explain to Ren why Sean was so certain that all they were doing was fucking.

"It's not that he doesn't want a relationship," Gabe said carefully as they walked down the street. It was really a gorgeous day—sunny and not too hot yet, with the most beautiful cloud-free blue sky overhead—and he couldn't even attribute any of that to the fact that he'd spent the last night in Sean's bed. "He got out of a really serious relationship a few years back, and I think he expects to feel a certain way when he's romantically interested in someone, because of that relationship."

Ren frowned. "It must have been pretty serious."

Sean and Milo had been *married*. At a fairly young age. There was no way it had not been extremely, life-changingly serious.

"Yeah, I think so," Gabriel said. "So that's why he thinks we're just going to hook up."

"He really believes that he just *wants* you?" Ren sounded skeptical. And frankly the same skepticism was echoed in Gabriel's own mind. He knew that what they were sharing wasn't just sex. The only difficulty was continuing to have that really good sex, while also carefully cluing Sean in to the fact that they weren't just friends with fucking awesome benefits.

"Yeah, it's complicated," Gabriel admitted.

"Complicated is trying to decide whose house you're going to hook up at. Or whether you're going to give a blowjob or a handjob, or whether you're going to get serious enough to actually fuck," Ren said. "This isn't just complicated. And it *will* blow up in your face."

Gabriel didn't want to believe Ren was right, especially when it had been going pretty good so far. They'd even made it mostly past Tony's speed bump without it derailing them. In fact, Gabe thought the necessity of working together had actually made Sean want him *more*.

Not that he was going to inform Tony of this fact; he was insufferable enough as it was.

"Maybe I can get him to fall in love with me back, before it does," Gabriel said optimistically.

Ren stopped in the middle of the sidewalk. "Back? Back? *Back*?" He sounded horrified. "Please do not mean what I think you mean."

The more he *did* think about it, the more right Gabriel thought it felt. Of course he loved Sean. He'd probably loved him for a long time. Maybe he didn't have a wealth of experience in this area, but he *had* been in love before, and while this didn't feel exactly the same as that, there was no denying that it felt deeper and stronger and the tug towards Sean so inevitable that it was amazing he hadn't realized it before now.

"I think I do," Gabriel said. "And it's not like you didn't know this was coming. You did. I did, now that I think about it. I never wanted it to be about *just* sex, and you said, *hook up with him, because it's hard to make it just sex*. Well, you were right."

Ren threw up his hands. "Officially, I give up on you."

"I kind of thought you gave up on me ages ago," Gabriel said with a laugh, because even though his cousin was seriously overdramatic, even Ren's fit couldn't ruin this day. The sun was shining and he hadn't *just* spent the night with Sean, he fucking adored him.

"That was on you ever having the capacity for being cool," Ren said. "But this is *worse*."

"Just because you don't have the capacity for it doesn't mean the rest of us don't want to fall in love," Gabriel said, and that was perfectly reasonable, right? He wasn't saying *Ren* had to fall in love—even if he even could, at this point—Gabriel just wanted to enjoy it.

"I have the capacity," Ren said in a clipped voice as they neared the lot. "I just choose *not* to."

"Yeah, that's all fine and good," Gabriel said with hesitation, "but sometimes I'm not sure you *get* a choice."

"You always have a choice," Ren said with steel in his tone.

Gabriel thought Ren was fucking crazy, but what else was new?

He pulled his keys out and went to unlock the door, but to his surprise, there were scratches on the stainless steel panel of the door—the panel that held the lock. Alexis' truck had had very similar ones, only a few weeks back.

"Shit," Gabriel said.

"What is it?" Ren asked, coming closer. "Did you decide you were being stupid?"

"No," Gabriel said, pointing to the scratches. "I think someone tried to break into our truck last night."

But Ren was already not paying attention—he was craning his head around the edge of the truck, clearly distracted by something else he'd seen.

Gabriel looked too, because anything that had given Ren that look on his face was something worth paying attention to.

There were wooden picnic tables scattered across the courtyard between all the different trucks. And on the very central one, someone had painted a message. Ren and Gabriel walked closer, his heart in his throat. Was this what Tony had been worried about the whole time? Thefts and vandalism?

It was worse than that. "Suck a dick," was the message, scrawled in bright purple paint, across the entire tabletop.

"Shit is right," Gabriel said with an unsteady exhale. "What the fuck is this?"

"I don't even *want* to suck a dick now," Ren said, his own voice not precisely steady, "and I always want to suck a dick."

"We're gonna have to clean this up." Gabriel pulled out his phone after glancing around and realizing they were the first owners here. This was their prep day, and he and Ren often were here by themselves for at least the first hour.

Tony needed to see this.

Tony just stood there and stared at the message.

His brother, Wyatt, stood next to him, a frown on his face, and the rest of the owners clustered a little ways back. Everyone's expressions were grim, but there was a healthy amount of disbelief thrown in. Gabriel knew how they felt. He'd felt safe here too, protected with their community, with the cushion of so many queer food truck owners gathered together. He'd always believed that they were stronger together than they were apart, and he knew Tony had believed in that idea too.

"Well," Ash said under his breath, coming up to stand next to Gabriel, "I guess I was wrong about needing security."

The semi-playful argument they'd had during last week's staff meeting felt a lot stupider with those words emblazoned across one of their picnic tables.

"I guess we were all wrong," Gabriel admitted.

"But how do we know," Ash continued, "that someone like Lennox isn't behind this shit? He didn't really seem all that comfortable with us . . . what did he call it? *Fucking around all the time?*"

"He might not be comfortable, but the guy wasn't homophobic. You know that, Ash."

Ash was still frowning though, like he didn't quite believe it. "I wish Tony would find someone else."

"Tony isn't going to find someone else," Gabriel said. "He said it at the staff meeting: the guy knows us, knows our trucks, knows the lot. Maybe he's a little uncomfortable with so many queer couples, but that shouldn't stop him from keeping us safe."

"Do you trust him?" Ash asked him, point-blank.

Gabriel wished that this day hadn't been totally derailed; he wished that Ash was actually asking him about Sean, not about Lennox. He wished they didn't even have to *talk* about this. But that option had come and gone.

"I don't know him, but I trust that he's going to do his job," Gabriel finally said.

Just then, the man in question arrived, wearing a sharp black suit, with a white shirt and a narrow black tie that he hadn't quite finished tying yet. Lennox was walking fast, but silent, people parting and letting him through, until he came to a stop right in front of the table.

"Glad you got here so quick," Tony said, extending a hand, which Lennox took quickly and efficiently.

He was putting on a brave face, Gabriel realized, but Tony was shaken, some of his confidence leeched away.

Gabriel had never understood it. So what if some of them *did* like to suck dick? Did that make them lesser people? Anger was pointless, because it did *nothing*, but it surged through him anyway.

"Oh great, our knight in shining armor is here to save us," Ash said, not even bothering to lower his voice.

"Ash," Gabriel warned, "this isn't . . . just *don't*, okay?"

Ash shot him a venomous look and stormed off.

A second later, Sean took his place.

Gabriel had wondered, before this clusterfuck had hit their lot, what it would feel like to see Sean for the first time since he'd left his house, early this morning.

What it would feel like to see him for the first time, *knowing* that he loved him.

These circumstances were definitely not fucking ideal, but Gabe still felt the same surge of love and affection and caring that he knew couldn't be mistaken for anything else. He wanted to comfort Sean when he felt sad, he wanted Sean's comfort in return.

In fact, he really wanted it *right* fucking now.

"Hey," Sean said softly, his eyes distressed. "Hey, Alexis told me that you found it. You okay?"

"Ren and I did, yeah," Gabriel said. He reached for Sean's hand, and to his surprise, Sean met him halfway, giving his fingers a reassuring squeeze.

"Lennox is gonna make sure this never happens again," Sean said.

"Don't tell Ash that," Gabriel warned. "He's really upset that Lennox is the guy Tony is hiring to take care of it."

They watched as Lennox looked over the scene, carefully touching the still-wet paint with the pad of his finger. His expression was normally difficult to read, but today, it was an impenetrable mask.

"You really think so?"

"Yes," Sean said with quiet confidence. "Yes, he is."

Gabriel searched for something he could say to distract from his own distress. Not let it leak over to Sean. "You think if Tony hires Lennox, he'll be able to find out if Lennox is his first name or his last?"

Sean chuckled under his breath. "Oh, I bet he will."

"Ugh, of course." It was stupid to be disgruntled about that, when their safe space had been invaded.

"Or maybe not," Sean said thoughtfully. "Lennox is practically a mystery in human form. You think he'd give the goods up that quickly? That easily?"

"Maybe you're right." Gabriel shot him a quick grin. "I bet it'll drive Tony crazy if he doesn't find out."

"That'll be fun to watch," Sean said. He hesitated. Squeezed Gabriel's hand again. "It was nice to wake up next to you this morning."

"It was nice you didn't kick me out. Sorry I fell asleep on you." He'd apologized for falling asleep so early this morning, but he did it again, because he did feel a little guilty about that.

"We were both tired," Sean said, dismissing the apology with a casual wave of his hand. "Maybe a repeat tonight?" He sounded so hopeful that Gabriel's heart leapt. He wanted, more than anything, for Ren to be wrong. This wasn't going to be a disaster; it was going to be the best thing that ever happened to him.

Gabriel wasn't all that surprised that the next evening, the normal Saturday night event at the lot, turned into something a lot bigger. A lot of the owners must have told their friends and invited them to come out for the band that was playing—and they must have invited their friends too.

It was packed, and there was a supportive smile wherever he looked.

The tables were all occupied, more people spilling into the grassy area between the seating area and the semi-circle of food trucks. There was even a crowd towards the front, by the stage Tony had had built for the bands that played weekly.

But the one table that wasn't occupied was the one that had been vandalized. Instead of cleaning it off, Lucas had taken one look at the still-drying paint and had said only three words: "Could've used glitter."

Tony had stared at him, and Lucas had shrugged. "We all enjoy sucking dick, don't we?" he'd asked, like it wasn't intended to be an insult, scrawled across their property. "I don't intend to pretend otherwise."

"Do you really . . ." Tony's voice had dropped low, so low that Gabriel, setting out his bins of plasticware and napkins for the day, had barely been able to hear him. "Do you really think we should keep it? I was going to clean it, and if that didn't work, throw it away. We don't need a constant reminder that someone invaded our safe space."

"But it happened," Lucas said firmly. "We can't pretend it didn't. We should *own* it."

Gabriel had turned away, uncomfortable by the intimacy in the gaze shared by his two friends as they embraced.

He was also not surprised when the next time he saw the table, the words hadn't been scrubbed off, but were permanently adhered with a thick layer of glitter, with a few bright rainbows up and down the legs. Rainbows that matched the style of the ones that Lucas liked to doodle on the blank toes of his Converse.

"Looks good."

Gabriel glanced up and Sean was standing there, his eyes glued to the table and its subtle sheen in the firelight, sitting in its place of honor.

"I was surprised, I guess," Gabriel said, "but it makes sense."

Sean shrugged. "I was lucky enough that when I came out, my mom didn't care. I think she even knew before I did that I was gay."

"I wasn't even the first person in my family to come out," Gabriel said. "My brother, Luca, did first. Shocked the hell out of Nonna, but she recovered. Thank God, too, because then I did, and then Marco, our youngest brother."

"And Ren, of course," Sean said in a teasing voice, like he knew that him mentioning Gabe's cousin in this context would bother him. But Gabriel knew now that Sean had *never* been interested in Ren—except to drive him crazy enough to give in.

"Ren was scandalizing everyone forever," Gabe said. "I think he enjoys it."

It had never occurred to Gabriel that, for Ren, it was about anything else other than enjoying himself and life, but after their conversation yesterday morning, he had to wonder. Had someone broken his cousin's heart, and he'd never realized it?

Had nobody ever realized it?

He thought about asking Ren, but it was clear from what he'd said that he wouldn't talk about it.

"Someday," Sean said, smiling as he took a few steps closer to Gabe, "someday he is gonna meet someone who makes him reconsider everything."

Gabriel couldn't help but think Ren had *already* met the person who'd made him reconsider everything. But he didn't want to betray his cousin's confidence, so he just nodded. "Yeah, that's gonna be a day," he said.

"Lennox was prowling around right as it was getting dark," Sean said, changing the subject. "Did you see him?"

Gabriel nodded. He had, off and on all day. And he'd seen some of what had to be Lennox's employees, all in seemingly identical dark suits, prowling around, checking the cameras that they'd been putting up around the perimeter of the lot.

"I guess we're gonna have to keep it in our pants on the lot now," Sean said with a dimpled grin. "There won't be any more dark corners to make out in."

"It's alright," Gabriel said, putting an arm around Sean's shoulders and tugging him closer. "I'm perfectly happy to make out in your bed. Or on your couch. Or in your kitchen."

Sean smiled. "Yeah, I bet you are," he teased.

"Hey, as long as the making out is part of it, I'm satisfied," Gabriel said. Which was the honest-to-God truth. He didn't want or need more, just Sean pressed up against him, loving every moment.

"I could use a little more *satisfaction* right now," Sean said, wiggling a bit.

"You're incorrigible," Gabe said, but suddenly he wished they *could* go back to that dark corner and he could get Sean off, without anyone else knowing.

But with Lennox and his people skulking around, Sean was probably right; those days were over.

"I guess we should enjoy the music," Sean said mournfully. "You want to grab a beer?"

"You closed for the evening?" Gabriel wondered.

Sean nodded. "Everyone's here for the band. And the beer."

"I left Ren holding down the fort," Gabe admitted, "but you're probably right. We can close down. Alexis always stays open late, and so does Tony."

"The blessing of having employees," Sean said.

"You could get one," Gabriel said. He knew Sean sold enough that he could afford it.

Sean shot him a look. "And put them *where* exactly?"

"I'm not sure, but it's something to think about. You can't do everything, forever," Gabriel said.

Sean didn't argue, just gave a thoughtful *hmmm* to Gabriel's suggestion.

"I'm gonna tell Ren to close up," Gabe said, pulling out his phone, and shooting Ren a quick text. He looked up, and Sean was staring at him, expectantly. "You wanna go grab a beer and a dance?" he asked casually, like his heart wasn't in his goddamn throat. Because sharing a drink and definitely sharing a dance wasn't what hookups did. But they hadn't been doing what hookups did for awhile now. Honestly, Gabe wasn't sure they'd *ever* done what hookups did.

But Sean didn't argue or look conflicted at all. He just grinned, brightly. "That sounds great," he said. "The music sounds great tonight."

Gabriel didn't say that it wouldn't have mattered if the music sounded like a toddler pounding on a toy drum set, he would've still wanted to dance with Sean.

"Yeah," he agreed, hand sliding down Sean's back, resting right in the small of his back, feeling the heat of his skin through the thin fabric of his t-shirt. They wandered over to where Tony was pulling beers.

"Hey," Tony said glancing up at them. "It's a great night, isn't it?"

"It is," Gabriel agreed. "I'm glad we do this."

"I'm glad we're *still* doing this," Sean added.

Tony grabbed them two beers. "It's gonna take more than a little bit of bullshit to scare us away."

"The glitter looks great," Sean enthused. "Honestly, I love what you did with it. It never would have occurred to me to turn it into a celebration."

Tony's smile was soft and sweet. The kind of look that Gabriel would never have imagined he'd wear, once upon a time. "That's all Lucas," he said. "He didn't want us to be ashamed."

With Sean's skin only a thin layer of cotton away from his hand and the wonder and awe of his feelings cresting through him, Gabriel thought to himself that he'd never been less ashamed in his life.

If he thought Sean wouldn't panic and freak out, he'd tell him how he felt. He wouldn't waste a single moment; he'd tell him *tonight*.

"And we're not," Sean said, sounding just as certain as he'd ever been about anything.

"How's the new menu item coming along?" Tony asked casually, changing the subject. "Ren mentioned you guys were working on it."

"It's going good," Gabriel said. "It's not what I expected it would be, but I think . . ." He glanced over at Sean, who was still smiling. "I think it's better because it's not what anyone would expect."

"I think so too," Sean agreed.

"You two seem to be on the same page recently . . ."

But that was all Tony got out before Sean interrupted him. "Tony, we said we'd take care of it, and we are."

Gabriel was surprised at the vehemence in Sean's voice. He hadn't expected that at all. Tony clearly hadn't either.

"Uh, okay," Tony said. "I wasn't saying . . ."

"Yeah, you were," Sean said, again not letting Tony finish. "You wanted to remind us that we still need to come to an agreement over who's going to keep the name. I know. I think about it every day, okay? I know Gabriel does, too."

He didn't. Not really. He thought about it every once in awhile, the ugly thought intruding in the happiness he'd found, and every time it showed up, he pushed it away, because he didn't know how to deal with it.

He'd *never* known how to deal with it.

But he was not going to be stupid enough to *say* that, especially not now.

"Alright," Tony said, his expression smoothing into a charming smile. "I trust you guys."

"You should," Sean retorted.

"Hey," Gabe said, fingertips brushing against his back. "Come on, let's have that dance, okay?"

"Yes," Sean said, and his smile was back. Brighter than ever. "Let's do that."

They set their beers on a nearby table, and Gabriel was pleasantly surprised when Sean was the one to take him by the hand and tug him onto the makeshift dance floor.

The band that Tony had found for the night was a little more honky-tonk than they usually got, but Gabriel found himself really enjoying it, and the lead singer's rainbow cowboy boots.

The song wasn't particularly up-tempo, but slow enough that it felt right for Gabriel to wind his arms around Sean's waist and pull him close, moving along to the beat. They'd been slightly more circumspect around the lot—ever since the first night, when they'd barely been able to keep their hands off each other—but there was a crowd tonight. If anyone saw them, Gabe decided he didn't care.

"This is nice," Sean said with a soft sigh, as his head rested on Gabriel's shoulder. "Really nice, actually."

"We did duck out on the six-month anniversary party early," Gabriel pointed out. "It feels good to celebrate that we're still here. Still going strong."

Sean pulled back, his eyes deep and dark in the shadows of the evening. "Better than ever," he agreed as they moved to the music together.

It was the perfect moment—and of course Gabriel had to ruin it by opening his big fat mouth and sticking his foot in it. "Did you mean it?" he wondered, before he could stop himself.

"Mean what?" Sean asked, sliding his fingers under the hem of Gabriel's t-shirt, making him shiver as they danced up his spine.

"That you think about it all the time?"

Sean still looked baffled.

"The name," Gabriel said. "You told Tony you think about it all the time."

"Oh," Sean said. "Yeah, actually," he added. "Sometimes I think if I could just think about it long enough, and clearly enough, I'd come up with the solution we'd both be happy with. Because . . ." He hesitated. "I don't want to lose this."

"I don't want to lose it either," Gabe said seriously.

"We'll get there," Sean said confidently. His entire hand pressed against the damp skin of Gabriel's back and he tensed, then relaxed into his touch. "Fighting with you was really fun, actually, but it turns out this is more fun."

"Orgasms usually are," Gabe teased.

Sean's gaze was serious. "And you give such good ones," he said.

He was wading right into the deep end—or maybe he'd been there long enough that the shock of it had worn off already—but he leaned in and kissed Sean anyway. And Sean didn't hesitate, he kissed him right back, their lips moving together in a woozy rush. It was hot, because kissing Sean couldn't ever be anything else, but there was a soft sweetness to it, a lack of rushing, that warmed Gabe's heart.

The frantic heat of the last few times they'd fucked had been glorious, but this felt even better. Not like they were just racing to the inevitable end, but like he and Sean were savoring every single moment.

Sean broke the kiss first, resting his head back on Gabe's shoulder. They were barely swaying with the music now, but it didn't matter. Gabriel's heart still felt so full it might explode. "You still going with me tomorrow?" he asked.

"Of course." Like Gabriel would let anyone else go with him. He'd already planned the restaurant supply stores they'd go to, and the really great Asian fusion place that was near one of them. They'd make a day of it. A *date* of it, if he had any say in the matter.

"I can't believe I used to think you were a stubborn asshole." Sean chuckled under his breath.

"I can't believe you think I'm still anything else," Gabriel retorted. It *was* kind of selfish asshole territory, pushing them both into this dating thing, without even telling Sean about it, especially when he'd been so clear about what he'd wanted.

But he was a grown man, wasn't he? If he didn't like any of it, he could pull back. He didn't have to cuddle in closer, burrow so near that if Gabriel could tuck him inside, he would.

"You're a lot of things, Gabriel Moretti," Sean said quietly. "But meatballs notwithstanding, you're anything but an asshole."

"I could . . ." Gabriel licked his lips. It felt like such a risk, telling him now, about the name he'd picked out, about the plans he'd made, about how he'd rather cut off his own arm than take away something that Sean cared about, like he did his ex-husband.

But what if Sean was still operating under the assumption that when they figured their shit out, it was over?

Deep down, Gabriel didn't really believe that was true. Sean had even said that what they were doing was more fun than arguing. But how long would that last?

What if he woke up one morning and knew, once and for all, that Gabriel could never fill Milo's shoes? The same way Gabriel knew it?

Gabe couldn't let him go, not just yet. If he did, and it ended, he was going to end up just as bitter and bereft as Ren, and that was a cautionary tale if he'd ever seen one.

"What?" Sean asked softly. "What is it?"

"Nothing," Gabe said. "I just wanted to say I could make you pancakes tomorrow. Blueberry. If you wanted."

"How did you know that was my favorite?" Sean sounded absolutely delighted.

"I know more than you think," Gabriel said.

CHAPTER ELEVEN

Sean didn't think he'd look forward to the Sunday he'd agreed to go shopping with Gabriel, but it turned out by the time Sunday morning rolled around, he wasn't sure he wanted to even let the guy out of his sight.

Especially if he kept making him the best blueberry pancakes he'd ever tasted.

And the way he'd danced . . . and the way he'd blown him later that night when they'd come back to his townhouse. Sean shivered just thinking about how wonderful it had been.

Even more shocking was the fact that this was Gabriel. *Gabriel freaking Moretti.*

What would he have done, way back when, if he had known that under all his stubborn bluster, Gabriel was like this? If the guy who had thrown a meatball in his direction was also the same one who left him limp and weak-kneed each and every time they touched?

Sean wasn't sure.

Truthfully, he didn't feel sure about much right at the moment, except that Gabriel's pancakes were extraordinary. But even as he sat at the breakfast bar, comfortably hip to hip with Gabe as they ate breakfast, he felt like the ground was shifting underneath him.

It felt like things were changing, and he didn't know how or why. All he knew was that when Gabriel teased him, saying he was still an asshole, a week ago, he might have agreed and *meant* it. But now? He couldn't. He just knew better.

He'd never really had just a hookup partner before, though, so maybe this was just what it felt like when you added in the *friend* to the *friends with benefits* equation. Because he knew that before, he and Gabriel had definitely not been friends. Co-workers, maybe. Verbal sparring partners, definitely. But now Sean couldn't deny that they'd ventured into a real, genuine friendship.

He wouldn't be voluntarily spending his day off with Gabriel if they weren't. And he wasn't just *letting* Gabriel come with him, or taking Gabriel with him because he needed the help—he was actually looking forward to spending the day with him.

"You're quiet over there," Gabriel said.

"Just really enjoying these pancakes," Sean said, taking all the thoughts that were currently making him uncomfortable and shoving them in a box. He couldn't deal with any of this right now.

Gabriel's smile was as bright as the morning sun filtering in through Sean's kitchen window. "Really?"

"Yeah," Sean responded. "You're a really good cook, you know."

The flush went from Gabriel's cheeks down his neck, where it disappeared under his t-shirt collar. Sean was charmed, and even vaguely turned on, even though they'd just had *very* satisfactory handjobs in the shower less than an hour ago.

"Thanks," Gabriel said, standing and grabbing their plates to take to the sink. "I'm not. Not really. Just runs in the family, I guess."

It annoyed Sean more than he wanted it to that Gabriel didn't understand that he was naturally gifted in the kitchen. He was naturally gifted in a lot of other ways too, and he was totally confident about those. He could make Sean sob with pleasure by barely crooking a finger. But whenever Sean tried to tell him how good a cook he was, he just brushed it aside.

Maybe that was part of becoming Gabriel's friend, he thought as he grabbed his keys and wallet, being offended on his behalf instead of just *offended*.

"I've got a whole list of places we can hit," Gabriel said as they got in Sean's car. "And," he added, with a trace of that blush returning to his face, "we can grab lunch at this Asian fusion place by one of them that I think you shouldn't miss."

Sean couldn't figure out why Gabriel would possibly be embarrassed about introducing him to a great new restaurant. Maybe he was feeling a little odd about this evolution in their hookup relationship too. Friendship didn't come naturally to everyone.

"Hey, that sounds awesome," Sean reassured him. "I can't wait. We just ate breakfast and I'm stuffed, but if I wasn't, I'd want to head there first thing."

Sean typed the address Gabe gave him into the GPS on his phone and plugged it into the car's system.

"Really?"

"Really," Sean said. "I mean, we're experimenting with our own Asian fusion, aren't we? But I'd hardly call us experts."

"Right," Gabriel agreed, relaxing into the seat more. "I almost forgot about that. We need to finish that recipe up today, I guess."

"I was going to make the nuts tonight," Sean said. "You could stay, after, and help me?"

"I'd really like that," Gabriel said, even though Sean had been struck by a momentary worry that this was a *lot* of time to spend together. What if Gabe got freaked out or felt pressured? But it felt like the opposite instead, when he agreed. Like the most natural thing in the whole world.

Sean told himself to stop second-guessing everything and just *enjoy* it.

By the time they made it to the fusion place for lunch, they had a good haul in the back of Sean's Outback. New spatulas and sauté pans for Gabriel, and he'd helped Sean pick out a new-to-him flat-top grill that he could install and plug in right where he'd had the original, bulky press that had been fine for starting out, but was severely limiting him now.

As they walked into the cute little hole-in-the-wall place, Sean's mind was racing with all the new things he could add to the menu, now that he had the ability to make them.

"Hey, Moretti!" An Asian guy with a nose ring and a shock of blue mohawked hair came around the corner and greeted Gabe with enthusiasm. "It's been ages since we've seen you around here."

"Yeah," Gabe said, falling into the hug like it was second nature. Sean hung back a little, awkward because he hadn't realized that Gabe was such good friends with the guy who ran the place.

Why had he assumed that Gabriel wasn't comfortable with friendships? He had so many, and Sean *knew* that. He'd just wanted to think Gabriel wasn't just uncomfortable with *him*.

"Been busy," Gabriel said. "You know we opened that food truck lot, right? Down by the Coliseum?"

"Yeah, yeah, I'd heard," the guy said, leading them into the restaurant, and seating them at a prime table, right by the kitchen. "It's going good, yeah?"

"Great," Gabriel said as they sat down. "Sean here owns a truck that parks there, too. We've just been out looking at a couple of restaurant supply stores, seeing what kind of used stuff they're carrying."

"I know Gabe is all about the Italian all the time," the guy said, smiling at Sean, "but you definitely don't look related."

"We're not," Sean said, chuckling.

"Mac," the Asian guy said, shaking his outstretched hand. "It's good to meet you."

"I do wraps. Like salad wraps and stuff. Always looking to expand my ideas and my horizons, you know," Sean said. Though from a quick glance at the menu, this guy was already brilliant. His mouth was watering just reading the descriptions. And the smells coming out of the kitchen? Sean had already determined that he was going to end up ordering half the menu and taking it home for leftovers.

"Oh, you see any decent fryers?" the guy asked.

"A few," Gabriel said, pointing out the last place they'd been by name, and telling Mac that they'd had a few good ones for sale.

"Great, thanks," he said. "I'll check them out. You guys both want the iced tea?"

"I definitely want the iced tea," Gabriel said. He smiled at Sean. "And so do you, it's fruity and not too sweet and fucking incredible."

"Alright, then," Sean said. "It sounds like I'll want the iced tea."

Mac laughed, and patted Sean on the shoulder. "Gabe here won't steer you wrong."

When Mac went off to grab their drinks, Sean asked, "Where did you meet him?"

"He had a food truck, at first, right when I came to LA," Gabriel said. "He was a kind of mentor to me, when I was first getting started. And then he got this place, and got out of the truck business."

"Is that something you'd ever want to do?" Sean wondered.

"No way," Gabriel said with an emphatic shake of his head. "Luca, my brother, he's in charge of the family business back in Napa, and I'm not interested in being his little bitch."

Sean raised an eyebrow. "He's a little overbearing, some-times," Gabriel explained. "You know how older brothers can be."

"I don't, actually," Sean admitted. "I don't have any. Or any younger ones, either. Just me and my mom."

"You were better off," Gabriel said, leaning closer. "I felt like I was suffocating. Too many brothers and sisters and relatives."

"Maybe." Sean wasn't convinced. But he could see Gabriel's side of it, and he could see how growing up in the middle of so many people, all of whom had a vested interest in you being a certain way, would make being your own person hard.

Sean could see that he was still struggling with that. Still reliant on Nonna's recipes. Still uneasy about his own obvious skill. Still hesitant to make his truck his own.

"What should we get?" Gabriel said, changing the subject, which Sean was fine with. They'd not argued at all, except for a little friendly, flirty banter when they'd been wandering the aisles of the supply stores.

"God, everything looks amazing," Sean said, which was true. He was still skimming the appetizer section of the menu, trying to decide if he wanted the Korean barbecue gyoza or the avocado egg rolls.

"Can I . . ." Gabe stammered. "Can I make some suggestions? I know Mac said I'd take good care of you, but I *would*."

Sean knew it was true; he'd never doubted it for a second. And *that* was a development that made him squirm uncomfortably in his chair.

"Of course you can," Sean said, nudging him with a grin. "I was hoping you would. Otherwise I'm going to order everything on this menu and gain fifty pounds."

Gabe shot him a cocky look that Sean *swore* a year ago had been completely unattractive, but now made his blood race. "I think we can work it off," he said.

"What should we order, then?" Sean felt eager, almost gluttonous. And not just for the food.

It was so sexy to see Sean like this: open and laughing and eager.

When he'd first arrived in Los Angeles, and they'd met, Gabriel hadn't known what Sean was dealing with. Nobody had known. But looking back, Gabe could see the effects of his grief. He'd been quieter, more withdrawn, a smile coming way less readily to his face when someone said something funny. He'd been suffering, and Gabriel hadn't even known. Had probably thought—and definitely *said*—more than one unkind thing, all because he hadn't had a clue what Sean was dealing with.

But over the last two years, he'd begun to come out of his shell. He'd formed friendships, he laughed now, just as easily as breathing, and he was vital and vibrant and so alive that Gabriel found he couldn't even tear his eyes away.

"Fine, I guess," Sean said with a laugh. "I guess we can get the drunken noodles, if you insist."

"Here's the thing," Gabriel said, "these aren't just any drunken noodles, they're *life changing* drunken noodles."

Sean raised an eyebrow. "What if I'm not in the mood for something so drastic?" he wondered, a teasing lilt to the edge of his voice.

It was almost embarrassing how much Gabriel wanted him to be—and in the mood for not just life-changing drunken noodles, but for life-changing relationships.

He could hear Ren's voice in his head, telling him not to screw this up, and Gabriel knew that he couldn't. That he *shouldn't*. But with every day that went by, it felt worse to not tell Sean the whole truth. That they'd never just been hooking up. That Gabriel had more feelings than he knew what to do with. That the friendship—and everything else—developing between them felt like the most important thing in his life.

Most of all, that he should have changed his truck's name the morning after Sean had told him why he couldn't.

After they put in their order—*including* the drunken noodles—with Mac, Sean leaned back in his chair, an expression of bliss on his face as he sipped his iced tea. "You're looking rather serious," he said.

"Food this good requires contemplation," Gabriel said.

"You should do something like this," Sean said unexpectedly.

"What, open a restaurant?" Gabe laughed. "If I wanted to do that, I'd just go beg for a job back from my brother." Which sounded *terrible*.

"No," Sean said. "Some kind of fusion stuff. You've got the chops, you know, you could do it."

"Fuck with Nonna's recipes?" The very idea felt sacrilegious. Luca would come down from Napa and murder him. Slowly. Nonna would probably return from the grave to cheer Luca on.

"See?" Sean said. "That's exactly what I mean. Was doing what we did with the Thai wrap, *fucking* with her recipes? No, it was using her meatballs to make something different. Something awesome. I think there's no greater compliment out there than putting your own spin on something."

"You don't think I should make meatball hoagies anymore?" Gabriel was incredulous. He'd made his reputation on those sandwiches. They were praised, all over the city. People came from an hour away when they were craving one. And yet, at the very same time, the idea of being able to step out of the very tiny box he'd created was enticing. It was seductive.

Ren would love it, because he was bored to death with what they were doing.

Frankly, Gabriel could admit that sometimes he was too.

And wasn't that part of the reason he'd wanted to branch out on his own? So he could be his own man? Make his own choices?

"I think you should, but I think you should explore other stuff too," Sean said. He pointed to the steaming plate of dumplings a waiter deposited on their table. "Like I'm pretty sure that traditionally they don't fill gyoza with bulgogi."

"They don't," Gabriel agreed.

"I'm not saying, change everything. I'm saying . . . just think about it, okay?" Sean said.

"Just because you're excited to redo your whole menu doesn't mean you need to redo mine," Gabriel teased lightly as he opened his chopsticks, using them to grab a dumpling before Sean ate them all.

"You'll be adding something new tomorrow," Sean said slyly. "I'll send over the wraps and the veg in the morning, by the way. And we've still got to finalize the spiced nuts."

It was easy to switch gears; to focus on the new shared item they'd both be selling.

"How many meatballs do you think you'll need?" Gabriel wondered.

"How many do you *think* I'll need?" Sean teased.

"I'll send Ren over with a couple hundred," Gabe said. "That should last you for a few days, at least. And I can have him make the glaze too, if you want."

"That'd be great," Sean said gratefully. "I'll probably be up late, working on the nuts. Trying to get them right, and then trying to make enough to last us a few days."

"Don't worry," Gabriel said, reassuring him, "I'll help. I said I would."

"Right." Sean shot him a grateful look. "I appreciate it a lot."

"Hey, it's partly my dish, too, right?" Gabriel said, reaching out and clasping Sean on the shoulder. "Don't want to make you do it all."

More food arrived then, the drunken noodles releasing a cloud of delicious steam, and the kimchee fried rice mounded in a delectable pile. The shrimp kung pao glistened in its sauce.

Sean stared at the food, entranced as it kept arriving.

"Think you ordered enough?" Mac said, appearing with a sly grin on his face. "Or should you get more to go?"

"Hey!" Gabriel's outrage mingled with Sean's laughter.

"The food looks incredible," Sean said, reaching out with his chopsticks, spearing a shrimp and popping it in his mouth. "*Tastes* incredible."

"Thanks," Mac said warmly.

Gabriel had a feeling that he'd get a text from his old friend later, wanting to know what was going on between him and Sean. After all, he'd never brought a guy here before. But bringing Sean? Had felt like a total no-brainer.

"Do you want to go to any more stores?" Sean asked after they'd finished shoveling most of the food into their mouths. "Or are you good?"

"Actually, I've got a few more things on my list," Gabriel said. He didn't, not really, but he was unwilling to cut their afternoon short. Even if he'd already committed to helping Sean, that was *work*, and this was . . . well, it wasn't work. "Technically," he added, "it's Ren's list."

Ren *had* been whining about some of their equipment lately, but then Ren liked to bitch about everything. Still, it wasn't technically a lie.

"Alright," Sean said, not looking disappointed in the least. "I'm down for more."

"I just bet you are," Gabriel teased, and Sean laughed.

And Gabriel thought to himself that if he could hear that sound every single day for the foreseeable future, he'd be a very lucky man.

A few hours and two stores later, they were almost back to Sean's townhouse when his phone rang, and Gabriel saw Tony's name flash across the screen.

"Hey, Tony," Sean said, clicking answer on the car's screen. "What's up?"

"Just wanted to check in, because I'm putting in some signage orders," Tony said, sounding distracted like he actually *was* at the sign shop. "I thought you might both want one for your new mashup."

"Yeah, we do," Gabriel said, without thinking.

"Oh, Gabe, you're there too," Tony said, sounding surprised. "I didn't realize . . ."

"He was just helping me with something," Sean interrupted.

Like he didn't want to go into the details with Tony, Gabriel thought. And how could he blame Sean for that? He didn't even want to go into the details with Tony. But it stung, anyway.

"Right," Tony said, with an edge of a leer to his voice. "I just bet he was helping you."

"Tony," Gabriel cut in. "We want the signs."

"Right, right, alright. I'll have them make some up. Can you text me what you want it to say?"

"Sure," Sean said. "We can do that."

"A lot of *we* in this conversation," Tony added.

"Thanks to you," Sean retorted. "This was your whole idea, remember?"

It had been, originally, and God knew Gabriel hadn't been a fan of it at first either, but it had been growing on him, doing this with Sean. To the point where he was actually really looking forward to shutting everyone's interfering asses up with their great dish *and* getting to brag about the sales next time they all met at the Funky Cup.

"Oh yeah, I remember," Tony said. "How could I forget?"

"Ugh," Sean groaned after Tony hung up. "Sometimes I really don't know why I like him so much."

"You're not alone," Gabriel agreed with a grumble of his own. Why did it feel like Tony was always a stupid comment away from destroying all his hopes?

If you were honest with Sean, he wouldn't be, Gabe's conscience added unhelpfully.

"Well, I guess we better come up with something," Sean said as he pulled into his driveway. "You got any bright ideas?"

"Yeah, I've got a few," Gabriel said, and right after Sean shut the car off, leaned over the console and captured Sean's mouth with his own.

They hadn't kissed since the shower this morning. They'd barely touched, and Gabriel hadn't realized how much he'd missed it.

But the way Sean groaned into his mouth and opened up, the kiss went from slow and sweet to so much hotter in an instant.

For a long minute, and then another, they kissed, Gabriel not even giving a shit that his neck was at a weird angle that would probably give him grief later, or that his knee was digging into the hard plastic of the console or even the fact that his phone was buzzing with what were almost certainly Tony's texts, wondering where their description was.

Then Sean broke off, a bright smile on his face, his eyes sparkling. "I wanted to do that all day," he confessed.

"Me too," Gabe said softly. He considered saying more. *Wanted* to say more, but then Sean's phone rang again, and the moment was broken.

Sean opened the door as he answered the phone. "Tony," he said, a clear note of exasperation in his tone. "We said we're getting it . . . *okay*, fine, we'll get it faster, then."

He hung up as he unlocked the door, Gabriel close behind him. "He is so goddamn impatient," Sean complained as he pushed the door open. He stormed into the kitchen, clearly really annoyed by whatever Tony had said on the phone. "He actually had the nerve to tell me that he didn't have time to wait for us to get our hands out of our pants."

"Oh, well." Gabe laughed nervously. "It's like he's got a freaking camera on us, or something."

"Right?" Sean flopped onto the couch. "I guess we better come up with something now, before he decides to show up on my doorstep."

"I think we could go with something simple like, *Thai meatball crunch wrap,*" Gabriel suggested, sitting down next to Sean and starting to type on his phone. "We'll need a description, too."

"I'll text you over a list of the ingredients," Sean said. "And we'll need a price."

"Oh, shit, right." Gabriel scrubbed a hand over his face. "I guess we'll have to fudge that. I don't have my laptop with the pricing spreadsheet here."

Sean looked up at him, surprised. "You have a pricing spreadsheet?"

"Well, yeah. Don't you?" Gabriel asked.

But Sean just shrugged. "Not really," he said. "I mean, I know the idea behind it. Cost of your raw materials, cost of your time, times the multiplier you've picked." He looked contemplative. "I just wouldn't have expected it out of you, I guess."

"We wouldn't have a string of successful restaurants without a pricing structure," Gabriel admitted. "And it's not really *mine*, it's something I borrowed from Luca and fussed around with, honestly. But yeah, I do think it helps."

"I should do that too," Sean said with a resigned sigh. "I know I should. Just . . . there's only so many hours in the day, you know?"

"I could help you with it," Gabriel offered, before he could stop himself. He shouldn't be insinuating himself into Sean's life before he told him the truth. What he really needed to do was take Sean's hand in his and confess everything. That he'd liked him from the very beginning, but now, those feelings had morphed into something so much deeper and stronger. *Like* had become *love*, so easily that Gabriel wasn't even sure where one ended and the other began.

But the sudden anxiety blooming in his stomach stopped him.

"Thank you," Sean said, and paused. "You're just really great, you know?"

"I thought we agreed I was a stubborn asshole still."

"Yeah, that ship has definitely sailed," Sean said wryly.

"Well, what should we do about the price? Tony will need it today, and I don't have the spreadsheet. We could use something on my menu as a jumping-off point?"

"Yeah," Sean said. "I like that idea."

They compared the price of Sean's wraps to Gabriel's rolls, and made some adjustments for the vegetables, subtracting out the cheese cost, and Gabriel was really pleased with the number they came up with. It lined up with some of his other menu items and fell right in the middle of Sean's offerings, too.

Ten minutes later, they had sent the text to Tony containing everything he needed for the signs.

"Well, that's done," Sean said, his eyes glimmering with mischief. He leaned in, brushing his nose against Gabe's playfully. "What should we do now?"

There was nothing more that Gabe could possibly want than to take Sean up on his clear offer. His dick was half-hard in his jeans, and his blood was still pumping from the kiss in the car. But it was getting late in the afternoon, and if they wanted to finalize everything for the new wrap, they needed to focus.

He didn't usually like to leave anything to the last minute, but the enticing promise of getting his hands all over Sean had distracted him the last few days.

"We should really get everything set up for tomorrow," Gabriel said reluctantly, standing up.

Sean gave an exaggerated sigh, and joined him. "I guess you're right, though my idea sounds like a lot more fun."

"It definitely would be," Gabe agreed.

"I'll go get the ingredients together for the first batch of nuts," Sean said, turning towards the kitchen. But then, he turned back. "Hey, you know what would be great?" he said. "If you grabbed some stuff from our trucks, and we made a few more test runs here, before tomorrow."

What Gabriel wanted was to stay, but he had to admit that it was a good idea. "Sure," he said. Sean was already grabbing a pen and a pad from the kitchen, and scribbling down a long list of things. "Plus," he said, glancing up, "anything you might need from yours."

"Right," Gabriel said, leaning in close to Sean so he could see what he was writing. The pen, which had been moving at light speed only a moment before, hesitated on the page and Sean glanced up at him, eyes wide.

"Oh," Sean said, and for a split second, Gabriel didn't know what he was saying. But then Sean reached up and pressed his mouth to Gabe's. The kiss was just as hot as it had been in the car, maybe hotter, because then Sean was pushing him against the wall between the kitchen and the living room, devouring him like he couldn't ever get enough.

Gabriel was just about to say *fuck it* to the entire plan and reach for Sean's dick, because it was hard and rubbing against his thigh and he could only take so much temptation without succumbing to it—but then Sean pulled back, and just stared at him, breath coming in choppy, uneven pants.

"Sorry," he said after a long moment. "Sorry, you were just there and well . . ." He shrugged, like it was hopeless. And it was, because Gabe was hopelessly charmed.

"The way I'm thinking," Gabriel said, "the sooner we get done with this work stuff, the sooner we can revisit that."

"Right, right," Sean said, flushing all the way up his neck to his cheeks. "I just . . . you were right there and well, it's hard to get enough, isn't it?"

Gabriel had been with plenty of guys where it hadn't been so hard to get enough. But with Sean? It felt like that would never happen. And maybe, Gabe thought with a quickening of his heart, Sean was on the exact same page.

"I'll go, then," Gabe said, plucking the list out of Sean's hand. "Before we decide we really *can't* get enough." He leaned in and brushed a kiss across Sean's scruffy cheek. It felt unbelievably soft, like down, and he turned to go before he could be tempted into staying.

"I'll get the nuts started," Sean said with determination in his voice. "My keys are hanging on the hook in the entry. Pink jelly ring, for the truck lock."

"I'll be back soon," Gabriel promised.

He was, actually, back pretty soon. It wasn't a long walk to the lot from Sean's townhouse, and he gathered everything they needed quickly, throwing it in one of the Food Truck Warriors canvas bags he had floating around.

He was back on Sean's doorstep thirty minutes later, giving a quick knock on the door before opening it and walking in.

"In the kitchen!" Sean called out, as Gabe walked through the downstairs towards the back of the house and the kitchen.

"That was quick," Sean said as Gabe set the bag on the counter and began to unload it.

"Found everything I needed fast," Gabriel explained. Didn't want to add that he'd hurried on purpose. Figured that was probably self-explanatory, because it felt like they could barely keep their hands off each other.

"Good," Sean said. He had a huge metal mixing bowl out, and was stirring some nuts in a sticky spicy-smelling substance. "I've just got this ready to put into the oven."

"How long does it bake for?" Gabe asked, already looking forward to convincing Sean that using the time to make out would be the best use of it, but he was already turning towards the sink, flipping on hot water, and washing out the metal bowl.

"Ten minutes, give or take," Sean said, "but I've got to flip them around occasionally so they don't burn."

"Well, *that's* disappointing," Gabriel said, coming up behind him at the sink, putting his arms around Sean while he washed the bowl out. "I was kinda looking forward to taking a break."

Sean turned and flashed him a smile. "I thought you *just* took a break."

"A break with you," Gabriel said. "That's the only kind that matters."

He watched as Sean's fingers hesitated on the sponge, and unexpectedly he turned, soapy fingers trailing up Gabe's arms. The look in Sean's eyes was full of trust and an undeniable affection. Gabe felt his breath catch in his throat. This was going to be the moment. He could feel it, deep down, in his bones. Sean was going to take a deep breath and he was going to confess everything. How this had started only as sex, but had become so much more. He was going to tell Gabriel . . .

And then the alarm on Sean's watch went off, blaring practically in his ear. Sean flinched and then slipped out of Gabriel's arms, and went over to the oven, peeking in and using a towel to grab the edge of the cookie sheet to shake the nuts around.

"How do they look?" Gabe asked, after he'd recovered from his disappointment.

"Good," Sean said. "Coming along, anyway. We should know if there's any adjustments that need to be made in the next couple of minutes."

"Alright," Gabe said. He turned towards the plastic container of meatballs he'd set on the counter earlier. It made sense to work on the wrap now, and get everything prepped for tomorrow's sales, so they could enjoy themselves later.

Gabriel wasn't very good at delayed gratification, but for Sean, he could get better. For Sean, he could do anything.

CHAPTER TWELVE

SEAN WOKE UP WITH the smell of roasted nuts in his nose. For a long moment, he couldn't remember falling into bed or even falling asleep.

He *could* feel the warmth of Gabriel's body next to his though, and it made him smile, because Gabe had stayed again.

Rolling over, he saw the trail of clothing on the floor of his bedroom, and the events of the night before began to filter back through his mind. The first batch of nuts had been a disaster—tasty but the spices were totally wrong for the rest of the wrap, which Gabriel had practiced constructing a few times, making sure that he knew exactly how to do it, so he could also teach Ren how to do it.

Then, on the third batch of nuts, Sean had finally gotten the balance of salty to sweet right, only to realize that his second bag of peanuts he'd bought had started to go rancid, and he'd need another one.

Gabriel had run out again, having to try three different grocery stores to find what they needed, and by the time Sean had been satisfied with their stockpile to use for the next week, it had been almost ten, and while he'd been undeniably eager earlier to fall into bed with Gabriel, when they'd actually done it, they'd both barely had the energy to strip down, before falling asleep almost immediately, exhausted.

Sean did remember setting the alarm for eight, an hour before they needed to be at the lot, but when he glanced at his smart watch, he saw that it was just past seven. Still, despite the early hour, he felt well-rested and incredibly energized. More than ready to face whatever the day held.

He slipped out of bed, and went to the bathroom, brushing his teeth and peeing, before returning to the bedroom.

Gabriel's eyes were open, the warm brown of them making Sean shiver with anticipation. "Good morning," he said, his voice gravelly from sleep still.

"It is a good morning," Sean said.

"Better than last night, in any case," Gabe said.

"I . . ." Sean knew he shouldn't apologize; nothing that had happened last night—none of the many, infuriating delays—had been his fault. But he'd been just as disappointed as Gabriel. The kisses they'd shared had left him buzzing with anticipation.

But regret was nothing if you couldn't keep your eyes open.

"Don't you dare apologize," Gabriel said, grinning. "Besides," he said, sliding out of bed just as Sean returned to it, "there's plenty of morning before we have to be at work."

"Forty-seven minutes to be exact," Sean said.

"I do like how ambitious you are," Gabriel observed, dropping a soft kiss on his cheek. "I'll be right back."

Sean waited with an increasingly breathless anticipation as he heard the bathroom door shut behind Gabriel.

He'd seen the toothbrush that Gabe had brought. Had seen it sitting next to his, in the holder, and had been pleasantly surprised at his own reaction.

He hadn't exactly expected that he'd freak out. But things were changing between them. Sean wasn't stupid enough to deny that. But he wasn't sure what they were morphing into, or if he should press pause while he figured out what he felt about that.

Except, the brutal honest truth was that he knew exactly how he felt, and all he felt was joy.

It was just really fucking nice not to be alone. Maybe, Sean thought, it would have been easier if that was all it was. A body to warm his bed on lonely nights, but the problem was that he'd never really wanted that. The only man he'd ever wanted since Milo was Gabriel.

So it was very hard to pin all of this on loneliness.

"You look like you're thinking way too hard."

Sean glanced up and saw Gabriel standing there, naked except for a pair of boxers, riding low on his hips, his tongue flicking out to wet his lower lip.

"Maybe you should come over here and make me stop," Sean teased.

Gabriel stared at him a moment longer and then was on the bed, climbing onto him with a grace that belied his size. He cupped Sean's cheek with one hand and it was shockingly tender, considering the way Gabriel was grinding his hardening dick against Sean's own, sending a rush of anticipatory pleasure through him.

For a second, Gabe just hovered there, lips right above Sean's, and he felt himself aching for it, straining to get closer, to that thrusting cock, and to his mouth, and to the man himself.

Then Gabriel kissed him, and it was hot and sweet and reverent and a whole lot dirty, his tongue delving deep, his mouth echoing the same minty flavor of his own.

"Fuck," Gabriel said, and Sean could already feel him breathing hard, his heart racing a mile per minute as he pressed a palm to it. "God, I want you so much."

"I want you too," Sean said, feeling a little bashful about just how much. Sex had never felt like an imperative before, but with Gabriel? It was life or death.

"I want to be inside you again," Gabriel said, and his voice had gone hushed. His eyes were worshipful as he slid a hand down Sean's body, towards the edge of his briefs. "But more than anything, I want what you want."

"I want that too," Sean said. He couldn't say anything else. The desire was so strong, it felt like it was going to wash over him in one suffocating wave. There was so much, he felt like he was going to choke on it.

He couldn't remember ever feeling its equal.

Even with Milo.

But before that thought could even fully register, Sean pushed it away again. He couldn't deal with that right now.

Gabriel's fingers on his cock, smoothing the wetness on the head down further, as he gave him a firm stroke, were all he wanted to deal with.

Pushing himself up, Sean kissed him again, their mouths sliding together again and again, until he was lost in the sensation, barely even registering Gabe letting go of his cock and the sound of the drawer in the bedside table opening.

He relaxed into the feel of Gabe's thumb sliding inside him, wet and welcome. He knew him now, and trusted him, and didn't doubt for a moment that Gabriel would make him feel good. The first time had been so extraordinary, and even if it hadn't been, he knew the man now, in a way that he hadn't necessarily then.

Gabriel slid a second finger in alongside the first, and Sean groaned at the stretch, desperately craving more of it.

"Come on," Sean begged. "I'm ready, I'm . . ."

The fingers paused inside of him and Sean's eyes flicked open, only to find Gabriel staring at him, pupils blown, the expression on his face a mix of tenderness and raw desire. "You're going to be ready when I say you're ready," Gabriel said, leaning down, and brushing a kiss across his mouth. "I want it to be good for you."

"I'm with you, aren't I?" Sean said, before he could stop himself. It seemed like with the pleasure short-circuiting his system, the filter between his brain and his mouth had seemingly disappeared. "It's always good."

Gabriel smiled, but didn't say anything, but *thankfully*, moved his fingers again, delving deeper until it felt like they were pressing right against that spot that never failed to make him see a whole universe of stars. Until he was pleading and incoherent, his cock leaking onto his stomach, so hard he felt like he might come the moment Gabriel touched him.

But he didn't, just grabbed a condom from the drawer, and then *finally*, after it was on, began to slide inside of Sean.

He was still big, but this time there wasn't even that moment of uncertainty, of doubt that it would really work, that it would fit. He just slid right in, delving so deeply that Sean knew his eyes were wide and unblinking, just letting the intense feeling crest over him.

"Fuck you feel so goddamned good," Gabriel ground out, his head dropping to Sean's shoulder as he began moving. Sean's hands reached up, tracing down Gabe's spine, fingertips digging into his damp skin, wanting him closer, *needing* it in a way that he didn't really recognize.

And then Gabriel was moving faster and harder, and Sean could only hang on for the ride, feeling his cock slide between their bodies, catching on Gabe's stomach, and that was all it took for him to slide right off the edge into oblivion, crying out as he clenched around Gabe's cock.

"Oh, god," Gabriel moaned right after him, shaking in Sean's arms as he followed right after him.

As their heartbeats calmed and he began to come back down to reality, Sean had two immediate overriding thoughts: *one*, he could stay here forever, just like this, and *two*, he couldn't possibly, not at all.

What was he *doing*?

He'd promised Gabriel just sex. He'd insisted to him that it couldn't be anything else, because nothing had felt like it had with Milo.

There was no possible way that Sean hadn't loved Milo with every bit of his heart. He'd known that, before, when Milo had been a laughing, perfect figure next to him. At their wedding. On their honeymoon. During the many nights they'd just relaxed on the couch, throwing popcorn into each other's mouths and watching the trashiest reality TV they could get their hands on.

But what he felt for Gabriel was so intrinsically different, he'd not even seen it coming, and now that he did, he didn't even know what to do with it.

Was it friendship? Was it, somehow, impossibly, *love*?

Sean didn't know, and he was kind of freaking out.

Because whatever this was between them, it was no longer just sex.

Maybe it had never been just sex.

"I . . ." Sean took a deep breath. "I gotta get up. The alarm is gonna go off any second."

Gabriel was probably too worn out, riding on a wave of endorphins to recognize the panic in Sean's voice. But he heard it in his own, and wondered, with a pang somewhere near the vicinity of his heart, how Gabriel could have missed it.

Rolling off Sean, Gabe just gave him a carefree grin. "I thought we had forty-seven minutes. I'm pretty sure we only used thirty-nine of those, and maybe sixteen seconds, for good measure."

It hadn't even been close to forty-seven minutes, which Gabe probably knew, but Sean wasn't going to bother addressing. He was too full of the panic suddenly streaking through him.

"I just . . . I gotta get in the shower. Get ready. Get the nuts packed up to go. We've got more than normal prep this morning, you know."

"I know," Gabriel said. He did not seem particularly eager to get up.

But Sean knew he couldn't stay in bed a moment longer.

"I'll be in the shower," he said, and got up and left. And he immediately missed the warmth of Gabriel next to him.

By the time Sean got to the lot an hour later, he was still feeling uneasy.

Gabe had helped him pack up the nuts and had given him a brief kiss when they'd parted, telling Sean that he was headed home to shower and change and then he'd see him at the lot.

Gabriel had apparently not noticed Sean's uneasiness, probably because his own mood had been playful and happy, like his regular innate charm was simply bubbling out of him this morning, too plentiful to control.

Sean hoped that had nothing to do with him, but he was afraid it did.

Somehow, they'd gotten embroiled in this *thing*, and they were already deep in the middle of it before he had even realized it was happening.

Sean stared across the way at Gabriel's truck, where Tony was putting up the sign, chatting casually with both Gabe and Ren. Tony had done his first, commenting briefly on how glad he was that they'd figured something out.

He'd initially been afraid that Tony would continue the teasing from yesterday, because Sean could *not* handle that right now, but he'd apparently gotten the memo that Sean was busy and didn't want to be bothered, because he'd posted the sign next to Sean's menu, on the side of his truck, and had moved on to Gabe's almost immediately.

But Sean?

He couldn't seem to dismiss his own bad mood. Instead of working, he was just standing here, *stewing* in it.

Finally he decided that he'd go outside, take a picture of the new sign and post it on Instagram, hoping to drum up some interest in his followers for the new dish.

He was getting the shot framed just right when he heard a voice literally *growl* behind him. Except this was Los Angeles, and as far as Sean knew there weren't actual *bears* running around.

Sean turned, and there was a man standing there, staring at his truck. Specifically at the *name* written along the top of the menu, the red letters bright and cheerful against the white background.

"Can I help you?" Sean asked, even though he really didn't want to. He was already in a bad mood and he could tell this guy was just going to piss him off more.

"I think you sure as fuck *should*," the guy growled again.

There was something so familiar about him, Sean thought as he took a step closer. The dark hair, with the threads of gray already beginning at the temples, and the handsome face, with the dark, intense eyes. He looked so painfully similar to someone, Sean *knew* he should know, but he couldn't quite put his finger on it.

"Excuse me?" Sean retorted. He'd been nice before, but he wasn't sure how long he could keep up the facade.

"You stole my brother's name," he said bluntly, pointing first at Gabe's truck, and then at Sean's.

It was only then it hit Sean who this was. This was one of Gabriel's brothers. This had to be Luca, the eldest. The one that Tate had mentioned visiting last summer, the one that made things hard for Gabriel.

Taking a second look, it was obvious. The facial structure was the same. That was Gabriel's hair, just less shaggy, and more precisely cut, and with the gray. And that attitude? Definitely explained the gray. Also explained why the guy's arrogance had felt so familiar. The antagonism radiating out of Luca reminded him so much of how Gabriel had used to be, back at the beginning.

He'd had to learn it from somewhere.

"I didn't steal anyone's name," Sean said in a measured, surprisingly calm voice. "We both ended up with it, kind of by accident."

Luca's brows slammed together. "Then you should have changed yours."

The resemblance was so staggering now, that Sean couldn't believe he hadn't seen it right away. He crossed his arms over his chest. "Yeah, I don't think so. And while you're at it, maybe you should actually *talk* to your brother about what's going on, because we're dealing with this."

"If you were dealing with it, you would have already fixed it," Luca said inflexibly. And that, Sean thought with frustration, was really an adjective that could describe all Morettis. Even Gabriel.

"You mean *I* would have changed my name, right?" Sean said. "Because that's what you're really saying."

"Gabriel has paperwork. He could sue you for copyright infringement. He *should* have sued you for copyright infringement."

Why was Sean not surprised that the very first thing Luca had done was drag out the threat of lawyers?

He sighed. "You're really just embarrassing yourself now. Go talk to Gabe. He'll explain the whole thing."

Luca looked absolutely apoplectic, and it filled Sean with a lot more satisfaction than he had any right to. "He will. He will explain the whole thing, and then we will come back here, and you will agree to change your name."

"I don't think you understand," Sean said stiffly, annoyed, "I'm not changing it. We've talked about this."

"With Gabriel?" Luca had the nerve to sound shocked at this.

"*Yes*," Sean said.

"But if you had talked about it, then this would all be fixed."

Sean ground his teeth together, deciding it was just about time for him to lose his temper. "Maybe *you* should talk to him," Sean said, giving him a little wave that had the desired reaction of making Luca's jaw clench visibly. "Go on! I hope you have a good brotherly talk!"

Luca looked like he wanted to say something else—well, more like he wanted to say *a lot* more things—but he shot Sean one more searing glare, and stormed off in the direction of Gabriel's truck.

Maybe Sean should have felt a little bit guilty about sending Luca over to his brother, all primed for an argument, but he didn't. It was cowardly, and he *definitely* should have felt ashamed, but Sean felt like he needed some space and some time to think. Things were changing between them, both as slow as molasses and so quick it felt like he'd just *blinked* and they were different.

If Luca wanted to go over to Gabe's and distract him for a morning, or even for a whole day—and while he was at it, let Gabe inform him of what was *really* going on, then Sean wasn't going to stand in their way.

"It's the most beautiful fucking day," Gabriel half said, half sang as he sank, wrist-deep, into an enormous bowl of meatball mixture.

"You're absolutely disgusting," Ren muttered.

"Yep!" Gabriel wasn't denying it. He couldn't. He was too happy. Maybe he hadn't quite told Sean the whole truth, but he had a feeling that when he did, Sean wouldn't run. He'd give Gabe one of those sweet, slightly crooked smiles, like *of course* Gabe had fallen in love with him and *of course* he'd fallen in love with Gabriel back, and tell him to get over here, so they could kiss.

Their first kiss as a real couple. The first kiss when Sean knew Gabe loved him, and Gabe knew Sean loved him in return.

He could already taste it, could feel Sean's passion when he took him to bed that first time.

"Should I leave you alone with those meatballs?" Ren asked, raising an eyebrow. "'Cause you keep mixing them that way much longer and they're going to get jealous of Sean."

Maybe he had been kneading the mixture a bit suggestively. Gabe shot his cousin a sheepish look. "Maybe Sean should be jealous of *them*."

"You have a real problem," Ren announced as Gabe removed his hands and went over to the sink to wash.

"Actually I've got the opposite of a problem," Gabe said. "Sean's crazy about me, and we both know, despite your insistence that it's a mistake, that I'm crazy about him."

"No," Ren said firmly, "you have a *real problem*."

"I really don't," Gabriel argued, certain to his core that Ren could only be talking about his epic love with Sean. He finished scrubbing his hands, and flipped the water off, grabbing a paper towel before turning to find the meatball scoop.

They had a ton of meatballs to bake off today, even more because he needed to send Ren over with a bunch for their new Thai wrap.

But before he could find the scoop in the clutter of tools scattered across the counter, he saw Ren's face out of the corner of his eye.

He was staring out the front window. At the real problem, rapidly approaching.

Luca was here.

"Well, shit," Gabriel said.

"I *said* you had a real problem." Ren shook his head. "Like you and Sean could ever constitute a *real* problem. On the other hand . . ."

"Luca is a massive pain in the ass?"

"A massive pain in *your* ass," Ren said with a succinct nod. "I think I'm gonna take my break now, if you don't mind."

"Hey, wait," Gabriel called out, but Ren had already shed his apron and was vanishing out the back door.

Just in time for Luca to stop in front of the truck, and eye him through the front window. He looked pissed—okay, he usually looked a bit pissed, but he looked way more pissed than normal. And it occurred to Gabriel then that the last time Luca had graced them with his presence had been last summer. Before the food truck lot had opened. Which meant that he'd never met Sean, and he'd never seen his truck. The truck that had the exact same fucking name as Gabriel's.

Knowing how Luca felt about intellectual property—it was nearing a fanaticism with him, he'd once camped out in a neighboring restaurant's dining room, arguing for hours that they had stolen Nonna's red sauce recipe.

Having tasted both, Gabriel had been pretty sure they had too, but the only one who had really, truly cared was Luca.

He had probably seen Sean's truck, and now he was going to lose his shit.

Gabriel sighed, and pulled his apron off. So much for a really good day.

By the time he made it around the truck to stand face to face with Luca, it was clear that he had *already* lost his shit.

His jaw was tight, his arms crossed over his chest, wearing one of those ridiculously tight t-shirts that showed off the biceps and pectorals that he'd worked so hard for. Personally, Gabriel thought he looked stupid, showing off like that, but that was Luca for you. Always in your face. Never surrendering.

Gabriel had told Sean that he'd left Napa and the family businesses because it had felt like he was lost in the midst of so many people who all wanted to tell him what he should do, but mostly, he'd left because of Luca.

Luca didn't want to just interfere in that friendly, familial way that so many of his brothers and sisters and various family members did. He wanted to tell Gabriel what to do, and exactly how to do it.

"Gabriel," Luca said, inclining his head a fraction. A hug was out of the question; they were much more likely to start brawling than embracing. Gabe wasn't proud of how bad the relationship with his brother had gotten, but he also refused to take any responsibility for it. If Luca wanted them to be friends, then he'd need to be a lot less Luca-like.

It seemed, from the way he'd shown up today, without announcing he was coming, that kind of change was not forthcoming.

"Luca," Gabe responded tightly. "I didn't know you were coming."

"I wanted to surprise you," Luca said.

Except they both knew that Luca showing up, out of the blue, was hardly a good surprise. It was much more likely that he'd decided not to tell Gabriel because he hadn't wanted to be talked out of coming.

"We're busy this week," Gabe said, which was not a lie, because they were busy *every week*.

"I'm only here for the day," Luca said. "And I'm glad I came, because *this*"—he thrust out a hand, gesturing in the direction of Sean's truck—"is what I've found."

Gabriel did not even try to explain, because the explanation wasn't something that Luca would ever accept.

Luca had come out on his eighteenth birthday, almost belligerently, like he'd halfway expected the family to kick him out, even though he'd spent the prior eighteen years being an absolutely model Italian son. But even after that, Gabe had never heard even a whiff of him dating anyone. Luca was too contained to fall in love. He would drive whoever he fell in love with absolutely insane within the first week.

And none of that would even matter anyway, because Luca would never make time for a relationship in the first place. He'd dedicated his whole life to running the family restaurants. He worked from dawn to midnight, nearly every day, without a single complaint, acting like that was *normal*.

Gabe knew he could never comprehend him putting business aside, or not changing the name because he'd been afraid of losing Sean.

"You're not even going to try to explain this?" Luca challenged, the edge of his steely tone growing impossibly harder. "I cannot believe you have *let* this go, for at least six months."

"Two years," Gabriel said, because the problem was that he'd always enjoyed waving the red flag in front of Luca's face. Maybe that might be why they didn't get along. That was definitely why Ren had seen his brother and then run. He'd grown up with them; he knew the kind of damage they inflicted on each other.

"Two years?" Luca stared at him in disbelief. "Are you insane?"

"It's not a big deal," Gabriel said, even though it was impossible now to downplay it. It had been impossible from the moment Luca had spotted Sean's truck. "We're working it out."

"That was what he said," Luca said. "But I couldn't believe you would be that *stupid* to not immediately take action to deal with the situation. To deal with *him*."

"I did take action. I threw a meatball at him."

Luca stared at him, unbelievably stunned into at least a momentary silence. "You threw a meatball at him. What are you? Ten years old? This is a *business*, Gabriel, which I have tried very hard to remind you of, over and over again. You have to take it seriously. Morettis don't play around."

Whenever Luca said that—and he said it often—Gabriel wanted to punch him in the face. They were not all the same. Just because they had the same last name did not make them identical. He was not, *thank God*, the same as Luca. Every single time Luca assumed he was, he wanted to kill his older brother slowly.

Painfully. Or maybe just so spectacularly that Luca never made the same mistake again.

"I wasn't playing around," Gabriel said, hating the defensive tone he heard in his own voice. "I was serious. I took it seriously. I even came up with a new name. Registered it and everything. But it's complicated. I couldn't just . . . I couldn't just do it, not like that."

"Not like what?" Luca said in a hard voice. "Not like the smart, intelligent businessman I know you're capable of being?"

It hurt. It always hurt. The biggest reason that Gabriel had left Napa was that there was never any wiggle room. You were either a clone of Luca—and his brother Marco was on his way there—or you were nothing.

Gabriel had been so sick of being nothing.

But even being nothing didn't hurt as much as Sean's voice, breaking through the red haze in his head. "You had a new name?"

Gabriel looked up and wanted to punch his brother more than he'd ever wanted to in his whole life. Because the betrayal on Sean's face cut deep. "You had a new name," he repeated, "and you didn't bother changing it? Not all this time?"

It was the last thing that Gabe had ever wanted Sean to find out. That he could have circumvented this whole problem, almost from the very beginning.

But without the problem, he'd always reasoned, what purpose would there be for Sean to talk to him? To bicker with him? They'd go back to being passing acquaintances, and Gabriel had never known how to face that. Which was why, instead of doing something about it, he'd let the situation fester for so long. Why the paperwork had sat, unused, in his desk drawer.

"I . . ." Gabriel didn't know what to say. *How* to say it. He'd imagined this going so differently. He'd imagined telling Sean that he loved him, that he wanted to be with him, and that, *hey*, by the way, on a completely unrelated note, he'd decided to rebrand his own truck.

But now Sean was staring at him, anger blooming in his expression, and Luca was staring aghast at both of them.

It was terrible.

"I was right all along," Sean said unsteadily, "you were just . . . you're just the selfish asshole I always thought you were." He turned and stalked off, almost certainly satisfied that his parting bomb had hit Gabriel with as much destructive force as possible.

Because Sean knew him now, and he had to know that the thing he dreaded most, the person he tried so hard not to be, was the selfish asshole. Was Luca.

"Good," Luca said, straightening. "Then you will change your name and put all this behind you."

Gabriel just gaped at him. "*No*," he said. "This conversation is over. I don't care where you came from, *hell maybe*, but I'm done talking to you about this."

Luca's brow furrowed. "What? You can't . . ."

"I can." Through the hurt, Gabriel at least felt a strength of purpose. He'd messed up with Sean, maybe forever. But he could still tell Luca to fuck off. Save a tiny fraction of self-respect.

"I still . . ."

Gabriel didn't let him finish. "I've got the money in the bank to pay your investment off. I'll write you a check today."

"But I don't . . ." Luca trailed off. For a moment, for only a split second, he actually looked human. Like he might care. Like he might actually give a shit about Gabriel, the *person*, his *brother*, and not just what Gabriel might bring to the family name. But then that all disappeared, and that cold, hard asshole mask was back in place. "Fine," he said. "Fine, if that will make you happy, I will take the money and go. I was just trying to protect the family. You know that."

Gabriel rolled his eyes. "Someday," he said, "you're going to wake up and it's gonna be a real bad day for you, because you'll realize that the only one who's ever failed to protect the family is you."

CHAPTER THIRTEEN

Gabriel waited all day to go find Sean.

It helped, a little, that they were crazy busy, just as he'd told Luca they would be.

It had helped, a little more, to give Luca that check and send him on his way with a very final *fuck off*.

It had helped, even more, that Luca had clearly been unhappy about it.

But even still, Gabriel had spent the day barely able to keep from staring across the way, at Sean's truck. He'd had a line more than once, and Gabriel had hoped he was selling as many of the new wraps as they were.

Ren had had to make another batch of glaze, and by the end of the day, they were running low on both the prepped vegetables that Sean had sent over, and the nuts that they'd finished together last night.

"Well," Ren said, stretching his back with a little moan. "That was hardly your beautiful day."

"I don't know, telling Luca to fuck off felt pretty beautiful to me," Gabriel said, even though he didn't feel quite as confident about it as he sounded.

Luca might be mean and more than a little controlling, but he was undeniably great at this. What if all the success Gabriel had experienced over the years was because of *him*?

"I wish I could've seen it," Ren said.

"If you hadn't run away, you would have," Gabriel teased him.

"I just didn't want to get caught up in the crossfire of your Moretti bullshit," Ren said practically. "It's always safer to be far away when the two of you face off."

"We're not *that* bad," Gabriel said, but he knew that they could be, sometimes. And after this, the likelihood of their relationship improving was not likely.

"You're just too much the same," Ren said.

"What?" Gabriel couldn't believe that Ren honestly thought that. "We're nothing alike."

"You're *exactly* alike," Ren said, leaning against the counter. "You both think you're goddamned right all the time. Both think you know best. And both think you know the best way to express your brotherly affection. In this particular situation, I can tell you that you're both fucking wrong."

Gabriel didn't say anything for a long moment. "That wasn't all he was doing . . ." he finally started to say, but Ren held a hand up.

"Maybe he blundered into this thing between you and Sean, but he didn't know it was even happening," Ren said. "He didn't *mean* to. And then you bit his head off."

"I did not," Gabriel said sulkily. Except he had.

"Yeah, alright," Ren said, clearly not believing him.

"He just . . ." Gabriel made a frustrated noise. "He just walked in and fucked everything up, you know? Like he usually does."

"Except," Ren said, "at least this time he didn't do it on purpose?"

"Fine," Gabriel grumbled. "He didn't do it on purpose."

"You two love each other," Ren said sagely. "You just express it in such different ways. Ironic, considering you're practically the same person."

"Is that enough?" Gabriel asked, annoyed that his cousin would not shut up.

"I think so. So are you really changing the name again?" Ren asked as they began the long task of cleaning up.

"Yes," Gabriel said shortly. "I should have done it ages ago. But . . ."

"But you were too desperate to get Sean to notice you," Ren finished for him. "I get it. But you know, you could've just *told* him you liked him, instead of continuing to tug on his pigtails."

"Maybe." Gabriel was still not convinced. And he was definitely not convinced that when he went over to Sean's truck that he would want to see him at all.

This whole time, he could have taken steps to help Sean pre-serve the memory of his husband—not because Milo meant anything to him, but because he meant so much to Sean.

If he was in Sean's shoes, he'd be pissed as hell at him.

"You could still tell him," Ren said speculatively, as he scrubbed down the grill. "You *should* tell him."

"What happened to *love is a choice*?" Gabriel wondered.

Ren sighed. "It is, and you made it, and he makes you happy. You make him happy too. I don't think he really was, before. But you know what? This isn't always how it works out."

Gabriel was dying to ask his cousin how it hadn't worked out for him, but he didn't, because if Ren wanted to tell him, he would.

"I don't think he was happy, either," Gabriel pointed out instead. He felt, like he had from the night that Sean had told him about Milo, the pressure to keep Sean's secret. Because if Sean had wanted any of their friends to know, he'd have told them.

It didn't change anything that Gabriel sure as fuck thought that they should have known ages ago. It wasn't his call.

"Well, he is now, or he *was*," Ren said. He sighed and stood up, giving the edge of the flat-top grill a final wipe. "Which means that you should get your ass over there and start apol-ogizing. Definitely start groveling."

"I will." Gabriel stacked the last of the packed containers away in their fridge. "I'm helping you, first."

"No, you're procrastinating because you're afraid he's going to be really fucking mad at you," Ren said.

Ren was not wrong. But it wasn't just that.

Gabriel didn't think he could seek out Sean if he was going to see that look of betrayed trust—the one that had sliced him to pieces—on his face again.

"I don't know much about love," Ren continued casually, "but I know that it isn't always easy. Things aren't always as simple as you hope they'll be."

"He might not forgive me even if I change the name, now," Gabriel said.

"He might not. But," Ren glanced up at him, a glimmer of a smile on his face, "I think he'll *want* to, and that's what matters."

Ren had a lot more faith right now than Gabriel did, and that was a scenario that he'd never imagined, not in a thousand years.

It was the one that convinced him that he couldn't hide out any longer, hoping that maybe Sean wouldn't be quite so pissed, that maybe he might even come seek *Gabe* out.

But Ren was right.

Even if Sean was pissed, he wouldn't be so pissed that he wouldn't want, deep down, to forgive him.

His love might be dented and a bit bruised by what had happened, but Gabriel knew, in his bones and in his blood and in every way that fucking mattered, that Sean *did* love him.

That knowledge was what gave him the courage he needed to propel him out of his truck and across the lot towards Sean's.

He could see Sean's face in the window, brow furrowed as he scrubbed at something, cleaning up after a long day. He hadn't seen Gabriel yet, but Gabe thought he could see the strain of the day on his face.

Finally, he looked up and a whole range of emotions crossed over it when he saw Gabriel. Longing and frustration and anger and hurt and resignation—but right when Gabe despaired that maybe Sean didn't love him after all, there it was. Begrudging maybe, but it was there, glowing soft and warm in his eyes.

He turned and walked down the stairs, coming around the corner of his truck.

It was late, everyone else had closed up for the night, and he didn't see anyone else, which was *right*, because nobody else had the right to hear this conversation.

"Hey," Gabriel said, "I came over because I wanted to let you know that Luca is gone."

"Good." Sean's voice was short, but there was relief in it too. "Does that mean he's not going to sue me now?"

Dread rushed through Gabe. He'd known that Luca had made things difficult for Sean before he'd come over to deal with Gabriel, but he hadn't realized that part of Luca's threats had included lawyers. God, that must have freaked Sean out.

"No, no, no," Gabriel said as quickly as he could, the words spilling over each other in his eagerness to set the record straight. "No, never. That . . . Luca is insane. That was never an option, never."

Challenge joined the relief in Sean's expression. "Good."

Gabriel wondered if that was all he was going to say. "And I wanted to apologize. I should have changed the name, way back when, the first night you told me about Milo, and why you didn't want to change yours. It was the right thing to do, and I just didn't."

"I told you not to," Sean said. He didn't sound as angry as Gabriel had expected. "I mean, I suppose I should be pissed as hell at you. You had an out for our problem the whole time and you didn't tell me. I guess you were probably pretty amused when I told you that I thought about it every day, trying to find a way out of our stalemate."

"I . . . *no*," Gabriel said, and he reached out for Sean, but he stepped out of his reach. The challenge in his eyes flashed again. Okay, so maybe he wasn't super pissed, but he also wasn't quite ready to make up yet. Gabriel could understand that.

"No," Gabriel repeated. "I didn't laugh at you. I wasn't *amused*. I was sick, to be honest, because I didn't know what to do."

"You didn't know what to do?" Sean sounded incredulous. "You had a name change all ready to go!"

"I know," Gabriel said, shame washing over him. "But . . ." He took a deep breath. "I know you're mad about that, and you deserve to be . . ."

But before Gabriel could get even more of his apology out, could even attempt to grovel a little bit, Sean interrupted him, pacing back and forth in front of his truck, like his feet couldn't stay still, not while he unloaded about what he *did* feel.

"I'm mad about that, a little, but what I'm really fucking pissed at is that you just *stood* there and let your brother just roll over you."

"I took care of him," Gabriel inserted. "I told you, I took care of it. He won't be around again. I don't owe him another dime, not for his investment, not for *anything*."

"Do you really think I give a fuck if he comes around here again? Yeah, his threats were a little scary, how could they not be? But I knew, *knew*, you wouldn't let him sue me, I knew we could work it out, but . . ." Sean shoved a finger into Gabriel's chest. "But you just let him walk all over you. You *let* him."

That was the last thing Gabriel had expected that Sean would be pissed about. "Luca and I, we have a complicated relationship," he said carefully. "We always have."

"What's complicated is all of this," Sean said, gesturing to the air between them, the same air that had crackled with tension the very first time they'd met and continued to crackle still. "And now I'm wondering what we're even doing, who you even *are*, this guy that I'm . . . I'm all mixed up about."

"Mixed up?" Gabe found that he was the one gaping in shock now. "You're *mixed up*?"

"Yes," Sean said tightly. "I said we were just going to get naked and I thought that was all it was . . ."

"It's not all it was," Gabriel said. "It was never about that for me." It was terrifying to continue, especially considering the look on Sean's face—the utter confusion, like he truly didn't know what they were doing. "I never just wanted that. I thought you were on the same page I was. I think you *are* on the same page I am."

"What page is that?"

Gabriel reached for him, and this time Sean didn't fight him, just tucked himself into his embrace. For a second, he just held him, the man he'd come to love so much. There was a little bit of terror, because how could there not be? But there was hope too, and it was a live thing inside him, blossoming into something incredible. How could Ren have ever said this was a choice? It had never been a choice.

"I love you," he said softly. "Maybe that's too much for you to hear, but I do. I think I might have loved you for a long time. Long before I even knew what this was."

For a very long moment, Sean was silent, but the unmistakable feeling of him tensing in Gabriel's arms was enough of an answer.

Sean slipped away from his grasp and turned his head. He couldn't even look at Gabriel. Couldn't even meet his eyes. "That's . . ." His voice shook. "That's never what this was supposed to be about. I *told you*."

"I know you did," Gabriel said, trying not to let the disappointment and hurt leak into his voice. It wasn't his fault that Sean didn't know what he was feeling. And maybe Gabe should've been less sure that Sean loved him, but he *knew* he did. The same way he knew how to make Nonna's red sauce, and how to make the best meatballs and the best ziti that anyone had ever tasted.

He'd never been as sure of anything in his whole fucking life.

"I wasn't being cute or funny or playing hard to get when I told you," Sean said, sounding wretched. "It just . . . it *felt* different with you, than it did with Milo. I loved him, loved him with everything in me and I just don't know . . ." He took a shuddering breath. "I don't know if I can feel that way about you."

Maybe even then, Gabriel should have believed what he was telling him. But he also knew about pain and how you could carry it with you, even long after you thought you'd set it down. How it could hold you back, even when you wanted to be set free.

Maybe Sean thought he didn't love him, because he didn't know how to let himself.

The other option was just not one that Gabriel would accept, because he'd felt the warmth and strength of Sean's affection and care himself, and he'd *known* it wasn't just one-sided. Sean had never pushed him away, not once, he'd only drawn him closer and closer, until it felt like Gabriel's heart was beating right next to his.

"You already feel that way about me," Gabriel said, and *yeah*, maybe it came out a little cocky. But he *was* cocky, about this anyway. He'd won Sean's love, even if Sean didn't know it, and that was one of the greatest, if not *the* greatest thing, he'd ever done in his life.

"I don't want you to get your hopes up," Sean said carefully. "I don't know what I feel."

"It doesn't matter," Gabriel said, reaching for him again, but Sean took a step back, and then another one.

"Your feelings and my . . . well, I don't know what I feel. Not even close. Because of that, at least, maybe we should take a break from each other, at least for a little while," Sean said, like he wasn't in the process of trying to burn down Gabriel's world. All his hope, beginning to crumble, a little bit at a time. Because what if he never realized how he felt? What if he was just as sure as Gabriel was? What if this was the stalemate that ended up killing them?

He'd been so sure that the stupid fucking name would be the end of them.

But what if it was something more insidious, something buried a lot deeper, something that Gabriel couldn't fix as easily as filing new paperwork and ordering a new sign for the truck?

What if it was Sean's history with his dead husband that had doomed them before they could ever begin?

Gabriel already knew he couldn't fight a memory, which was why he had deliberately never done it. And he wasn't going to start now.

Not when Sean had been so fucking clear. He'd even said the words. He'd told Gabriel how much he'd loved Milo, and when Gabriel had given him the opportunity to move on, to tell *Gabriel* how much he loved him, he'd refused to say it.

Gabe's throat closed up.

How could one person be so fucking right and so completely fucking wrong, all in the same moment, about the exact same thing?

But Sean was right; what they needed was a break from each other.

He turned, and without saying a single word, walked away.

It turned out that, no matter what, he was always going to give Sean what he wanted. Even if it was the totally wrong fucking thing.

There was nothing that Sean thought could possibly hurt worse than the moment he'd opened the door of the apartment he'd shared with Milo and the look on the police officer's face had ruined his life.

But this felt second to that. Watching Gabriel walk away, the muscles of his back tight and strained as he left.

Left *him*.

Except that Gabriel wouldn't have, he'd never have left his side, if Sean hadn't pushed him away. He *loved* him.

How did you even respond to a thing like that if you were genuinely sure you didn't know how you felt? It would have been betrayal of the very worst kind to *lie*, and say that he knew. It would have been somehow even worse to tell Gabriel that he loved him back.

He hadn't known what to say or do, flayed bare by Gabriel's simple confession. Space had seemed like a very good idea, and something that Sean desperately needed, until he watched Gabe walk away, and then it felt like the very worst.

Sean picked up his glass and drained his drink in one gulp.

Shaw, the bartender, shot him a sympathetic look. "Hard day?" he asked.

It had started out so great. Even after Luca and the sudden shock of finding out that Gabe had had a plan this whole time, it still hadn't been so bad. The new wrap had sold like crazy, and he'd almost been too busy to agonize. But as the afternoon had worn on, he'd been sure about one thing: he hadn't really been angry at Gabriel. Surprised, maybe, and dismayed at how easily Luca had pushed him around. But not *angry*.

"Weird day," Sean said instead.

Shaw began to pour him another drink, even though Sean hadn't intended to order another. It felt too much like falling into old habits that he'd sworn to himself that he'd never revisit again. But, as he watched Shaw's fingers move so confidently through the motions, what would be the harm of it?

What he really wanted was to talk to someone. Not just *someone*. One of his friends. Maybe Tony or Lucas or Tate. Even Ash, though he was rarely as sympathetic as the others. But how could he, when they didn't know the whole story?

He'd have to lead with, "By the way, I have this dead husband that I've never mentioned to any of you," and Sean wasn't stupid or even remotely drunk enough to believe that was a great way to start anything.

Of course, that was exactly how it had started with Gabriel.

Even thinking his name ached.

Sean took the glass from Shaw's hand. "Thanks," he said.

Shaw leaned over the bar. "You know, I've been told I have a good ear for problems, and you, my man, look like you have a real problem."

He couldn't help but sigh. He *did* have a problem. "What would you do if you found out that a friend of yours had a whole history that you didn't know about?"

"Did this friend lie to me about it?" Shaw asked, straightening and starting to wipe out drying glasses. "Or did they just omit the details?"

"Isn't lying by omission a form of lying?" Sean wondered.

Shaw shrugged. "I think it's whatever they decide it is," he said.

"They?"

"You're talking about *your* friends, aren't you?" Shaw was smart; Sean had always known this. But he hadn't realized it until he narrowed in on the thing that he'd only vaguely hinted at. "And you're the friend who wasn't honest."

"I . . ." Sean took another drink. "I wasn't. I . . ." It still wasn't easy talking about this; probably because he *didn't* talk about it. Not for years. "I was married, before I came to Los Angeles."

"Divorce?" Shaw asked casually, like he already had this pegged. And maybe he thought he did, because no doubt a lot of sad people who passed through this bar had had their hearts broken from a relationship that just hadn't worked out.

"He died," Sean said.

Shaw's eyes flew to his. "Oh shit. I'm sorry, I didn't . . ."

"You couldn't have known," Sean said heavily. "Because I didn't tell you. I didn't tell anyone. I told myself I was starting over. That I was moving on, the way my therapist wanted me to do, and in a lot of ways, I *was."* But now, looking back over the last two years, Sean wasn't sure that was what he'd been doing at all.

"You told Gabriel, didn't you?" Shaw guessed.

"I did . . . not long ago," he admitted. "I thought he should know, before we . . . well, before we got naked together."

"I knew you guys were up to something," Shaw said.

"I stupidly thought we were just hooking up. I even told him that was all it was, because well, how could it be anything else? I knew how it felt to fall in love. To love someone so much I wanted to spend the rest of my life with him. The way I felt about Gabe? Totally different."

"But no less intense, right?"

"Well . . ." Sean hesitated. Because Shaw was right. It had gotten intense, right at the end. He could remember this morning, when everything had felt so sunny and right and perfect and it had felt like his heart would beat out of his chest, just so it could follow

Gabe. He'd known things were changing. But he hadn't thought it was *love*.

Because he knew what that felt like.

"Love doesn't always feel the same," Shaw said kindly.

"I don't know if what I feel for Gabe is even love," Sean said. "And wouldn't it be worse if I told him it was, and it turned out that it wasn't? I couldn't . . ." His voice broke, remembering the way Gabe had looked tonight. "I couldn't do that to him."

Shaw leaned a hip against the edge of the counter. "And doing what you did tonight was better?"

Sean felt suspicion bloom inside of him. "How do you know what I did tonight?"

"Listen," Shaw said, setting the clean glass down. "It's not very hard to be a student of human nature when you're a bartender, especially when it's for your group. You guys have patterns. For awhile, after you showed up and after the group started coming together, y'all had one pattern. And you kept to it, together and apart, most of the time. But then, a few weeks back, you came in with Gabriel and broke your pattern. You drank something else. It was just the two of you. And you weren't fighting."

"We weren't." Sean licked his lips, tasting the alcohol on them. He remembered just how much they hadn't been fighting. That night had been the first glimmer that there might be something more between him and Gabriel.

"And now you're back, and to be frank, you look pretty fucking miserable, and you're drinking more than you have in the last six months," Shaw said, gesturing to the half-full manhattan in front of him. "And even without all that, you're drinking the same drink you two drank together. Now, I'm not here all the time, though God knows it feels like it sometimes, but you didn't drink those before, and you haven't had one since the night you two were here."

Put together, it was rather damning.

"You're really too smart for your own good," Sean said, letting out an unsteady exhale. "You're right. We had a fight. Or not a *fight* necessarily." There hadn't been yelling. Didn't there need to be yelling in a fight? "But something. Something . . ."

"Something you're not happy about." Shaw finished his sentence even as he pulled two beers.

"I don't think either of us are happy about it," Sean said wryly. Maybe he should have gone to Tate. Or Tony. Or Lucas. Or even Ash. But Shaw had been a good listener.

"Then that's something, isn't it?" Shaw pointed out. "It was clearly not just the two of you getting naked. Because I promise, the getting naked Ren does has *never* brought him to my bar, looking like he might cry."

"We'd all be doing a lot better if we were more like Ren," Sean muttered.

"Yes and no," Shaw said. "Honestly? I think he sleeps like a baby, after. But to answer your question, your *first* question, I think it's never too late to tell your friends your history. Maybe you didn't share it before. Maybe they won't be happy about it. But I think you already know that you should. Even if it's hard."

Shaw was right; he already knew what he should do.

"And," Shaw added, smiling now, "I have it on good authority that Tony and some of the others are out by the fire pits right now."

"What? Are you psychic now, too?" Sean wondered.

"They came in before you," Shaw said. "And if I know them at all, they won't leave until they've had a few drinks."

Shaw was right about that. Sean had a feeling that Shaw was right about a lot of things.

"I guess if they've had a few drinks, maybe they'll be less pissed," Sean said, fumbling with his wallet as he pulled a twenty out of it and slid it across the bar.

"It's on the house," Shaw said with a quicksilver smile and a shake of his head. "Just do me a favor."

"Go tell them?"

Shaw nodded decisively. "They're good guys. They care about you. I promise."

Sean didn't even need Shaw's promise to believe it. He already *knew* it, which is why it had been so dumb to omit this detail about his life. Why, after so much time had gone by without him telling them, he wasn't sure how to remedy the situation.

He slid off the stool and picking up his drink and his twenty, walked towards the outside patio. Pushing open the door, he immediately spotted Tony and Lucas and Tate and Chase, all clustered around one of the smaller fire pits.

"Hey," Tony said, when he glanced up and saw Sean approaching. "I don't think Gabriel's here. I didn't see him after we closed up."

It occurred to Sean that Gabriel wasn't the only one who'd assumed there was more going on in their relationship than just getting naked. Maybe everyone else had seen what Gabe had. Maybe the only one blind here was Sean.

But he had to be sure, and how could he possibly be sure?

"I'm not . . . we're not together," Sean said awkwardly. He sat down next to Tony, hating that somehow he'd begun to feel like his friends were strangers, all because he hadn't been as honest as he should have been. "I think he's actually kind of mad at me right now, actually."

"Why?" Tony asked.

He'd been so determined when he'd marched out here, after Shaw had given him the push he needed. But now, with Tony and Lucas and Tate and Chase looking on eagerly, his words dried up.

"I . . . I . . ."

Tate shot him a sympathetic look and then squeezed his boyfriend's hand. "Chase and I have actually got plans, so we'd better take off."

It was clear from Chase's confused expression that they *didn't* have plans, but Tate was giving him an out, in case he didn't want to share his confession with quite so many people.

"We'll see you guys tomorrow," Lucas said.

After Tate and Chase had disappeared out the side door, Tony leaned in. "So, why is Gabe mad at you?"

"I think a better question is why *isn't* he mad at me," Sean said wryly. "But before we get into all that, there's something you should know first. I was married, before, when I lived in Portland. Milo died two years before I came here, and that's actually one of the big reasons I moved to LA."

Sean knew lots of people judged Tony. They thought of him as stupid and callous and good for a laugh but nothing else. But his expression went solemn and he reached over and squeezed Sean's hand. "God, man, I am so sorry. I had no idea."

"That must have been so hard," Lucas said.

"It was," Sean agreed. "But it's better. So much better. Coming here, it was the best decision I ever made. I met you guys, I wasn't so alone anymore, I found a new calling. It was great for me."

"And you met Gabe," Tony said.

Sean wanted to take back everything nice he'd ever thought about Tony. *But,* he reminded himself, *this is why you came out here, so you could talk to him. To figure out how to fix this fucking mess.*

"I did." Sean took a deep breath. "I told him, at the beginning, that we should only hook up, because I knew what love felt like and I thought what I was feeling wasn't romantic."

"Ouch," Lucas said. "No wonder he was all worked up about it."

"Yeah." Sean regretted so much of what he'd done, knowing now that Gabriel had had feelings for him this whole time.

"But you meant to be kind about it," Tony said, reaching out and squeezing his hand again. "You were *trying* to do the right thing. Trying to make sure that his expectations didn't exceed your own."

"Yeah, well, I think they did, whether he meant them to or not, and then I made a total hash of it."

"How?" Lucas wanted to know.

"It was just supposed to be a hookup, but I guess, looking back, it never really was. I mean, we *did* hook up, but we did lots of other stuff too. We hung out, and did things together and he slept over, and *well*, I can see why he thought things were changing. Why my feelings were changing."

"Is it impossible to believe they might have been?" Tony asked. His tone was kind, but Sean still shied away from the thought. He couldn't have been wrong. Not about this. Love was something he *knew* something about. He was familiar with the first flush of it, and the comforting everyday middle of it, and also the end of it, when it felt like your world was going to fall apart because you'd lost it.

Also, though he'd tried to avoid this thought during the entire thing with Gabriel, he couldn't avoid it any longer. Falling for Gabe, for *anyone else*, felt like an intrinsic betrayal of everything Sean had felt for Milo.

It wasn't like he actually believed that Milo wouldn't want him to move on. He'd been twenty-five when Milo died. Nobody should spend the rest of their life alone, and Milo would've been the first person to say that.

But that rationalization was hard to accept *now*.

It had only been four years. Surely that wasn't enough time to mourn someone he'd loved as much as he loved Milo.

"Not impossible," Sean said. "But . . . difficult to accept."

"I believe it." Lucas' voice was kind and warm, full of empathy. "It'd be a hard thing, to move on." He glanced over at Tony, and Sean could see the love in his eyes that he was intimately familiar with. "I don't think I could do what you did."

There'd been a time when Sean hadn't thought he could do it either. But in the end, he hadn't had a choice.

"Like I said, some unexpectedly good things came out of it. I moved here. I started my food truck, which was something I'd always wanted to do, but I couldn't, not until I'd gotten the money from Milo's life insurance. And I met you guys. Honestly, I'm happy again. Or," Sean added with a wry twist of his mouth, "I *was* happy again, before I fucked this thing up with Gabriel."

"How exactly did it get fucked up?" Tony wondered.

Sean thought he could talk about how and why and whose fault it was for a hundred years. But really, maybe it was simpler than that. "He told me he loved me, and I said I didn't know how I felt."

"Ouch," Tony said.

"Hey," Lucas said, nudging his boyfriend's side with an elbow, "he was trying to do the right thing."

"By breaking his heart?" Tony wondered. "I can't imagine . . . well, I can't imagine what it would feel like if I said I loved you, and you didn't say it back."

"Um," Lucas said. "That *is* what happened."

"Oh." Tony laughed. "Well, obviously we aren't good role models."

"I think you are, actually," Sean said. "Maybe you didn't get it right at first, but you got there. Things aren't always perfect."

"You mean, like you and Gabriel?" Tony asked pointedly.

"Yeah," Sean said. "I . . . I really *don't* know how I feel. I can't lie to him. Not about this."

"No, you were right not to," Lucas said reassuringly. "It wouldn't have been right to lie."

"But then what do I do?" Sean didn't want to sound so upset, but he *was* so upset. He'd hurt Gabriel, who he knew he cared about at the very least as a friend. He'd broken them apart, just when things had felt so damn good.

"Are you scheduled to be part of the festival next week?" Lucas asked.

The festival? For a second Sean wasn't even sure what he was talking about. Then it hit him. The City of Food Festival, that they were closing for. That he'd forgotten to even register for, even though he'd fully intended to.

Gabriel had obviously distracted him more than he'd even realized.

"Uh, no, actually," Sean said, feeling embarrassed because they'd all talked about it at the staff meeting, but instead of registering he had . . . well, he had gone home and obsessed over whether he should invite Gabriel over to fuck. "I totally forgot."

Lucas shot him a sympathetic look. "Well, then it's an easy decision. Close for a week. The lot's closed anyway. Go somewhere. Think about Gabe. It's hard to do when he's right here, you know? But maybe some space will help you figure out what you *do* feel for him."

"What if I don't love him?" Sean asked, because it was his worst fear.

Worse even than telling him that he did, and realizing later that it was just lust.

Worse than the guilt he'd feel moving on from Milo.

"Then you don't," Tony said. "But I think I speak for Gabe here when I tell you that he'd want you to figure out for sure, before you talk to him." He nudged his boyfriend. "And Lucas is right. It's hard to know, when Gabe is right there. He's a big guy, you know? Takes up space."

Sean knew exactly what Tony meant. Gabriel was louder-than-life, full of passion and noise and excitement. It was hard, even when they were parked on opposite sides of the lot, for him to *not* think about Gabriel.

At least, to think about him in any kind of objective way.

"Is there someplace you could go, for the week?" Lucas asked.

Sean had thought, initially, that if he was going to be closed for the week, he'd just take a nice long staycation. Not set any alarms and sleep in. Work on some of his new menu ideas. Maybe even go to the beach for a day.

But then it occurred to him that maybe he *did* need to get away. Like really get away. And the thought of the beach tugged at a thread inside him.

"Yeah," he said. "Yeah, there's a place I can go."

Maybe he couldn't ask Milo for his advice, because Milo was long gone, but maybe going to the place where he'd scattered his ashes would bring him some kind of clarity.

"Great," Tony said, clapping him on the back. "I think you should. And don't wait til the weekend, when we're officially closing."

"You're sure?" Sean was surprised; Tony was very adamant about the fact that they needed to be open on all the days that they had agreed to be. It didn't look good for customers when they showed up to visit the lot and noticed half the trucks were closed.

"I'm sure," Tony said. "I want you to get your shit straight, okay? Gabriel is a friend. You're a friend. I don't want to see either of you suffer."

It occurred to Sean, much later, after he'd returned home to a cold dark townhouse, that Tony was willing to take this gamble because he was sure, as sure as Gabriel had been, that Sean loved him.

That everything would turn out as beautifully as it had turned out between Tony and Lucas. Between Tate and Chase. But that wasn't how life worked. Sean had discovered that the hard way.

And he was afraid he was about to discover it all over again.

CHAPTER FOURTEEN

Gabriel showed up the next morning, determined that he was going to make things right.

Only to walk over to Sean's truck and discover that it was closed up tight, with a handwritten sign, posted in the window that stated they wouldn't be open for the next ten days.

"What's this?" Gabriel said as Tony walked by. Looking casual, but if Gabe knew Tony at all, *knowing* it wasn't. "Did you have something to do with this?"

"All I know is Sean decided to go away for awhile, take a trip," Tony said. "He said he needed to think about something."

Gabriel felt like crying. Sean had said that they needed some space, but it had never occurred to him that he would mean they needed *this* much space.

He'd thought a couple of days, at worst, and then Sean would come waltzing in, with a huge grin on his face and a love confession tumbling out of his mouth.

Because one thing that Gabriel was more sure of than ever was that Sean loved him. He couldn't feel all of this for someone who didn't feel it back; it just didn't feel *possible*.

"So he left," Gabriel finally said. He wanted to pour out the whole horrible story, but from the sympathetic expression on Tony's face, he had a feeling he'd already heard most of it.

"He left," Tony said. He reached out and gave him a reassuring pat on the shoulder. "But he's gonna be back, okay? And I think maybe it'll be good for both of you that he went."

"Good from a *you'll have some time to get over each other* point of view or good from a *he'll have something to say that you want to hear* point of view?" Gabriel asked.

But Tony didn't give anything away; just looked regretful. *Sorry.* And that was definitely way fucking worse.

"I don't know," he finally said. "I think the only person who can answer that question isn't here right now."

"Ugh, you're fucking useless," Gabriel moaned.

"But *hey*," Tony said encouragingly, "you know what Sean being away for a week means?"

"That I'm going to be miserable and drunk the whole week?"

"That you have time to figure out what you want to do with your truck," Tony said.

"What? I mean, I have the new name," Gabriel said. "I already picked it out. I have the logo done and everything."

"Yeah, I get that," Tony said. "But I just thought maybe it's time for you to do more than just re-name yourself, you know? Maybe think about a total rebrand."

Before Gabriel could ask Tony to explain what the fuck that even meant, he'd strolled off, whistling obnoxiously.

Like he'd just set up everything to his own fucking satisfaction.

Gabriel went storming back to his own truck, in a mood that was not only increasingly bleak, it was increasingly pissed off.

"You look like someone peed on your lawn," Ren said, when he stomped up the stairs and into the truck.

"Worse than that," Gabriel said, leaning against the bulkhead. "Sean's gone and Tony's decided that it's okay for him to interfere."

"Is that really a surprise?" Ren asked. "Tony lives to interfere. And it's not like he hasn't, already." He gestured towards the sign hanging in the window, advertising their new special, the wrap that Gabriel and Sean had invented together. "The good news is that at least that particular interference was profitable."

"He told me while I'm re-naming myself, maybe I should think about re-branding," Gabriel said, hating how wretched he sounded. "What the fuck is wrong with what I'm doing now?"

"Maybe there's nothing wrong with it," Ren said, "and maybe everything is wrong with it."

"What do you mean?" Gabriel asked suspiciously as he washed his hands. As much as he'd like to throw a fit, he couldn't, because there was a shit ton of work to do. And more of it, now, because Sean had left, leaving Gabe's truck as the only one who was selling the new special.

That also meant that Gabe was going to have to figure out the sourcing for the wraps and for the vegetables. He was already internally groaning thinking about it.

"I mean, you've been doing what Nonna did, and what Luca does, and what your parents do, forever," Ren said. "That doesn't mean that's all you're capable of."

"You sound like an annoying combination of Tony and Sean," Gabriel complained as he dried his hands.

"I probably do, because they're probably right," Ren said. "By the way, don't worry about stocking up, because while you were over gnashing your teeth and re-breaking your heart over at Sean's truck, he had his daily delivery re-routed over here."

"Really?" Gabriel was pleasantly surprised.

"Just the stuff we needed for the new wrap," Ren confirmed. "It needs prepping, which'll be a problem and a half, but if we rush, we should be fine."

"Alright," Gabriel said, and couldn't believe he'd been so upset when he marched in here, he hadn't spotted the boxes of produce, much more plentiful than their normal delivery, sitting in the corner, ready to be prepped for the day's meals. "I guess I'll get started on this."

"I've got the meatballs today," Ren said, gesturing to where he was already mixing them up in the big bowl. "And I'll start the red sauce in a minute."

Normally, Gabe would've protested. He *always* made the sauce. That was what he did. Nonna had forced him to memorize it early on, because the recipe hadn't ever been written down.

"Please," Ren added when he glanced over and saw Gabriel's confusion. "Do you really think I don't know the recipe?"

"I don't know what to think," Gabriel answered honestly. "I'm a fucking mess right now."

"You're not a mess," Ren said firmly. "But you are at a crossroads, and that means you've got to decide what you want to do next."

Gabriel looked over at his cousin. His best friend, if he was being perfectly, totally honest with himself. The only person he trusted more than he trusted himself.

"I don't think that's right," Gabriel said. "I think it means that *we've* got to decide what we want to do next."

Ren's face broke into a huge smile, totally authentic, no deliberate charm to be found. "Really?"

"Really," Gabe said firmly. "I finished buying Luca out, so I own this now, and well, I kind of think *we* should own it."

"I won't argue with that," Ren said.

And even though everything was falling apart, it also kind of felt like the beginning.

Sean had thought he'd feel a lot differently if he ever came back to Oregon. Especially if he ever swallowed all his misgivings and not only came back to Oregon, but went to the place that he and Milo had loved to visit together.

Cannon Beach was laid out like a particularly busy labyrinth, already buzzing with people clogging the streets even though it wasn't even ten in the morning yet.

He could've flown in—Cannon Beach wasn't a long drive from Portland, where the airport was. But he'd driven, because he thought he'd need the alone time to figure out how he was going to face this place.

He leaned against his car door and let his eyes drift across the busy streets. The cafes that he and Milo had shared so many meals in, the shops they'd browsed through, buying little trinkets and framed photos for the wall of the condo they'd shared in Portland.

He'd kept them all, but he couldn't face displaying them, even two years after Milo had passed, so they were still sitting in boxes, stacked in the closet of the spare bedroom.

Someday, Sean had always promised himself, he'd unpack them and hang the pictures and set the driftwood and the blown glass pieces on his mantle and the coffee table.

Or maybe, he never would, not now. Not when he'd apparently moved on and hadn't even realized it.

Guilt that Sean didn't want to feel, guilt that he *rejected*, swamped him anyway.

It had been two days since he'd left Gabriel and Los Angeles, and he still wasn't sure what the origin of the guilt was. Was it because Gabriel had told him he loved him and he hadn't been able to say it back? Or was it because deep down, he'd *felt* a reciprocal feeling, and the very idea of moving on, of moving *past* Milo, was intolerable?

Must not have been too intolerable considering how tightly you were clinging to Gabe, his conscience supplied, even as he tried to silence it.

So he felt guilty about both, then. He regretted how much he'd hurt Gabriel. He regretted how easy it had been for him to fall into a new relationship with him.

How much he'd *wanted* it, even as he'd tried to claim otherwise.

Sean pushed away from the car. He'd come here, he might as well swallow down his pain and all this interminable guilt, and do what he'd come here to do.

Except, as he walked down the street towards the first set of shops and restaurants, a few blocks from the beach entrance, he still didn't know what that was, exactly.

Was he asking whatever was left of Milo for forgiveness? Was he figuring out what he felt for Gabriel?

Maybe, Sean thought, staring in the window of the Celtic-themed store that Milo had adored, he should start by figuring out what he was even doing here.

"Sean!" Tara stuck her head out the open door. "I thought I saw it was you!"

He and Milo had spent so much time in this store, his husband deciding that despite all the clear indications otherwise, deep down he *must* be Irish, that they and the owner had become friends.

He hadn't seen her since before Milo had died, the last time they'd come to the coast for a long weekend, staying in the family cabin that was usually available for them.

Sean wasn't staying there this time; he wouldn't be able to bear it. Milo's mom, Lacy, was a wonderful lady, and he missed her, but he wasn't sure he could face her. Surely she would be able to tell, just by looking at him, that he'd moved on, and he couldn't do that to either of them.

Tara would have heard of Milo's passing from Lacy, but he was still unprepared for her big, tight, undeniably fierce hug when he stepped into the shop.

"I heard about Milo, I am so sorry," she said, her voice thick even though it had been four years.

But the thing was, standing in this place, letting his gaze drift over the CD display and the hand-knit Arran sweaters and the dusty fake Christmas tree, dotted with claddagh and dancer ornaments, he felt like it had been more like four days, not four years.

"Yeah," Sean said when she let go. Her eyes were a little watery, and he found his own matched.

He blinked hard and looked away. He'd underestimated how hard this was going to be. He'd underestimated how much he'd been *needing* to do it.

"What have you been doing?"

"I actually . . ." Sean cleared his throat. "I actually moved to California. To LA. I'm running my own food truck and well . . ."

He didn't want to say he was doing good, but it was on the tip of his tongue anyway.

"You're doing good?" Tara went back to the unpacking she was doing, carefully unwrapping boxes of glass claddaghs, the light flashing as she set them in the window display. "I can tell you are. And I'm so glad. I was worried about you."

"I'm . . ." Sean hesitated again. Should he apologize? Obviously she'd known why he hadn't been back. "I'm really good, actually. Moving helped."

"And a food truck!" Tara exclaimed. "That's so cool! What are you selling?"

"I've got a bunch of different kinds of wraps," Sean said. "You know how I used to sell them at the cafe I worked at?"

"Yeah, in Portland," Tara said. "I'm so glad you did that, because I know how much you loved it."

"I did. I *do*," Sean said.

"That's so great," she said enthusiastically. "I'm so proud of you." She reached over and gave him another quick hug. "And you're back! Just for the weekend?"

He'd reserved the hotel for the week. He didn't have to be back in LA until next Sunday, but he hadn't been sure if he'd want to spend a whole seven days here, without Milo.

Even if he needed it, he wasn't sure he *wanted* all that time off.

"For a couple of days, at least," Sean said.

"Then you'll have to stop by," Tara said confidently. She glanced down at his hand. "I see you aren't wearing your claddagh ring anymore. In the market for something new?"

Milo had bought him a sterling silver one, way back when, when they were still dating, and he'd stopped wearing it after his death. Even the thought of turning it around, proclaiming himself to be single again, had hurt too much.

He would be alright with buying another one—maybe even buying one for Gabriel, if he could get up the gumption—but then he'd have to decide if he was single or if his heart was taken.

And even if he did figure out how to make that difficult decision, he'd have to make sure it didn't feel too much like something he and Milo had shared.

"I'll think about it," Sean promised. "I wouldn't buy one anywhere else, that's for sure."

Tara grinned. "I'm glad to hear it."

"It was so good to see you again," Sean said, and discovered that he *meant* it. "Business seems to be great still."

"Can't ever complain about the tourists," Tara said, voice dropping as a pair wandered into the shop. "Bless them, really."

"That's the right attitude," Sean said with a chuckle under his breath. "I'll stop by again, alright?"

"You'd better!" Tara called out as he exited the shop.

After leaving Tara's, he walked down the main street towards the beach. This wasn't where he'd scattered Milo's ashes, along with his family—that was further up, out of town, along one of the impossibly tall cliffs overlooking the ocean—but he could still feel the warmth that was Milo touch his heart as he looked out over the crashing waves.

Maybe he didn't know why he'd come, or what he was looking for. Or even why he felt that inexorable pull of guilt, but he felt like he'd made the right choice.

Even though he wasn't sure right now, by the time he returned to LA and to Gabriel, he'd know the right thing to say.

"You said you wanted to spend your week off drunk and bored, but even then I thought you were kidding," Ren said as he slid onto the barstool next to Gabriel's.

He held up a hand for Shaw, who poured him a manhattan and set it in front of him.

Ren picked up the glass, taking a long sip.

Gabriel had already known that coming to the Funky Cup was not really *hiding* per se. There were too many people they knew that came here. Too many friends who would gladly tell on him if Ren asked them. And that wasn't even taking into account the fact that they counted the owner and the bartender in that particular category.

"I didn't want to spend the night at home." *Alone*, Gabriel added as an afterthought. Ren had been out, Gabriel had assumed with a hookup, but it must not have worked out because here his cousin was, ready to bust his ass again.

He'd been bored and lonely and tired of scrolling through Netflix, looking for something to watch. So he'd come out here, not because he'd expected to see Sean, but he'd at least expected to see one of the guys. But it seemed they were all packed up and at the festival downtown.

Gabriel sighed into his manhattan. "If you tell me I'm pathetic, we're not ever talking again."

"Now, that might be tough," Ren said with a glimmer of a smile. "Because," he added, pulling a small notebook out of the pocket of his jeans, "we've got a new menu to plan."

"Ugh, *now*?" Gabriel still felt a momentary panic slice through him whenever he thought about departing from the well-worn but beloved recipes that Nonna had passed down.

"We only had the special on the menu for a few days," Ren said. "But the only thing that beat it in sales was the meatball sandwich. And it gave our specialty a real run for its money."

"Really?" Gabriel knew they'd sold a lot of the Thai wraps, but it had never occurred to him that they'd sold *that* many.

"Of course, it might be because Sean wasn't around to cut our sales in half, but . . ." Ren glanced over at Gabriel, like he was afraid even saying the guy's name would unhinge him even more, "but he was only closed for two days this week. I don't think that affected things that strongly."

"Oh, good," Gabriel muttered into his drink.

"The point is that people wanted to buy other things from us. They're willing to be flexible. So that just leaves us one question."

"What's that?" Gabriel wished that as much as he'd wanted company, Ren had left him alone. He didn't want to revisit why everything he was doing needed to be changed. It was bad enough that Sean wasn't sure he loved him after all. He was losing his security blanket, too, and it hurt more than he'd expected that it would.

"How do you want to be flexible? What do you want to keep? What do you want to add?" Ren grabbed a spare pen that was sitting on the bar top and opened his notebook. It was, surprisingly, not empty, but already scribbled with ideas.

"I want to keep something from Nonna," Gabriel said firmly, realizing just how much he meant it. "I don't know what that is, but *something*."

"You altered the meatballs and added them to the Thai wrap," Ren said thoughtfully.

"You want to keep the meatball recipe?"

"I also think we should keep the meatball sandwich," Ren said. "It's a bestseller. I like the idea of innovating, but I don't think we should throw everything out."

"I . . ." Gabriel thought for a second, and realized he'd been about to say that he loved that idea. They could do a thousand things with meatballs. Hadn't he always bragged that Nonna's meatballs were the best, and also the most flexible thing she'd ever made?

Why couldn't they take that idea and run with it?

"You love it, I know," Ren said, his smile suddenly growing brighter. "I'm a genius."

"Modest, too," Gabriel teased, elbowing him in the side.

"Hey, I call it like I see it," Ren said, flipping a page and making a notation on the top which read, *Menu*.

He watched as Ren wrote down meatball sandwich as the first item, and then the Thai wrap underneath it.

"I'm not sure Tony's going to let us keep that on the menu permanently," Gabriel said. "And what about Sean? We did that together. We can't claim it for us, permanently."

"No reason why you can't convince Tony," Ren argued. "You know how convincible he can be."

Ren was not wrong. Gabriel nodded.

"*And*," Ren added, "I think when Sean comes back, he's either going to want to give you anything you ask for, or he's going to feel so fucking guilty, he'll give it up without a fight."

"I don't *want* him to give it up without a fight," Gabriel argued. "I want . . . well, you know what I want. I want us to share it."

The sympathetic look on Ren's face hurt worse than the uncertainty Gabe felt deep down.

"He may not feel the same way about it as you do," Ren said carefully.

"I know," Gabriel said. Hesitated. "But keep it on there. I want to serve it. We'll figure out this whole fucking mess when he comes back."

"Alright," Ren said. He tapped the pen against the paper. "What else?"

What else could they serve with the meatballs?

"We should do a spicy cranberry meatball," Gabriel said. "Like those we used to have out at Christmas, you know? In the crock-pot?"

"Like a play on the cocktail weenie," Ren said with excitement, jotting that idea down.

"Never say the word *weenie* again, please," Gabriel said with a laugh punctuating his warning. "I'm begging you."

Ren laughed too. "Fine. But the idea's solid."

"And stroganoff meatballs," Gabriel said, a world suddenly opening up in his brain, so many ideas suddenly filtering in that he could barely register them all. "We could do them up in a sandwich roll, like the one we already have."

He listed three other ideas, Ren scribbling and nodding along, and then he paused, realizing something.

"If we do this," Gabriel said. "We're going to need to change the name on the truck. The one I picked out, it isn't going to work anymore."

"It won't," Ren agreed. "What about . . . well, what about Balls and Buns?"

"Oh my god," Gabriel said, a little shocked. "*Lorenzo Moretti!*"

But Ren was grinning unrepentantly. "When did you become such a prude?"

"Tony is going to kill us," Gabriel said.

"Hey, it's accurate, isn't it?" Ren said, with a sly smile. "We've got meatballs, and we're still going to have some in buns. The traditional style, of course, and then that banh mi you were just talking about. And the stroganoff. Those are all balls in buns."

"Somehow I don't think that's going to convince Tony to like the idea," Gabriel said. But at the same time, he knew Tony would secretly—or maybe not so secretly—laugh his ass off about it.

"It's a good thing we're not really considered a 'family destination,'" Ren said.

Gabriel rolled his eyes. "You might think you're the prince of dirty talk, but before Tony settled down, he would've given you a real run for your money. He hooked up with everyone."

"Hey, if a guy that looked as good as Lucas was interested, I'd think about it, too," Ren pointed out.

"Liar," Gabriel teased.

Ren flashed a smile. "I said I'd *think* about it, not that I'd actually go for it."

CHAPTER FIFTEEN

Sean had been holding out hope that by the time he made it to the overlook, the special one, the spot where a short hike from the road, you'd get the best view of Cannon Beach, he would *know*.

But the problem was, he hadn't really believed it before, and he still didn't believe it now. Milo was dead and gone. Just because Sean and Lacy had scattered his ashes here didn't make him any less *gone*. It didn't matter that Sean had been standing here when Milo had proposed. Or that they'd gotten married only a half a mile away, at the family's beach house.

Milo wasn't here. He couldn't tell Sean how *he* felt or what Sean should be feeling.

Sean hugged his arms around his chest, the outside of his windbreaker damp with morning fog combined with the spray from the water hitting the rocks below.

He'd spent the last few days in Cannon Beach avoiding this place, sure that he would feel either wretched or enlightened when he came here. But truthfully, all he felt was very silly.

Collapsing down onto a fallen log, he ignored the cold that seeped through his jeans as he stared out at the sea, still feeling ridiculous.

Of course Milo was not here.

But now that he had come to that inescapable conclusion, there was nothing else to do but *face* it.

He'd moved on, even if he hadn't wanted to—and he'd done it the whole time while pretending that it was nothing but sex.

But Sean had known. Why else had his body and his heart and his brain been so adamant that it *had* to be Gabriel? Why had he been so sure that it could only be him, and nobody else?

If he'd just wanted to get off, all he'd have needed was a guy he had even the barest sexual interest in, and there had been a handful of those over the years. He'd always brushed them off, giving himself the excuse that he wasn't ready, that he wasn't looking for something so transient that it'd end in a few hours or a few days.

But that was the very offer he'd made to Gabriel. They'd get naked, and nothing else—even though there had already been so much between them that was fully clothed.

Maybe they'd spent two years bickering, but they'd also spent those two years becoming friends. Even as they both had claimed otherwise.

But looking back? Trying to see things clearly?

Sean scrubbed a hand over his face, his skin numb from the cold and from the epiphanies that kept revealing themselves.

They'd been friends.

The antipathy between them had faded almost immediately into a snarky, sweet, almost flirtatious banter. They'd revolved around each other, even before that inevitable day when Tony had forced them to actually confront the thing between them.

The only thing that had ever truly kept them apart.

And, Sean realized now, the only thing that kept them together, too.

He'd been so upset, Sean thought, as he stood, shaking off the cold and the damp from the log, about everything else, that he hadn't really thought about why Gabriel would have a new name for his truck and hold on to it and not use it—when it was the one thing standing in their way.

But he'd done it because it was the one thing that held them together, when otherwise they might have drifted apart.

It was impossible to forget what Gabriel had said. He'd told Sean that he'd loved him, and he'd said *I think I might have loved you for a long time. Long before I even knew what this was.*

Maybe Gabriel wasn't alone.

Maybe he'd had these . . . Sean guessed they were *feelings,* because why else would he feel like his heart was beating out of his chest when they even looked at each other? Why else would he feel like he'd *die* if he didn't get his hands on him right away? And it was the only explanation for why he'd stood there, pained and shocked, when Gabriel had told him he loved him.

If they weren't feelings, there was no fucking way he'd still feel that same sick feeling *days* later. A *week* later.

He'd come to terms with the fact that it wasn't going to go away.

But he hadn't come to terms with the fact that he could have fallen in love again.

Five minutes later, he was still staring into the ocean, wishing that his brain, so cooperative only a few minutes earlier, would allow him to accept this.

Except, he realized, watching the crash of the waves, it wasn't his brain at all, was it? It was his heart.

That was when he heard it—the sound of steps, the crush of the moss and the twigs breaking under their weight.

He knew he wasn't the only person who came here. Later, long after he'd said yes to Milo's proposal, he'd joked about how he'd been terrified not that Sean would reject him—but that someone would interrupt them.

Turning, Sean saw the last person he'd expected to find.

Not Milo, but another pair of kind dark eyes that were intensely familiar.

"Sean!" Lacy exclaimed with surprise. "I'd heard you were in town—Tara stopped and told me the other day, but I hadn't realized you'd . . ." She took a deep breath as she walked closer to him, her hands shoved deep in her bright pink parka's pockets. "I hadn't realized you'd come here. But of course you would."

Maybe Milo wasn't looking over this place, but someone else was. Someone who was still living and breathing and was more than capable of offering any judgment that Sean deserved.

The very first thing he had to do was apologize.

He hadn't known she was here, at the beach house, but of course he could've called her and let her know. She'd have come for him, to see him again. After all, it was the first time he'd been back in Oregon since he'd left.

They emailed sometimes. The occasional text message or phone call. He kept in touch, because the man he'd loved had loved her, and because, over time, he'd discovered that he loved her too.

That particular realization had not hit until the aftermath of Milo's death.

It seemed he was doomed to make these mistakes over and over again. Clueless until confronted, like a two-by-four to the side of the head, about what was actually true.

"I'm so sorry," he said in a rush, walking up to meet her, to wrap her up in a long hug. "I should've told you I was coming."

She tugged him down towards the log.

"It's fine, Sean," she said reassuringly. "Please don't worry about it. Though, honestly, hearing you were around, it made me think about Milo. And every time I do, I come here."

He was fairly certain that she couldn't know that this was the log he and Milo had been sitting on when he proposed. But he sat down anyway, because it wasn't like he hadn't already *tried* sitting on it, desperately trying to bring her son back to life.

And worst of all, not even because he still mourned him as desperately as he had after his death, but because he wanted Milo's permission to love someone else.

"I'm surprised you took the time away from your truck during such a busy season," Lacy said, still gripping his hand. It *was* cold, and hers was warm, but it was more than that.

"I . . ." It should have been harder to decide to confess everything he'd been hiding. But the truth was, he'd come here looking for answers, and maybe Milo hadn't magically appeared, and there hadn't been any signs, but maybe this was what he'd been waiting for. "I came because I needed to," he admitted.

Lacy's eyes softened further. He could see more lines around them, and on her forehead, than she'd had at their wedding, than she'd had when they'd first met, so many years earlier. Losing your only son would probably cause more than a few extra wrinkles.

"I'm sorry you aren't doing better," she said, squeezing his hand. "I thought you were . . ."

"I was," Sean said with a resigned sigh. "I really was. But . . . I don't know how else to tell you this, but I think I'm . . . I think I'm moving on."

Tears appeared in the corner of Lacy's eyes, her gaze still undeniably sympathetic. "Darling," she said, "did you think that you wouldn't?"

He'd known that he would, someday. He'd been a young man on the day Milo died. Nobody would ever fault him for eventually finding someone else to love, even himself. But he hadn't expected that it would be so soon. Or that it would feel so effortless.

So different.

Because that was his issue, wasn't it? He felt totally different about Gabriel than he'd felt about Milo.

Maybe, like Shaw said, love was different. But what if what he shared with Gabriel was stronger or sexier or *better* than it had been with Milo?

He wasn't sure how he could ever forgive himself for that.

"I . . . I didn't expect to now. I didn't expect to with *him*," Sean finally admitted.

Her hand squeezed his again. "Can you tell me about it? Because I want to hear about him."

"Really?" Sean found he couldn't quite believe it.

"Really," she said firmly. "Sean, you deserve to find happiness. I know you had it with my son. And God knows, he was happier than he'd ever been in his entire life when he met you. A mother knows these things. But you're still here. You're still breathing. You deserve to have that again, don't you think?"

"I want to believe it." Sean looked out, all the way to the horizon, where sea and sky met. Where, if miracles were ever possible, he thought he might see Milo again, when he came here.

But maybe this was its own kind of miracle.

"Then you should believe it," Lacy said firmly. "Milo would have wanted you to believe it."

"I . . . I . . ." Sean swallowed hard, swallowed back his tears, thinking for the first time of Milo in ages, not as an abstract concept, but as the laughing, loving guy that he'd adored. The one who never wanted to hold him back. The one who was always supporting him and pushing him and encouraging him.

The very last thing Milo ever would have wanted was for Sean to spend the rest of his life alone.

"I think he would've really liked Gabriel, actually," Sean said. "I think he would've. I think he would've hated him, too, a little. The way I did, at first."

Lacy was smiling, even as he saw the tears drip down her cheek. "You didn't like Gabriel at first?"

"He owns a food truck, too," Sean said. Resigned, because while the specter of Milo wasn't around to ask, his mother was. And that was somehow even better. "We actually have the same name on our trucks," he added, and found *he* was smiling, too. Impossibly. "He didn't like it when I showed up in LA, and of course I wasn't going to change it, because it was always what Milo wanted, right?"

"Right." Lacy chuckled. "And so you argued with him about it."

"Oh my god, so many times," Sean said. Thinking of all those times when he'd kept the argument going because he hadn't wanted Gabe to turn and walk away.

How had he never realized that he hadn't wanted him to go because he *liked* him, not because he disliked him?

"You still haven't changed the name, have you?" Lacy asked.

Sean shook his head. "But I'm thinking . . . I've thought that maybe I should."

"Really?" For the first time since she'd appeared out of the mist, Lacy looked surprised.

"I fucked things up," Sean said succinctly. "I let him think that I didn't care about him. And then I left. There's no excuse for it, I was confused, yeah, but I wasn't so confused that I couldn't see that things were changing between us, that I was *feeling*. But I denied it, and I pretended, and I dragged him along." Sean shoved a hand through his hair, feeling the cold, damp moisture in the air. It felt totally different here than it did at the beach in California. And even though it was warm and sunny there, and usually the opposite here, at Cannon Beach, Sean thought he preferred this. It felt *right*.

"You need to go easy on yourself," Lacy said. "He was the first . . . since Milo?"

Sean nodded. "I didn't even realize we were in the middle of something, and then we *were*, and I couldn't handle it. It was easier to keep acting like it was nothing. Just sex." He blushed, realizing that he'd said *sex* to his husband's mother. But she just laughed, completely unconcerned.

"You're not even thirty," Lacy said conspiratorially. "You're allowed to want things. Even men. *Especially* men."

"Well, I wanted him," Sean admitted. "And I took him, and *god*, I shouldn't have. Not because of Milo, but totally because of Milo." Sean stood and began to pace again. "He deserves someone better. Someone who doesn't have to lie to themselves."

Lacy's words were kind, but they were firm. "I think the only person who gets to say what they deserve is Gabriel, and I think if you love him, then he's probably a very forgiving person. A kind person. A generous person. And he wouldn't want to hold this against you."

Sean remembered how Gabriel had tried to convince him. How his face had fallen when Sean had said that he needed space.

"He wouldn't," Sean agreed. "He's . . ." Sean grinned then, because a thousand different Gabriels paraded through his mind. Gabriels throwing meatballs. Gabriels teasing him. Gabriels laughing. Gabriels cooking, his confident capable hands constructing something delicious. Gabriels kissing him. Gabriels smiling, soft and sweet, when he thought Sean wasn't looking. "He's that and more," he finally finished.

Lacy was crying again, and impossibly still smiling, and she stood, joining him, looking out over the bluff where they'd scattered Milo's ashes. "He'd be so happy for you," she said softly. "Someone to love you when he couldn't anymore."

"You think so?" Sean looked out over the ocean, and for the first time, felt like he could believe it.

Lacy put her arm around his shoulders, pulling him in tightly. "I believe it," she said. "And I want you to come up here, during the slow season, and I want you to bring this new guy of yours. I told you this, on the worst day, and I want you to know it on the best too: you're family. You'll always be family."

Sean didn't have any more words. Just put his arms around her and hugged her tight and hard, wondering how he'd gotten so lucky to have a wonderful husband and a family who'd loved him, through thick and thin.

And then to get lucky enough to find someone else he could love. Who loved him back.

Sean knew in that moment that he wouldn't be waiting four more days to go back to Los Angeles. He needed to see Gabe, and he needed to tell him something.

Something important.

Something life-changing.

Something so wonderful that Sean didn't know how he hadn't done it before now.

Gabriel hadn't been able to bear going to the truck lot during the break week.

It was bad enough that it felt empty and barren without the people that usually frequented it, but without Sean? It felt even worse.

He felt even worse.

What were they going to do when he came back?

It was hard to keep hope alive when it had been over a week and the last thing Sean had said to him was *maybe we should take a break from each other, at least for a little while.*

Maybe Sean would come back to LA, and he'd have moved on. He'd greet Gabriel with regret in his eyes and reluctance to touch written all over his face. He'd say something like, "Space was good, and I think we might need more of it. Permanently."

"Are you . . ." Trailing off in a muttered curse underneath his breath, Ren snapped his fingers in front of Gabe's face. "Are you standing there, envisioning the worst again?"

"Again?" Gabe tried for an innocent tone but that ship had sailed, at least a few days ago. Probably after the tenth recitation of what he thought might happen when Sean came back.

"Again," Ren said firmly. "Why is it that it's always the worst-case scenarios you're fantasizing about? Who are you and what have you done with my relentlessly optimistic cousin?"

Gabriel leaned against the counter in the kitchen in their loft, where ingredients were strewn from one side to the other. Recipe testing was never a pretty business.

"He fell in love," Gabriel muttered. Then held up his hand. "And I really don't want to hear it, Ren, okay? It was a terrible idea. I never should have touched him. I know it."

He wasn't sure if Ren was right and he'd been *relentlessly* optimistic, but he'd generally taken on a positive view of things. Not much fazed him for long.

Before, Gabe had been so sure that Sean loved him too and was just scared, but a week later, after the feel of his touch had faded from his skin? Well, he *wanted* to still be that certain, but all that certainty was currently being crowded out by *reality*.

Gabriel did not like reality very much.

"Hey," Ren said, snapping again in front of his face, "come back to LA, and help me with this." He had a pan of meatballs on the stove, glazed with a variation of the mixture they'd used for the Thai wrap, that was meant for the banh mi sandwich. Strips of cucumber and carrot and radish were quick pickling in a bowl and Ren had just finished mixing up the spicy mayonnaise mixture that they were going to smear across the toasted bun.

Bun . . .

Something was tickling Gabriel's memory. Something he needed to be doing. His memory was spotty these days—at least where anything that didn't relate to Sean was concerned.

"Crap," Gabriel said suddenly. "I have to meet the sign guy at the truck."

"He has the new signage ready?" Ren said, carefully shaking the pan of glazed meatballs. "That was quick."

"They usually are, once the idea gets approved."

"Tony is going to murder you, slowly, for not telling him ahead of time."

"Probably," Gabriel said. Truthfully, the shock on Tony's face was one of the few things that gave him a lot of joy these days.

Though, the idea that he and Ren were revolutionizing their menu, *together*, using one of Nonna's famous recipes as the backbone, that made him feel all warm and fuzzy inside, too.

Even if everything went as badly as he feared it would with Sean, even if he never loved him, and Gabriel had to pine for him forever, at least he and Ren would have this.

"I'm going to have to leave in a few minutes," Gabe added, as he watched Ren carefully begin to assemble the sandwich.

"Well, at least stick around until this is done and you can try it. Decide if we need any more changes," Ren said, an edge of annoyance in his voice. "We've got two more recipes we need to finalize before we open again tomorrow."

"We'll get it done," Gabriel said, trying to find his confidence again.

"If you hurry back, we will," Ren said.

"I will," Gabriel promised.

Ren piled the meatballs onto the sandwich, then using his fingers, grabbed a handful of the picked veggies, and arranged them on top. Grabbed a spoon, and drizzled the spicy mayonnaise over the whole thing. With a flourish, he sliced through the sandwich, nudging Gabe's half towards him. He picked it up, making sure it wouldn't immediately fall apart—which unsurprisingly, customers really hated—but it stayed firmly together, and he gave silent props to Ren for learning the best way to construct these things.

The first bite was an explosion of flavor on his tongue.

The second, he started to parse out the individual flavors. The sticky savoriness of the meatballs, the shredded basil, the pickled vegetables, the creamy spiciness of the mayo.

"That is really fucking good," Ren said after he took a third bite and swallowed it.

"Yeah, it is." Gabriel set down his sandwich before he devoured the entire thing. Lifted his hand to give his cousin a high five. "Great job, dude. It's delicious."

"No changes?" Ren said after slapping his hand. "Really?"

"Seriously, it's perfect," Gabriel said.

Ren's eyes narrowed. "You're not just saying that, are you?"

"Would I?"

"Normally, *no*," Ren agreed. "But right now? I don't know, you're off your game. Sean fucked you up something fierce. That's what . . ."

"Yes," Gabriel interrupted him. "Yes, that's what falling in love does. I get it, okay?"

"I wasn't . . ." Ren looked really sorry. "Well, I *was*," he added. "But I didn't mean it that way."

"It's alright if you did," Gabriel said with resignation. "I know I was stupid. I know I threw my heart away, without really thinking it through. And you know what? I'd do it again."

"I know you would." Ren's voice had gone soft and quiet. "That's the kind of man you are."

Gabe had to look away before the emotion overwhelmed him. He didn't regret what he and Sean had had—he couldn't find it in himself to regret it—but he did wish that it had ended differently. He wished that they could find a way to be friends, maybe in the future. Even if it would hurt.

"I should go," he said. "The sign guy's gonna be waiting for me."

"I'm going to finalize the recipe and then clean up," Ren said.

Gabriel grabbed his wallet and his keys, and on the way over, grabbed an iced coffee from his favorite cafe. It was hot, *blazing hot*, an August day where it felt like the sidewalks might start sizzling any moment.

Gabriel turned the corner and came face to face with a lot that was just as empty as he'd envisioned it would be.

He skirted around the side instead of walking through the middle—he couldn't quite face Sean's truck, not just yet—and pulled his keys out, even though he was pretty sure the sign guy didn't need to actually get inside to replace the outside, rebranding and renaming his truck, finally. But he'd also ordered new shirts and new aprons, as well as new paper menus, and he hoped that he'd be able to stash them inside for the time being.

Glancing at his phone, he noticed that the guy was already ten minutes late. Gabriel told himself not to be annoyed, but he kind of *was*.

He paced in the truck, reassuring himself with the way everything still shone and gleamed, and was in one piece. Ever since the picnic table incident, Lennox had made sure that nobody was on the lot that didn't belong there. But he still worried—and Gabe *knew* Tony worried.

Otherwise, he wouldn't be having Lennox install that ridiculous security system.

Glancing out the front window, he wondered if he'd be able to see the cameras, or if they were so small and hidden, he'd have to guess where Lennox placed them.

Knowing Lennox, he'd be searching forever before he spotted one. That guy was a sneaky bastard.

But the first thing Gabriel saw wasn't a camera. It was the sign guy—and he was across the lot, talking to . . . *was that Sean?*

Gabriel stared, shocked. That was Sean's truck—or else it *had* been Sean's truck. The distinctive red and white was gone, replaced by a bright turquoise and an even sunnier yellow trim. He couldn't quite read the name from this distance.

Had he . . .? *No,* Gabe insisted to himself. He wouldn't have sold his truck and *given up*. Except . . . maybe he would have.

Gabriel, who had made himself a whole truckload of promises about how he wouldn't force the issue with Sean or push him or make him uncomfortable in any way, was down the stairs and out the door in a flash, practically *running* across the lot.

He didn't even bother to read who had bought the truck off Sean.

He only had eyes for the man he loved.

"Gabriel!" Sean didn't look upset to see him, or surprised, or any of the emotions that he'd expected. He looked *pleased*.

Gabe's heartbeat sped up—and it had already been racing from his run across the lot.

"What's going on?" he demanded. "Did you sell your truck?"

"Is that what you're so worried about?" Sean teased.

"*Yes*," Gabe said. "I'm . . ." He gestured at the sign guy, who was staring at both of them like they'd just grown second heads. "I don't want you to give this up, just because I was a stubborn asshole. I . . . I know I fucked it up. I know I pushed you too hard, but you can stay, right? I can be better. I can be . . . well, I can *try* to be quiet. I can do that, for you. I can do anything for you."

A smile played across Sean's lips. "You sure about that? I don't think I can see you being all that quiet, Moretti. It's not in your nature."

"I told you. I'd do it. For you." Gabe couldn't quiet the panic streaking through him. Sean was going to leave, he was going to go away again, and he would *never* get a second chance. Or a third chance. Or whatever fucking chance he was on.

Maybe it was selfish—it was definitely the stubborn asshole in him—but he wanted all the chances that Sean would give him. He'd take them all and give Sean back all the love in the world. At least all the love that Sean would accept.

"Yeah, you did." Sean glanced over at the sign guy, who was staring at both of them still. He reached out and signed the paper on the clipboard he'd extended in his direction. "Thanks," he said to the sign guy. "Sorry I kept you a little bit longer, but I think we're done here."

"Yeah," he said. "No problem. My next job is just over there." He gestured in the direction of Gabriel's truck. "So if you need anything else . . ."

"Wait," Sean said suddenly. "Wait. You're . . . who's your next job?"

The sign guy shot Gabriel a look that clearly said, *it's this crazy dude, right here.*

"You didn't," Sean breathed out, looking blown away. "You *did.*"

"I said it," Gabriel said. "I said I'd do anything for you. I should've done it an age ago, when I first looked into it, but I was selfish. I wanted . . . it kept us together, you know? It kept us talking and arguing and *god*, I liked that too much."

"I did too," Sean said, and Gabriel's heart was splintering. Was it possible for a heart to break from too much hope? Too much happiness? Or was it his heart being remade? Reforged with the belief that he'd finally done the right thing?

He glanced and now that he was closer and not completely distracted by the fact that Sean was here, *now*, he could finally see the name. Wrap It Up, the logo on the truck read.

It was perfect. Not as perfect as Sean, but that was a high bar.

"But," Sean continued, before Gabe could get his brain on the same page and ask if all this meant what he *hoped* it meant, "truthfully, I liked this even better." He fit into Gabriel's arms like they'd been made to hold him. Sean smiled, and leaned in, brushing a quick kiss across his lips. "I'm sorry, I made a huge mess out of things. It sucked to watch you walk away. It sucked to be the one who made you do that. But I couldn't keep going like I was . . . I needed to get my head on straight."

Gabriel held his breath. "Is it?"

"Yes," Sean said with a nod. "It's never been on straighter. And now so is my heart. I . . . I wanted to come back and tell you that I was wrong about so many things. First, I never should have been so goddamned stubborn about the name. It's just a *name.* So I changed it," he said, gesturing behind Gabe. "I'm not going anywhere. I'd rather cut my arm off than sell this truck. You aren't getting rid of me that easily."

"I changed mine too," Gabriel said, with a sheepish grin, fingers tightening on Sean's arms. "Or I *am* changing it. I . . . I guess I should have asked you first. But it felt like the *one thing* I could do to prove to you that I was the right guy. That I love you."

"You know what? Ditto." Sean grinned wildly, looking as happy as Gabriel had ever seen him. Happier, *lighter,* so much more alive. If Gabriel hadn't loved him before, there was no way he didn't love him now.

Gabriel kissed him then, because he didn't want to hear what he was sorry for. He'd already heard everything he needed to hear, even if Sean hadn't said it out loud.

He loves you, just the same way you love him. His heart *did* break then, reforming around the knowledge that even though nobody could ever know what the future held, it didn't matter, because they had each other now.

"Wait," Sean gasped, moving back a half step. Gabriel reached out for him, but Sean held his hand up. "It's important that I say this. I mean it when I say I fucked this up."

"I don't care," Gabriel said.

"But *I* care," Sean said tenderly. "You deserve the apology and you deserve to hear everything that I couldn't say before."

"Okay." Gabriel shoved his hands in his pockets so he wouldn't interrupt him again.

"I love you," Sean said, and Gabriel was unprepared for the way the words hit him. He'd *known* them, believed in them even when Sean had claimed he was wrong. But to hear them now? It was like the dawn of a spring day, even though it was the height of summer, and the air was so hot and dry. "I think I loved you a long time too, I just couldn't face it. I . . . I didn't think I'd ever really move on, but I did, and I didn't even realize that I'd done it. I couldn't *let* myself realize it. But every moment I spent with you, it was like you were showing me how to live again. I wanted it, I craved it, craved *you*. But even then, it was never just getting naked."

"Hey, I'm happy to get naked with you anytime," Gabriel interrupted, because he couldn't quite help himself. The joy was bubbling out of him, like a champagne bottle that had just been unceremoniously uncorked.

"I'm gonna hold you to that," Sean said seriously, and Gabriel laughed. "But I mean it, I love you. Today, tomorrow, every day in the future. Even if things don't work out, and I sure as fuck hope they will, but I'll always be grateful for everything you did for me."

"I was a selfish asshole. I *am* a selfish asshole. I didn't do it for you," Gabriel said, and reached for him again. This time Sean came willingly, sinking into his arms, head resting on his shoulder. "Well, I kinda did it for you."

"I know you," Sean murmured into his ear. "No matter what you might try to claim, I *know* you did it for me."

CHAPTER SIXTEEN

By the time they made it back to Gabriel's apartment, he felt overheated and overwhelmed.

"I'm sorry," Gabriel had said between hot drugging kisses they'd been trading in the shade by Gabe's truck. Gabe's *new* truck, which was now called something *wild* that was going to drive Tony around the bend. "I've got to head back to my place, at some point. Ren's finishing up the recipe testing for the new menu, and I promised I'd help him."

"New name, new menu, new recipes," Sean said wonderingly. Still shocked that they had *both* ended up changing their name—and not only had Gabriel taken the step that he'd sworn he'd never do, he'd re-envisioned everything he was doing.

It was brave or it was crazy.

Maybe it was a little bit of both.

"Yeah, well," Gabriel had blushed—or was that the flush from the heat and the arousal that Sean had felt pressed hard and hot against his hip? "Someone encouraged me to try something different. And I decided it was important to prove that I could."

"And Ren is helping you," Sean asked after Gabriel had signed the sign guy's paperwork, officially transitioning On a Roll to Balls & Buns.

Tony was *really* going to lose his shit. Sean couldn't wait to see it.

"Even better, Ren is doing it *with* me," Gabriel said as they'd begun their long, hot trek towards his place.

"Really?" Sean was thrilled for Gabe.

"He even came up with the name that's probably going to get me murdered," Gabe said with a sly grin.

"Yeah, I want to be there when you tell Tony," Sean said. "Promise me."

"You gonna be around tomorrow morning?"

Sean squeezed his hand. It was almost too hot to hold hands, but he didn't give a fuck. He felt like he could do *anything* now that he'd won Gabriel's heart—and Gabriel had won his own right back.

"Plan on it," Sean said. "Besides, I wouldn't miss this for the world."

"It's gonna be fun," Gabe said, holding the door open for him. "Come on, let's see how crazed Ren is by this point. I was supposed to be home an hour ago, and he keeps sending me texts."

"What kind of texts?"

"Oh," Gabriel said as he pushed the button for the elevator, "threatening ones, like he's going to quit, that he's going to move out, that he's going to leave me for someone who actually cares about the business, etcetera, etcetera."

"I didn't think Ren was that dramatic," Sean said.

"Ren's a Moretti," Gabriel said with a bright, happy grin. "Best get used to it, babe."

They were kissing again when the elevator arrived with a ding.

It opened and Ren was standing there, glowering.

"You two," he said flatly.

"Us two," Gabriel said happily. "We made up."

Ren rolled his eyes but he was smiling. "What a surprise. I'm so shocked."

"You're really not," Gabriel said. Ren stepped out of the elevator. "Where are you going?"

"Away," Ren said dramatically. "You're pissing me off."

"Well, I'm back now," Gabriel said, reaching out and stopping the elevator doors from closing. "Come back, and we'll get the last two recipes finished together."

"Together?" Ren asked suspiciously.

Gabriel shrugged. "Three sets of hands are better than two."

Ren stepped into the elevator, and after it dinged closed, rounded on them. "Just so we're clear, there is to be no disgusting or sappy display of affection. No kissing, no hugging, no *taking a break,* AKA retreating to the bedroom for a quickie, alright?"

Sean nudged Gabriel's shoulder with his own. "You said he was dramatic, not that he was such a drill sergeant."

For a second, Ren stared at him. And then he started laughing, like he couldn't quite stop. When he finally did, the elevator had reached the top floor.

"Honestly," he said, as they walked towards their apartment, "I've never had something I *needed* to be a drill sergeant about before."

"I gave him half the business," Gabriel announced proudly. He patted Ren on the back as he unlocked the door. "Officially, legally, the whole nine yards. I don't know why I didn't do it before."

"Probably because Luca would have blown a gasket," Sean muttered under his breath as they walked into the gloriously air-conditioned apartment.

"You're probably right," Ren said with a crooked grin. "Honestly, that makes it even better."

"It really does, doesn't it?" Gabriel said, letting go of Sean's hand and perusing the ingredients scattered over the counter. "Did you get the lingonberry jam?"

"Jam?" Sean asked, confused. "Did you decide to start serving scones?"

"We," Gabe announced proudly, "are going to be serving all kinds of meatballs."

"And all kinds of buns," Ren inserted slyly as he joined Gabe in the kitchen, sliding a glass jar of jam across the counter to his cousin.

"But not my *favorite* buns," Gabriel teased, shooting Sean a look that made it clear that when they were finally alone, he was completely committed to giving Sean everything he wanted—and more.

"Ew," Ren complained. "I thought I said *no disgusting or sappy displays of affection.*"

"You said it," Gabriel said with a lighthearted smile, "but that doesn't mean it's gonna happen."

"What's the plan for this dish?" Sean said, deciding that he might as well help, because like Gabe had said, three sets of hands *were* better than two. And he already knew what would happen if he ended up dragging Gabriel by his dick back to his bedroom.

Ren would make his life hell, for the near and the foreseeable future. And since he wanted to spend that foreseeable future with Gabriel, pissing off his cousin and best friend didn't seem like the best plan.

"It's a play on Swedish meatballs, but in a sandwich," Gabriel said, shooting him a grateful look, clearly pleased that Sean had changed the subject. "The meatballs, plus a savory gravy, and lingonberry jam mayo, and picked cucumbers and radishes to add crunch. All piled up on a potato roll."

Sean's mouth watered. "Uh, that sounds *awesome.*"

"Thanks," Ren said. "You really think so?"

"Uh *yeah*," Sean said. "This whole concept is brilliant. Using Nonna's meatballs to experiment with other dishes? It's awesome."

"It's partially thanks to you it happened at all," Gabriel said, shooting a particularly mushy glance Sean's way.

"What he really wants is to beg you to put the Thai wrap on his menu," Ren inserted.

"You showed me what was possible," Gabriel said, and sounded apologetic. Like he shouldn't take what had been undeniably a great idea and use it.

"I don't *own* that idea," Sean said. He'd moved into the kitchen now, and had taken the knife Ren had given him, and started slicing the cucumbers and the radishes for pickling. "We came up with it together."

"Yeah, but if we'd kept to my ideas, we'd have some kind of weird soggy wrap," Gabriel said, and the expression on his face—gratitude and admiration and *love*—made Sean weak in the knees.

Ren must have caught it too, because he growled a little. "What did I tell you two?"

"We weren't even touching," Gabe protested.

"Yeah, except you looked like you *wanted* to be," Ren insisted, and he was *not* wrong.

"I'm sorry," Sean said, even though he didn't feel all that sorry. But he saw enough of himself in Ren that he thought he might understand a little of what he felt. "We'll try to keep it under wraps."

Ren sighed, and set down his flat whisk, where he'd been prepping to make the gravy. "You don't need to apologize." He hesitated, like he knew *he* needed to be the one making the apology, but wasn't sure where to begin. "I'm really happy for you two, honestly."

Gabriel raised an eyebrow. "Really?"

"Really." Ren sounded certain now. "You two . . . it's kind of beautiful, actually."

Sean's gaze met Gabriel's and he couldn't disagree, because while there was weight there, and shared history, and a thousand ways they'd needled each other over the years, he knew that Gabe would never stop fighting for him. Or cooking with him.

"See," Ren continued, gesturing with the whisk, "that sort of shit is why I can't even be angry. You're so . . . so . . ."

"Adorable? Heart-warming? Wonderfully in love?"

Ren turned back towards the stove. "Sure," he said carelessly, casually, but Sean knew he didn't feel that way at all. The tense line of his neck said everything he didn't. "Really," he added, "I'm just glad you put poor Gabe out of his misery, because he was so far up his own ass, it was getting annoying."

Sean chuckled, and nudged Gabriel with his elbow. "I was pretty miserable without you, too. Missed you even when I didn't want to be missing you."

"If that's the cost of you being here with me now, then I'm glad you were," Gabriel said, and Sean couldn't resist anymore. He tilted his head and Gabe's lips met his.

"Ugh," Ren said, his word punctuated by a sharp rap on the front door.

Gabe lifted his head from Sean's slowly. "Who's that?" he asked.

"Probably the Girl Scouts selling cookies," Ren said, flicking the stove off under his pan of gravy and heading towards the front door.

"I'd like three boxes of Samoas and four of Thin Mints," Gabriel called out.

But then Sean tugged his mouth down towards his again, and for a second, they both got lost in the kiss.

There was no better evidence of this than the fact it took a very wry, very frustrated voice to jerk them out of it.

"I see you both finally did what you were supposed to."

Sean opened his eyes and pulled away from Gabriel.

Tony was standing in the living room, flushed, like he'd *run* the few blocks here. His blue eyes were twinkling with amusement, but his expression was flat. Emotionless.

"Yeah, about that . . ." Gabriel started to say, but Tony lifted his hand.

"Do you remember that contract you signed?" he asked.

Gabriel reached beneath the counter and gripped Sean's hand. "Yeah, I do."

"Do you remember," Tony said, beginning to pace, "that there was a clause about requiring approval for any and all name and branding changes?"

"Uh, sure?" Sean said, speaking up this time. If Gabriel was in trouble, he was in just as much trouble—because he'd changed his name, *too*.

Now he hadn't changed his to something that was guaranteed to make Tony's blood pressure rise, but he'd still done it without any approval whatsoever.

Tony's glare shifted, and then suddenly, he was grinning like he couldn't ever stop.

"You're *both* in trouble," he said, "but you, Gabriel Moretti, are a *real* pain in my ass. At least Sean picked something that won't have the family groups picketing me."

"What?" Gabriel asked innocently. "Is there something dirty about it? I'm serving balls *and* buns."

Tony threw up his hands. "You're lucky that I think it's absolutely hilarious and it's not like the family groups are coming around, anyway."

"Really?" Ren sounded just as surprised as Sean felt. He was sure that Tony was going to be way more pissed.

"Hey, fuck it, you guys are *family*, and it's absolutely brilliant. You're gonna have a line around the block." Tony paused, thinking about this for the first time. "Maybe I'll even end up hating you for outselling the rest of us."

"No way," Gabe said.

"Really?" Tony raised an eyebrow. "Why wouldn't I?"

"You said it," Gabriel said, but he wasn't looking at Tony. He was looking straight at Sean. "We're family. And even when family drives you crazy, you love them anyway."

"Damn straight," Tony said, but his voice had already faded away, because Sean realized he was right.

When he'd moved here, he hadn't had anything anymore. He'd felt empty and alone and unmoored. He hadn't even realized that had begun to change, but it had, and then when he'd woken up and opened his eyes to what was happening between him and Gabriel, it was impossible to miss what else had happened.

He'd found another family.

"I love you," he murmured to Gabe, and ignoring Ren's outraged squawk, reached up to kiss him again.

To read a bonus scene about Lennox finding out the new name of Gabe & Ren's truck, click here.

To continue the Food Truck Warriors series with *Full Speed Ahead*, Lennox and Ash's story, click here.

If you'd like to read more Morettis, check out Luca's story, the standalone grumpy/sunshine romance, *Sweet as Pie*.

INTERESTED IN READING MORE OF
BETH'S BOOKS?

CHECK OUT A FULL LIST OF TILES
BY SCANNING THE QR CODE
OR VISITING HER WEBSITE

WWW.BETHBOLDEN.COM/BOOKLIST

WANT TO FOLLOW BETH?

MAKE SURE YOU NEVER
MISS A RELEASE?

SCAN THE QR CODE BELOW
OR VISIT HER WEBSITE
FOR A SOCIAL MEDIA LIST,
NEWSLETTER SIGNUP,
AND SO MUCH MORE!

WWW.BETHBOLDEN.COM/ABOUT

www.ingramcontent.com/pod-product-compliance
Lightning Source LLC
Chambersburg PA
CBHW070406310726
48977CB00003B/579